Books should be returned or renewed by the last
date above. Renew by phone **03000 41 31 31** or
online *www.kent.gov.uk/libs*

Libraries Registration & Archives

ALSO BY ADRIENNE YOUNG
AND AVAILABLE FROM TITAN BOOKS

Sky in the Deep
The Girl the Sea Gave Back

Fable

ADRIENNE YOUNG

TITAN BOOKS

Fable

Paperback edition ISBN: 9781789094558
E-book edition ISBN: 9781789094565
FairyLoot edition ISBN: 9781789096224

Published by Titan Books
A division of Titan Publishing Group Ltd.
144 Southwark Street, London SE1 0UP
www.titanbooks.com

First Titan paperback edition: December 2020
10 9 8 7 6 5 4 3 2 1

A CIP catalogue record for this title is available from
the British Library.

Printed and bound by CPI Group (UK) Ltd, Croydon CR0 4YY.

FOR DAD

IT TOOK A WHOLE BOOK TO SAY GOODBYE.

40 . 25 . 3
144 . 24 . 4
228 . 21 . 2
3 . 16 . 5
86 . 21 . 11
112 . 29 . 3
56 . 16 . 7

ONE

That bastard was leaving me again.

Between the trees, I could see Koy and the others kicking up sand as they pushed off the beach. The skiff slid into the water, and I ran faster, my bare feet finding their way over twisted tree roots and buried rock on the path. I came through the thicket just in time to see the smirk on Koy's lips as the sail dropped open.

"Koy!" I shouted, but if he could hear me over the sound of the waves, he didn't show it.

I tore down the slope until I reached the foam left by a retreating wave and planted one foot in the wet sand before I jumped, my feet kicking as I flew over the swell, toward the stern. I caught the stay with one hand and crashed into the side of the hull, my legs dragging in the water as the skiff took off. No one offered me a hand as I pulled myself up and over the side with a curse under my breath.

"Nice jump, Fable." Koy took hold of the tiller, his gaze

1

on the horizon as he steered us toward the south reef. "Didn't know you were coming."

I raked my hair into a knot on top of my head, glaring at him. It was the third time in a week that he'd tried to leave me behind when the dredgers went out to dive. If Speck weren't drunk half the time, I'd pay him for the ride to the reef instead of Koy. But I needed a boat I could count on.

The sail snapped overhead as the wind caught it, jerking the skiff forward, and I found a place to sit between two leather-skinned dredgers.

Koy held a hand out to me. "Copper."

I looked over his head to the barrier islands, where the masts of trading ships tipped and swayed in the rough wind. The *Marigold* wasn't there yet, but by sunrise, she would be. I pulled the coin from my purse and, with gritted teeth, dropped it into Koy's palm. By now, he'd made so much copper off me that I'd practically paid for half of his skiff.

We picked up speed and the water rushed past, turning from the pale turquoise of the shallows to a deep blue as we pulled farther from the shore. I leaned back as the boat heeled, tilting so I could let my hand skim the surface. The sun sat in the center of the sky, and we had a few hours before the tide started to turn. It was more than enough time to fill my bag with pyre for trade.

I tightened the belt around my waist, checking each of my tools.

Mallet, chisels, picks, trowel, eyeglass.

Most of the dredgers had moved on from the east reef

months ago, but my gut had told me there was more pyre hiding in those waters, and I'd been right. After weeks of diving the stretch alone, I found the cache beneath a picked-over shelf, and the stones had filled my purse with coin.

The wind whipped around me as I stood, pulling strands of my dark auburn hair around my face. I took hold of the mast and leaned over the side, my eyes mapping the water as it raced beneath us.

Not yet.

"When are you going to tell us what you found down there, Fable?" Koy's hand tightened on the tiller, his eyes meeting mine. They were as dark as the blackest nights on the island, when the storms veiled the moon and stars in the sky.

The others looked up at me silently, waiting for my answer. I'd seen them watching me more carefully on the docks, and I'd heard their whispers on the beach. After weeks of light hauls on the reefs, the dredgers were growing restless, and that was never good. But I hadn't expected Koy to be the one to finally ask me outright.

I shrugged. "Abalone."

He laughed, shaking his head. "Abalone," he repeated. He was younger than most of the dredgers on Jeval, his toasted skin not yet wrinkled and spotted white from the long days in the sun. But he'd earned his place among them tenfold by stealing enough coin to buy the skiff and start his own ferrying trade.

"That's right," I said.

The humor left his eyes when they found mine again, and

I clenched my teeth, trying not to let the twitch at the corner of my mouth show. It had been four years since the day I was dumped on the blazing hot beach and left to fend for myself. Forced to scrape hulls in exchange for rotten fish when I was starving, and beaten for diving in another dredger's claimed territory again and again. I'd seen my fair share of violence on Jeval, but I'd managed to keep out of Koy's way until now. Catching his notice was a very dangerous place to be.

I stepped up onto the stern, letting the same wicked smile bleed onto my lips that had been painted on his back at the beach. He was a bastard, but so was I. And letting him see how scared of him I was would only make me easier prey. I'd had to find a way to stay alive on Jeval, and I'd lose a hand before I let anyone take my chance to get off. Not when I was so close.

I let go of the mast and the skiff flew out from under my feet as I fell back into the water. My weight crashed into the sea, the crystalline bubbles rippling up around me as I floated toward the surface and kicked to warm myself against the chill. The edge of the east reef touched the current, making the water colder on this side of the island. It was one of the reasons I knew there was more pyre down there than what had already been dredged.

Koy's boat shot away from me, the full sail curved against the cloudless sky. When it disappeared behind the barrier islands, I cut back in the opposite direction, toward the shore. I swam with my face in the water so I could measure the reef below. The pinks, oranges, and greens of the coral caught the

4

sunlight like pages of the atlas that used to lay unrolled across my father's desk. A bright yellow sea fan with a broken frond was my mark.

I came up, checking my belt again as I dragged the air in slowly, filling my chest, and then letting it out at the same pace the way my mother taught me. My lungs stretched and then squeezed as they emptied in a familiar push between my ribs, and I quickened my draw, sucking it in and pushing it out in spurts until I took one last full breath in and dove.

My ears popped as I carved through the water with my arms, headed for the brilliant colors glowing on the seafloor. The pressure hugged in around my body, and I let myself sink deeper when I could feel the surface trying to pull me back. A school of red-striped tangs pushed past, folding around me in a swarm as I came down. The infinite blue reached out in every direction as my feet landed lightly on a ridge of green coral reaching up like twisted fingers. I gripped the rock ledge above it, scaling down to the breach.

I'd first found the pyre when I was scouring the reef for crab to pay the old man at the docks to repair my eyeglass. The soft hum of the gemstone had found my bones in the silence, and after three straight days of trying to uncover it, I caught a lucky break. I'd kicked off an outcropping to surface when a shelf broke off, revealing a crooked line of basalt pocked with the telltale white clusters I knew so well. They could only mean one thing—pyre.

I'd made more coin off the traders on the *Marigold* in the last three months with this stash than I had in the last two years altogether. Another few weeks and I'd never have to dive these reefs again.

My feet settled on the ledge, and I pressed a hand to the rock, feeling down the curve of the ridges. The soft vibration of the gemstone hissed beneath my fingertips, like the stretched resonance of metal striking metal. My mother had taught me that too—how to listen to the gems. Deep in the hull of the *Lark,* she'd set them into my hands one at a time, whispering as the crew slept in the hammocks strung from the bulkhead.

Do you hear that? Do you feel it?

I pulled the tools from my belt and fit the chisel into the deepest groove before I hit it with the mallet, crumbling the surface slowly. Judging from the shape of the corner, there was a sizable piece of pyre beneath it. Maybe four coppers' worth.

The shine of sunlight on silver scales glittered above me as more fish came down to feed, and I looked up, squinting against the glare. Floating in the murky distance down the reef, a body drifted beneath the surface. The remains of a dredger who'd crossed someone or didn't repay a debt. His feet had been chained to an enormous, barnacle-covered rock, left for the sea's creatures to pick the flesh from his bones. It wasn't the first time I'd seen the sentence carried out, and if I wasn't careful, I'd meet the same end.

The last of my air burned in my chest, my arms and legs growing colder, and I hit the chisel one more time. The rough white crust cracked, and I smiled, letting a few bubbles escape my lips as a jagged piece of the rock broke free. I reached up to touch the glassy, red pyre, peeking out at me like a bloodshot eye.

When the edges of black began to push in around my vision, I kicked off the rock, swimming for the surface as my lungs screamed for air. The fish scattered like a rainbow breaking into pieces around me, and I came up out of the water, gasping. The clouds were pulling into thin strands overhead, but the darkening blue on the horizon caught my eye. I'd noticed the tinge of a storm on the wind that morning. If it kept the *Marigold* from reaching the barrier islands by sunup, I'd have to hold on to the pyre longer than was safe. I only had so many hiding places, and with every day that passed, more eyes were watching me.

I floated on my back, letting the sun touch as much of my skin as possible to warm me. It was already sinking toward the slanted ridge that reached over Jeval, and it would take at least six or seven more dives to get the pyre free. I needed to be at the other end of the reef by the time Koy came back for me.

If he came back.

Three or four more weeks and I'd have enough coin to barter for passage across the Narrows to find Saint and make him keep his promise. I'd only been fourteen years old when he dumped me on the infamous island of thieves, and I'd spent every day since scraping together the coin I needed to go and find him. After four years, I wondered if he'd even recognize me when I finally showed up knocking on his door. If he'd remember what he said to me as he carved into my arm with the tip of his whalebone knife.

But my father wasn't the forgetting kind.

Neither was I.

TWO

There were five rules. Only five.

And I'd been reciting them to my father from the time I was big enough to first climb the masts with my mother. In the dim candlelight of his quarters on the *Lark*, he'd watch me, one hand on his quill and the other on the green rye glass that sat on his desk.

1. *Keep your knife where you can reach it.*
2. *Never, ever owe anyone anything.*
3. *Nothing is free.*
4. *Always construct a lie from a truth.*
5. *Never, under any circumstances, reveal what or who matters to you.*

I'd lived by Saint's rules every day since he abandoned me on Jeval, and they'd kept me alive. At least he'd left me with that much when he sailed away, not once looking back.

Thunder grumbled overhead as we neared the beach, the sky darkening and the air waking with the whisper of a storm. I studied the horizon, watching the shape of the waves. The *Marigold* would be on its way, but if the storm was bad, she wouldn't be at the barrier islands in the morning. And if she wasn't there, I wouldn't be able to trade.

Koy's black eyes dropped to the net of abalone in my lap, where the purse of pyre I'd loosed from the reef was hidden inside one of the shells. I wasn't the stupid girl I'd once been. I'd learned quickly that tying the purse to my tools like the other dredgers did would only invite them to cut it from my belt. And there wasn't a thing I could do about it. I was no physical match for them, so I'd been hiding gems and coins inside gutted fish and abalone since the last time my haul was stolen from me.

I traced the scar at my wrist with the tip of my finger, following the vein of it like tree roots up my inner forearm to my elbow. For a long time, it was the only thing that kept me alive on the island. Jevalis were nothing if not superstitious, and no one wanted anything to do with the girl who had a mark like this one. Only a few days after Saint left me, an old man named Fret started a rumor on the docks that I'd been cursed by sea demons.

The skiff slowed, and I stood, hopping over the side with the net slung over my shoulder. I could feel Koy's eyes on me, the deep husk of his whisper at my back as I trudged up out of the shallows. It was every man for himself on Jeval, unless there was something to be gained by scheming. And that's exactly what Koy was doing—scheming.

9

I walked along the water's edge toward the ridge, watching the cliff face for the shadow of anyone following me. The sea turned violet with dusk, and the last gasping glitter of light danced on the surface of the water as the sun disappeared.

My callused fingers found the familiar crevices of the black rock boulder and I climbed, pulling myself up until the spray of seawater crashing on the other side hit my face. The rope I had anchored on the ledge disappeared into the water below.

I took the cracked abalone shell from my net and dropped it into my shirt before I stood, filling my lungs with air. As soon as the water rose with the crash of a wave, I jumped from the ridge into the sea. It was growing darker with every minute, but I took hold of the rope and followed it down into the shadows of the kelp forest, where the towering, ribbonlike strands reached up from the seafloor in thick, wavering threads. From below, their leaves looked like a golden rooftop, casting the water green.

The fish wound through the vines as I swam down and the reef sharks followed them, hunting for their suppers. The cove was one of the only places I'd been allowed to fish because the rough water made it difficult to keep the reed traps the other dredgers used in one piece. But the woven basket trap my father's navigator had taught me to make could withstand the crush of the waves. I wrapped the thick rope around my fist and yanked, but it didn't give, wedged by the push of the current between the rocks below.

My feet came down on top of the basket, and I braced myself against the stone, trying to kick it loose from where it was half-buried in the thick silt. When it didn't budge, I sank down, hooking my fingers into the woven top and jerked it back until it snapped, sending me into the slab of rough rock behind me.

A perch wriggled through the opening before I could get it closed, and I cursed, the sound of my voice lost in the water as I watched it swim away. Before the other one could escape, I pressed the broken lid to my chest, wrapping one arm tightly around the trap.

The rope led me back up from the seafloor, and I followed it until I reached the jagged overhang that hid in the shadows. I used my chisel to pry loose the stone I'd sealed with kelp, and it fell into my hand, revealing a dug-out hole. Inside, the pyre I'd collected for the last two weeks sparkled like broken glass. It was one of my only hiding places on the island that hadn't been found. I'd been sinking my fish traps in the little cove for years, and anyone who saw me dive here, saw me come up with my catch. If anyone thought I might be keeping my gems here too, they hadn't been able to find them.

When the pouch at my belt was filled with pyre, I replaced the stone. The muscles in my legs were already burning, tired from hours of diving, and I used the last bit of my strength to push toward the surface. A wave barreled in as I gulped in the night air, and I kicked myself toward the outcropping before it could suck me back under.

11

I dragged my weight up with one arm and lay back in the sand, catching my breath. The stars were already winking overhead, but the storm was moving toward Jeval fast, and I could tell by the smell of the wind that it was going to be a long night. The winds would threaten my hovel on the cliffs, but I couldn't sleep anyway when I had to keep my pyre or coin on me. My camp had been tossed while I slept before, and I couldn't risk it.

I slipped the wriggling fish into my shirt and swung the broken trap over my shoulder so that it hung against my back. Darkness fell over the trees and I found my way by moonlight, following the trail until it curved toward the crag and I leaned into the incline as the path grew steep. When the ground abruptly ended at a smooth face of rock, I fit my hands and feet into the holds I'd chiseled and climbed. Once I had my leg over the top, I pulled myself up and looked behind me to the path.

It was empty, the trees swaying gently in the breeze and the light shifting over the cool sand. I ran the rest of the way, until the flat ground dropped off sharply over the beach far below. The bluff overlooked the barrier islands, invisible in the dark, but I could make out the glow of a few lanterns swinging from the masts of ships docked for the night. It was the spot I'd sat every morning, waiting for my father's ship to return, even though he'd told me he wasn't coming back.

It took me two years to believe him.

I dropped the trap beside the fire pit, unbuckling my heavy belt. The wind picked up as I wrapped my hands around the thick tree trunk that hung over the cliff and shimmied myself up slowly. The ground dropped out from under me, and I looked down to the shore that lay at least a hundred feet below. The night waves were foaming white on the sand. Most dredgers were too heavy to climb out onto the spindly tree without the branches cracking and sending them to their death. I'd almost fallen myself once or twice.

When I was close enough, I reached up into the hollow at the joint of two swollen branches. My fingers found the purse and I swung my arm back, tossing it to the ground behind me before I climbed back down.

I started my fire and skewered the fish on the spit, settling into a comfortable groove in the rocks that overlooked the path. If anyone came snooping, I'd see them before they saw me. I just needed to make it to morning.

The coins clinked together as I shook the purse, spilling them onto the soft sand. Their faces shined in the moonlight as I counted, setting them in neat stacks before me.

Forty-two coppers. After what I would have to spend on skiffs, I needed another eighteen and I'd have enough to barter with West for passage. I had even set aside a little coin to keep me fed and sheltered until I tracked down Saint. I lay back on the ground and let my legs hang over the edge of the cliff, staring up at the moon as the fish crackled over the fire. It was a perfect, milk-white crescent hanging above me, and I breathed in the salty, cypress-tinged air that was unique to Jeval.

My first night on the island, I'd slept out on the beach,

too afraid to go up into the trees where the tents were pitched around burning fires. I woke to a man tearing open my jacket, searching my pockets for coin. When he didn't find anything, he dropped me on the cold sand and walked away. It took days for me to figure out that every time I fished in the shallows, someone would be waiting on the beach to take whatever I'd caught from me. I ate kelp for almost a month before I found safe places to forage. After almost a year, I finally had enough coin saved from cleaning other peoples' catches and selling palm rope to buy the dredging tools off Fret, who was too old to dive anymore.

The waves crashed angrily below as the storm winds blew in, and for just a moment, I wondered if I'd miss it. If there was something on Jeval that had become a part of me. I sat up, looking out over the night-cloaked island, where the tops of the trees moved in the dark like churning water. If it hadn't been my prison, I might even think it was beautiful. But I had never belonged here.

I could have. I could have made myself one of them, working to build my own small gem trade on the barrier islands like so many others. But if I was a Jevali dredger, then I wasn't Saint's daughter. And maybe even that wasn't true anymore.

I still remembered the hum in the belly of the hull and the creak of the hammock. The smell of my father's pipe and the sound of boots on the deck. I didn't belong on the land or on the docks or the cities that lay across the Narrows. The place I belonged was gone.

Miles away, where the moonlight touched the black seam of the horizon, the *Lark* lay beneath the waters of Tempest Snare. And no matter where I went, I'd never get home. Because home was a ship that was at the bottom of the sea, where my mother's bones lay sleeping.

THREE

I stood on the cliff as the sun came up, watching the *Marigold* down on the water. They'd arrived in the dark hours, despite the raging storm that had barreled in from the Unnamed Sea. I'd stayed awake all night, staring into the fire until the rain put out the flames, and my entire body ached with the need to sleep after three straight days of diving.

But West didn't like to be kept waiting.

There were already hordes of dredgers waiting at the water's edge when I made it to the beach. I'd been smart enough to pay Speck a month in advance for a spot on his skiff. He was lying on the sand with his hands folded behind his head, his hat set over his face. If you had a boat on Jeval, you didn't need to dive or trade because every dredger on the island needed you. Having a skiff was like having a pot of copper that never ran empty, and no one was more undeserving of luck like that than Speck.

When he saw me coming, he jumped up, smiling with a wide, rotten-toothed grin. "Mornin', Fay!"

I tipped my chin up at him, throwing my satchel into the skiff before lifting myself over the side. No one bothered to make room for me to sit, so I stood at the prow with one arm hooked around the mast and my hand closed over the purse of pyre inside my shirt. Koy's boat was already disappearing around the barrier islands ahead, packed full of so many bodies that legs and feet were dragging in the water on both sides.

"Fable." Speck gave me a pleading smile, and I glared at him when I realized what he was waiting for.

I worked the sail free, letting it unroll as he pushed us off. The dredgers asked things of me they'd never ask of one another. I was expected to just be grateful they hadn't drowned me as a scrawny child in the shallows, but the truth was, they'd never done me any favors. Never fed me when I begged for scraps or offered me a place to take cover during a storm. Every bite of food or piece of pyre, I'd worked for or nearly died getting. Still, I was supposed to be beholden to them that I was still breathing.

The wind picked up and we cut through the smooth morning water like a hot knife through tallow. I didn't like how calm it looked, the way the surface gleamed like newly fired glass. It was unnerving to see the sea asleep when I'd seen how bloodthirsty she could be.

"Word has it you've found a new pyre cache, Fay," Speck croaked, handing off the tiller and coming to stand beside me at the mast.

His breath stunk of home-brewed rye, and I turned my face into the wind, ignoring him. When I felt the others looking at me, my fist tightened around my purse.

Speck's hand went up into the air between us, his palm splayed flat before me. "I dinna mean nothin' by it."

"Sure," I muttered.

He leaned in a little closer, his voice lowering. "But there been talk, ya know."

My eyes cut over to meet his, and I studied him, trying to see what lay beneath the words. "What talk?"

He glanced back over his shoulder, and his silver braid of hair pulled from where it was tucked into his shirt. "There been talk about where you been keepin' all that copper."

The dredger sitting to my right shifted, his ear turning up to listen.

"If I were you, I'd stay out of that talk, Speck." I let my shoulders fall back, leaning into the mast. The key to dealing with the dredgers was to act as if you weren't scared, even when you were so terrified you had to swallow to keep the vomit down. Speck was harmless, but he was one of only a few on the island I didn't worry about.

He quickly nodded. "A 'course I do. Jus' thought you should know."

"Just thought you'd get another copper from me, you mean," I snapped.

Another smile broke on his face before he ducked his head and shrugged.

"You already overcharge me. I'm not paying you for gossip, too."

I gave him my back, letting him know I was done talking about it. I had at least three weeks before I'd have enough copper to barter for passage, but if the dredgers really were talking, I wouldn't make it that long.

Speck fell silent, leaving only the sound of the hull carving through the water and the whistle of the wind. The ribbed white sails of the *Marigold* came into view as we rounded the corner of the barrier islands, anchored beyond the outcropping of the farthest rise, and Speck gently slowed the skiff. I could see the square set of West's shoulders at the other end of the docks as he looked out over the water, a black silhouette before the rising sun.

I put one hand up into the air, spreading my fingers against the wind, and as soon as he saw it, he disappeared into the crowd.

Speck loosed the sail as we approached the dock, and before he could ask, I gathered the coiled rope in my arms and threw the lines out. The loop caught the post at the corner of the dock, and I hopped up from the deck onto the side, leaning back with my heels on the edge and pulling us in, one hand over the other. The wet ropes creaked as they stretched, and the hollow knock of the scull against the boat made Fret look up from where he was perched on his stool.

A reed-woven crate sat between his feet, filled with rare shells he'd foraged in the shallows. He'd lost his ability to dredge long ago, but he still traded every week at the barrier islands, selling things that no one else could ever seem to find. He was the first to say I'd been marked by sea demons, and he'd sold me his dredger's belt, forcing me to break my father's rules. Because as long as I lived, I'd owe him my life for both.

"Fable." He gave me a tilted smile as I climbed onto the dock.

"Hey, Fret." I touched his bony shoulder as I passed, looking over him to where West waited before the *Marigold* in the distance.

Dredgers were gathered along the narrow wooden walkway in the pale morning light, bartering with traders and fighting over coppers. Jeval was known for the pyre in its reefs, and even though it wasn't among the most valuable gemstones, Jeval was one of the only places you could find it.

And it wasn't just pyre the traders came for. Jeval was the only bit of land between the Narrows and the Unnamed Sea, and many ships stopped in for simple supplies in the middle of their voyages. Jevalis carried baskets of chicken eggs, lines of fish, and reams of rope up and down the dock, calling out to the crews that watched over the railings of their ships.

Shouting erupted ahead as I shouldered through a tightly packed group of men, and I ducked to the side when someone threw a punch. A fight broke out, shoving me to the edge of the dock, and an open barrel of mullein leaves rolled into the water, almost taking me with it. Two men jumped in after it, and I waited for the fighting dredgers to be pulled apart before I made my way past them.

As if he could feel me coming, West turned just as I pushed through the edge of the crowd. His waving, sun-bleached hair was pulled behind one ear, his arms crossed over his chest as he looked down at me with pale green eyes.

"You're late." He watched me pull my shirt free from where it was tucked into my belt and untie the purse. I glanced behind him to the horizon, where the bottom tip of the sun was already hovering above the water.

"By minutes," I muttered.

He stepped forward as I emptied the purse and six bulbous, white-crusted lumps of pyre rolled into my open hand.

He plucked the eyeglass from my belt and fit it to his eye before he leaned in, picking the pieces up carefully and holding them toward the sunrise so the light showed through the red gemstones. They weren't cleaned of the outer rock, but they were good pieces. Better than anything else the dredgers behind me were hocking.

"Looks like you hit that storm." I eyed the fresh tar drying on the hull of the *Marigold,* where a small crack marked the wood beneath the railing on the starboard side.

He didn't answer, turning the pieces over to check them again.

But that wasn't the only part of the ship that had taken a beating. High up on the mainmast, a girl sat back into a sling, repairing the leather straps that tied up the sails.

As a child, I'd lay flat on the main deck, watching my mother up in the masts of the *Lark,* a dark red braid swinging down her back like a snake and her sun-browned skin dark against the crisp white canvas. I blinked to clear the memory from my vision before the pain awoke in my chest.

"You've had a lot more to trade lately." West let the eyeglass drop into his hand.

"Lucky streak." I hooked my thumbs into my belt, waiting.

He reached up, scratching the blond scruff at his jaw like he always did when he was thinking. "Luck usually brings trouble." When he finally looked up, his eyes narrowed on me. "Six coppers." He reached for the purse at his belt.

"Six?" I raised an eyebrow at him, pointing at the largest piece of pyre in his hand. "That one's worth three coppers, easy."

His gaze travelled over my head, back to the dock of dredgers and traders behind me. "I wouldn't take more than six coppers back to the island with you." He fished the coins from his purse. "I'll give you the rest next time."

My teeth clenched, my fists tightening at my sides. Acting like he was doing me a favor by only partially paying me in trade made my blood boil under my skin. That wasn't how this world worked.

"I can take care of myself. *Ten* coppers or you can find someone else to trade with." I snatched my eyeglass from his fingers and held my other hand open in front of me. He'd give me the coppers because he didn't buy pyre from anyone else on Jeval. Only me. For two years, he hadn't bought a single piece from another dredger.

His jaw worked as his hand closed over the stones and his knuckles turned white. He muttered something I couldn't hear as he reached into the pocket of his vest. "You should trade less at once." His voice dropped low as he counted the coppers out.

He was right. I knew that. But it was more dangerous to have a stash of both pyre *and* copper on the island. Coins were smaller, easier to hide, and I'd rather have only one thing that others wanted. "I know what I'm doing," I said, trying to sound as if it were true.

"If you're not here next time, I'll know why." He waited for me to look up at him. The long days on the deck of the ship had painted his skin the deepest olive, making his eyes look like the jadeite my mother used to have me polish after her dives.

He dropped the coins into my hand, and I turned on my heel, shoving them into my purse before I tucked it back into my shirt. I pressed into the mob of Jevalis, swallowed up by the stinking bodies, and a lump tightened in my throat. The weight of the coppers in my purse made me uneasy, West's words sinking like a heavy stone in the back of my mind. Maybe he was right. Maybe . . .

I turned back, rising up onto my toes to see over the shoulders of the dredgers between me and the *Marigold*. But West was already gone.

FOUR

K oy was waiting in the boat when I stepped onto the beach.

The wind pushed his dark hair back from his face as he looked out at the chop on the water. The first time I ever saw Koy, he was swimming toward me from the shore so he could kick me off the sandbar I was fishing on. He hadn't taken his eyes off me since.

"Where are the others?" I asked, flicking a copper into the air and throwing my belt into the skiff.

He caught it, dropping it into the purse hanging from the mast. "Still working the traders."

We climbed into the skiff, and it drifted out of the shallows as Koy loosed the lines.

The wind caught the sail hard as soon as it opened, making the boat heel before it shot forward, away from the shore. I fastened my belt as Koy glanced back at me over his shoulder and his eyes dropped to my tools. He'd stolen from me before, though I'd never caught him. I'd had to change my hiding places several times, but someone always seemed to find them. The dredgers were rough and hard-edged but they weren't stupid, least of all Koy. And he had more mouths to feed than most everyone else.

His grandmother and two siblings were dependent upon him, and that made him more dangerous than almost anyone on the island. Being responsible for someone else was the greatest curse on Jeval, out on the sea, even in the Narrows. The only safety that existed was in being completely alone. That was one of the very first things Saint taught me.

Out at the barrier islands, the *Marigold* still sat before the dark backdrop of another storm brewing in the distance. This one looked worse than the first, but judging from the wind and the clouds, it would mostly play out before it hit us. Still, the *Marigold* and the other ships would probably stay docked until morning to be safe.

"What are you going to do with all of that copper, Fable?" Koy asked, tying off the line.

I watched the rope pull around the callused skin that covered his hand. "What copper?"

He looked amused, a sliver of teeth showing between his lips. "I know you're trading all that pyre you're finding. But I can't figure out what you're planning to do with the coin. Buy a boat? Start an operation with the traders?"

"I haven't been finding much pyre." I shrugged, twirling a piece of my hair around my finger. The strands were the color of tarnished copper in the sunlight. "No more than usual."

He grinned, leaning back into the bow so his elbow hung over the side of the boat. "You know why I've never liked you?"

I smiled back at him. "Why?"

"It's not that you're a liar. Everyone on this island is a liar. The problem with you, Fable, is that you're a good one."

"Well, I've always liked you, Koy."

He laughed as he pulled the sail and the boat slowed. "See? I almost believed you."

I stepped onto the side of the boat and dove in, crashing into the cold water and letting myself float back up to the top. When I broke the surface again, Koy was already leaving a wake behind him, headed toward the south reef. When he didn't look back, I swam in the opposite direction at a slow pace, trying to save my strength. My muscles and bones were still stiff and weak, but rest wasn't going to come anytime soon. Not with the dredgers paying me so much attention. The only thing I could do now was get the last of the copper I needed as fast as I could to leave this place behind.

I spotted the yellow sea fan and tightened my belt before I started working my lungs, inhaling and exhaling in a rhythm I had memorized. When the sharp tinge ignited between my ribs, I dove down, kicking toward the seafloor and sending the fish into a twist of glittering scales above me. I didn't waste any time lowering myself to the breach. The quiet hum of the pyre danced on my skin as I pulled the tools from my belt and got to work, hitting the mallet as hard as I could and working down a new line of rock. Most of it was just coral and basalt, but the smooth surface of a piece of pyre broke through about two feet down. It wasn't a big piece, so it would free more easily, but finding more could take me the entire afternoon. I pulled my arm back and braced myself on the reef as I brought the mallet back up. I hit the chisel squarely and the ping sounded underwater as a small chip broke off.

My hand slipped, slamming into the sharp edge as a shadow moved overhead, draping me in the dark. I jolted, dropping the mallet, and my heart kicked up, the air in my lungs waning. I whirled, pressing myself under the overhang of rock and gripping the chisel in my cold hand. A group of whale sharks were swimming over the ridge, weaving through the beams of sunlight casting down from the surface. I let out a stream of bubbles in a relieved laugh, the painful clench in my chest easing just a little. But I needed air.

I pushed off the rock, coming up between two of them and reached out to run my hand along the length of their smooth, spotted skin. Their tails flicked past me, and I smiled, kicking toward the puddle of sunlight wavering above.

But just as I reached the surface, something caught hold of my arm, dragging me back down before I'd even taken a breath. I yelped underwater, letting the last of my air escape as I thrashed to turn.

In the cloud of pivoting fish below, Koy's face was looking up at me, his hands clamped tightly around my wrist. I kicked, catching him in the shoulder with the heel of my foot and his fingers slipped from me. I swam as fast as I could toward the light, feeling the darkness creeping over my mind, and when I finally broke through to the air, I choked, my lungs twisting violently in my chest. The skiff was floating just down the reef, past a crest of rock so that I couldn't see it from below.

He'd followed me.

Koy came up in the next breath, launching in my direction. I tried to swim from his reach, but he took hold of my hair and wrenched me back to him.

"Where is it?" he shouted, his fist tightening. "Tell me where it is!"

I twisted, rearing my elbow back with a snap, and it caught him in the face. His fingers untangled from my hair, and I swam for the boat. Koy followed, cutting through the water faster than I could. By the time I reached the hull, he had ahold of my foot. I caught the lip of the stern and pulled against his weight, trying to get in. He yanked harder, a growl tearing from his throat, and I slipped, hitting the side with my face so hard that the light exploded in my head. I found the edge with my fingers again before I pulled myself back up and reached inside, my hand frantically looking for the scull. When I had it, I threw my arm back, hitting Koy in the head with the flat end.

He stilled suddenly, falling back into the water, and I hoisted myself into the hull, coughing. Koy's eyes rolled back into his head as he sank, a stream of red inklike blood spilling from his forehead. I let the lines down with clumsy hands, but as I reached for the sail, I froze, my breath catching.

I could still see him, sinking into the dark blue, just below the surface.

"You bastard," I groaned, dropping the scull and diving back in.

I hooked my hands under his arms when I reached him, hauling him back. I fought with his weight, almost tipping the boat as I lifted his limp body. Once I had his top half inside, I pulled his legs over one at a time and he rolled into the hull.

Every muscle twisted tight, the last of my strength wrung from my bones, and I retched, sending the saltwater I'd swallowed up my burning throat. I stood over Koy, my hands shaking. He was still losing a steady stream of blood, and I hoped he wasn't breathing. I hoped he was dead.

But I'd never been that lucky.

I kicked him hard, screaming, before I fell back onto the deck beside him, trying to catch my breath. I spit a mouthful of blood from my busted mouth into the water, looking back toward the island. My lip was cut open and my cheek was swelling, but I was alive. That was really all I could ask for.

I should have left him. Should have let him drown in the darkness. Why hadn't I?

You weren't made for this world, Fable.

I cursed, pinching my eyes closed as Saint's words echoed in my aching head. He'd said the same thing about my mother.

I snatched the scull from where it floated in the water and stood, pulling the sail in with weak arms. The line was heavy in my hands as I yanked, and when the wind caught the canvas, a single hot tear rolled down my cheek.

I didn't have three weeks. I didn't even have three days.

Beyond the crooked rise of the barrier islands, the *Marigold*'s sails were still rolled up against the storm gale blowing in.

If I made it to sundown alive, I had one chance to get off Jeval. And I was going to take it.

FIVE

By some twist of fate, the beach was nearly clear when I pulled the skiff ashore. Maybe Koy was telling the truth when he said the dredgers were still working the traders at the docks. Or maybe they were readying for the storm blowing in. Either way, there were only a few people to notice that I'd returned from the reef.

I threw the tangled nets over Koy's still body and grabbed my belt, hopping over the side and splashing down into the water. The first question anyone who saw me would have was what I was doing in Koy's boat alone. The second would be to wonder where Koy was.

I tossed the scull inside and put one foot in front of the other, taking my usual path to the cove where I kept my fish traps anchored. The sun was beginning to fall in the sky, the wind picking up. The crew of the *Marigold* would be preparing to set sail as soon as the storm passed.

A dredger with an armful of empty baskets eyed me as

I passed him, and I reached up to touch my lip with the tip of my finger. There was no telling how bad my face looked, and there was no way to hide it. As soon as someone found Koy, they'd put two and two together.

I found the path and cut south, toward the end of the longest stretch of sand. Once the sun fell behind the ridge, the beach was draped in shadow. I followed the trail up to the cliffs, watching behind me every few steps. But I stopped in my tracks as I came around the rocks, sucking in a breath.

My camp was ransacked, the few things of value or use I had, gone. Everything else was scattered in pieces over the sand.

Koy *had* been scheming. He took me out on an empty skiff to find my pyre cache while his friends tossed my camp for coin and pyre. But he hadn't counted on me getting back to the island alive. And whether or not he woke up in his boat, someone would have a knife in my gut by the time the storm hit the beach.

My eyes slid to the tree in the distance, my heartbeat faltering.

"Please please *please* . . ." I ran to it, jumping out from the cliff's edge to catch hold of the thickest branch and swinging myself up and over the trunk. My hand ran up the bark frantically, feeling for the hollow, and a cry slipped from my throat as my fingers caught hold of the purse. I clutched it to my chest. They hadn't found it.

I wiped at my eyes with the back of my hand, trembling as the image of the body floating on the reef came back to me. If I didn't hurry, I'd have my own feet tied to the coral, the cold seawater filling my lungs. My feet hit the rocks and I tore the hem of my shirt in one long strip before wrapping it tightly around the coin purse clutched in my palm. I tied off the end with my teeth. If someone was going to take it from me this time, they'd have to pry it from my cold, dead fingers.

Below, boats full of dredgers were headed to shore from the barrier islands. Almost every one of their faces was turned to the horizon, where black clouds were swallowing the rising moon. I scanned the water's edge for Koy's skiff and when I found it, my blood turned to ice, my skin prickling. It was there, pulled up onto the sand where I'd left it. But Koy was gone.

My eyes went to the darkening path. I couldn't go that way. Not without running into someone looking for me.

I turned into the wind and went upward instead, running over loose rock between rises of stone in a maze of dried-up riverbeds. I kept one hand to the wall, my bare feet struggling to find steady footing in the low light. The only way back down was the switchbacks, but the last time I'd taken that way was two years ago, when I'd fallen from the path and broke my leg. I'd almost starved to death, unable to get my own food or wood for a fire those first two weeks.

But right now, falling to my death sounded better than whatever Koy would do when he found me.

I bit down on my bottom lip as the walls opened up, the wind slithering into the cavern around me. I didn't hesitate, stepping one foot onto the narrow path with my breath held. The warm wind came up off the water, pressing me to the rock, and I tried to keep my eyes on the ground, one arm hovering out over the drop.

My bare foot came down on something sharp as I inched down the wall, and I recoiled, hissing. A drop of blood dripped onto the stone below, and I walked faster, not waiting until I reached the bottom to jump out onto the sand. I landed hard, rolling onto my side before I stumbled back to my feet and limped toward the beach.

The line of boats in the distance were docked for the night. I could smell the crisp burn of fish skin and fire smoke coming from the trees, which meant most of the dredgers were busy cooking their suppers. All except one.

Speck was lying flat on his back, already drunk on the rye he'd bought with the day's coin. The water came up over his bare feet, and his mouth was open, a crackling snore dragging over his throat. I gave him a light kick and waited, but he only made a gargling sound and rolled over, his face pressing into the sand.

"Sorry, Speck." I whispered, leaping over him.

But I wasn't sorry. While I was barely surviving the last four years, he was drinking enough rye to feed me for the length of my life. And he was my only way off the beach.

I waded out into the water quietly, dropping my dredging belt inside before I lifted myself into the boat and pulled up the small anchor, my heart racing.

"Fable!" a ragged voice rang out in the darkening light.

34

My head snapped back toward the trees, my face flushing hot. I pulled the anchor onto the deck and untied the sail.

"Fable!" My name tore through the silence again, lifting over the sound of the water.

The skiff drifted slowly as I took up the sculls. I'd have to row until the wind caught the sail, but I was out of time. Back on the beach, a figure burst through the trees.

Koy.

As soon as his eyes found me, he was running down the slope, kicking up sand behind him. Dark blood ran down the side of his face and neck, spreading onto his bare chest like an open hand.

I dropped the sculls into the water and pulled with a groan. Above me, the canvas of the sail was barely fluttering against the wind. I wasn't moving fast enough. My heart stumbled in a haphazard rhythm as Koy's boat splashed into the water behind me.

"Come on!" I screamed, willing the wind to come. "Come on!"

The sail snapped, bowing as the wind filled it, and the boom swung across the deck as the boat lurched forward, knocking me down. I crawled back to the stern, taking hold of the tiller. Behind me, Koy's skiff was turning about. The barrier islands were only barely visible, but at my back, Jeval was illuminated in the last moments of a fiery amber sunset. And Koy was gaining on me.

I was stupid for not leaving him in the water. I was stupid for getting on that boat with him alone in the first place.

It was my own fault that he'd been able to sneak up on me on the reef. And now, if he caught me before I got to the *Marigold*, I'd have no one to blame but myself.

You weren't made for this world, Fable. You want to prove me wrong? Get yourself off this island.

"Shut up," I rasped, the tears burning in my eyes as Saint's face conjured like a ghost before me. If I'd come this far only to die, I'd prove him right. A hundred times over.

I didn't slow as I came upon the docks. I stepped up onto the side and crossed my arms over my chest, jumping into the dark water with my belt and purse. When I came back up, Speck's boat crashed into the post, the crude wood scraping and cracking as I swam for the ladder. I pulled myself up the rungs and ran as soon as my feet hit the wooden planks.

"West!" I screamed his name into the dark as the *Marigold* came into view.

The ships floated silently in the bays, their lanterns flickering on empty decks. Behind me, Koy's footsteps pounded on the dock. Faster than mine.

"West!"

A figure appeared on the starboard side of the *Marigold*, and a lantern lifted to illuminate the face of a girl—the girl I'd seen up in the masts that morning.

"Fable!" Koy growled behind me, his voice like thunder.

The girl stared down at me wordlessly as I skidded to a stop beside the ship.

"Please!" I shouted, reaching up for the stowed ladder.

Her eyes went behind me, to Koy. She hesitated before she finally pulled at the ropes, and the ladder unrolled, slapping against the hull. I leapt for it, swinging out over the water and crashing into the side of the ship with my shoulder.

Koy slid on the dock, reaching for my legs, and I kicked him back, climbing the ropes with shaking hands until I was tumbling over the railing. I fell onto the deck hard, landing on my back and gulping in the air.

The girl stood over me, the lantern still swinging from her hand.

"What the hell are you doing?" West was suddenly behind her, his face almost invisible in the dark. He reached down, taking hold of my arm and yanking me back to my feet.

I went for my knife, opening my mouth to speak, but in the next breath, the cold, sharp point of a blade was pressed into the soft skin below my jaw. The girl was instantly at my side, a jeweled dagger clutched in her fist.

My hands lifted before me, and I went still as more figures came out onto the deck behind West. His furious gaze was fixed on me.

"Fable!" Koy's hoarse roar sounded again below, but West didn't budge. His stare didn't wander.

"Forty coppers to take me to the Narrows." I lifted my hand between us, where the heavy purse was still tied to my fist.

West stiffened, a storm of thoughts lighting in his eyes before he took hold of my arm again and shoved me backward. "Get off my ship."

I bit down hard on my lip, the sting of tears reigniting behind my eyes. I was going to have to give him everything. "Fifty-two coppers and two good pieces of pyre for passage," I panted. "Please."

"We're traders. We don't sell passage." West said, his hands clenching into fists at his sides.

That was a lie and we both knew it. Traders sold passage all the time.

West's eyes fell to my busted lip, and I watched the tick of his jaw. I could still feel the dried blood, tight over the skin on my face. "What'd you get yourself into?" He looked over the railing to Koy, who was pacing the dock below, waiting for me.

I reached back slowly, taking the knife from my belt. In one motion, I slid the blade between my palm and the purse, cutting it free before I pushed it into his chest.

"I'm not taking you anywhere," his voice ground like wet sand against stone.

I swallowed hard, grateful for the dark. I could feel the flush beneath my skin, the traitorous tears pooling in my eyes. "All right. There's at least one helmsman on these docks who will take fifty-two coppers." I clamped the blade of my knife between my teeth and slung one foot over the side, reaching for the ladder.

West's shoulders tensed, and he let out a long breath, his grip tightening on the rail. "Wait."

I froze, one tear falling down my cheek. He looked over me, to the other ships anchored down the dock before he turned back toward the water.

"West," the girl said, her tone tipping down in a warning.

The profile of his angled face sharpened against the moonlight as he looked at her. He cursed as he held a hand out to me. "Give me the copper."

My mouth dropped open. "What?"

"What?" The word was echoed by someone else on the deck I couldn't see.

West ignored him. "The copper," he said again, more slowly.

I jumped back down from the rail. "Fifty-two coppers and two pieces of pyre for passage to Ceros," I repeated the terms, the desperation in my voice not hidden.

"Done."

I took his hand into mine and shook on it, but the girl beside me was staring up at him, her head tilted in disbelief.

"You better not ever come back here, Fable!" Koy shouted, and I flinched as my hand fell from West's. "If I ever see your face on this island again, I'll tie you to the east reef! I'll watch the flesh rot from your bones!"

I watched him walk back down the dock, disappearing in the dark. It wasn't until I turned back to the faces of the crew standing on the deck of the *Marigold* that I realized what I'd done.

I'd made it off Jeval.

‹‹›

SIX

‹▲›

Lightning illuminated the clouds above the *Marigold*, splintering into a spiderweb of light. The edge of the storm reached the barrier islands in the dark, a cold mist blowing in with the wind. The ship rocked against it, the lantern swinging in the girl's fist as she held it up before her.

"Last I checked, we voted as a crew." Her gaze dragged from my head to my bare feet.

West ignored her, tossing my purse into the air, and a young man with spectacles caught it in both hands behind him. The lantern light reflected off the wide, round lenses as he looked up at me.

"I'm with Willa." Another man with dark hair pulled back from his face stepped forward. "I didn't hear you ask us if we wanted to take on a passenger."

I stayed in the shadow of the quarterdeck, clutching my tool belt to my chest. Four crew members stood before the mainmast, waiting for an answer from West. But he seemed to be measuring his words carefully, the silence pulling tight with the tension between them.

"It's fifty-two coppers." West looked at the girl.

She half laughed. "You can't be serious. What do we care about fifty-two coppers? We've never taken a single passenger on this ship in over two years, and I don't see why we should start now."

The man with the glasses stood watching, his eyes shifting back and forth between them. From the look of the ink-stained fingertips curled around my purse, I guessed he was their coin master. To him, it wouldn't matter that I'd just been a breath away from being gutted by Koy or that they'd been trading with me for the last two years. It was his job to make sure they didn't get involved in other people's business, good or bad.

"What is this, West?" A third man with skin the color of obsidian came down the steps beside me, one hand raking over his shaved head.

"It's copper," West snapped. "You have a problem with that?"

The girl they called Willa stared at West, her wide eyes expressionless. "Actually, I do."

West turned to the coin master, his irritation visible in the hard set of his jaw. "Divide it among the crew, Hamish. I won't report it. Drink your weight in rye when we get to Dern or buy yourself a new pair of boots. I don't care what you do with it."

That seemed to satisfy them for now, a hush falling over the deck. But the suspicion was still there in their side glances to one another. They weren't going to argue with pocketing my coin, especially if it wasn't going into the ship's log. But they didn't like the idea of me being on the *Marigold*, and they didn't care if I knew it.

"Fifty-two coppers, five ways," Hamish spoke beneath his breath, as if repeating the words made the decision final.

I glanced up to the two masts of the ship. I'd never been on deck or seen the rest of them, I'd only ever met West on the dock when they stopped in Jeval. From the looks of it, they crewed this ship with only five sets of hands, but a vessel like this should take at least ten crew members, maybe twelve.

"Four ways," West corrected. "I don't want a share."

Hamish gave a single nod, and I studied West's face, trying to read him. But there was no hint there of what he was thinking.

"You just said you took her on for the copper." Willa glared at him.

He met her narrowed gaze, jerking his head in my direction before turning on his heel. His boots knocked against the deck as he walked past them and disappeared through an open door.

Willa let out a long breath, watching the darkened archway before she finally looked back at me. I cringed as the soft lantern light shifted to illuminate the other side of her face. Her left cheek was raw and pink, the skin healing from a bad burn. It reached up the length of her neck and over her jaw, coming to a point.

I knew exactly what it was. I'd seen wounds like that before—a long knife held over a fire until the blade glowed and pressed to someone's face to teach a lesson. It was a punishment meant to humiliate you long after the pain subsided. Whatever crime she'd committed, she'd been made to pay for it.

It wasn't until I looked her in the eye that I realized she was watching me inspect the mutilation. "Come on." She dropped the lantern so that she was cloaked again in darkness and pushed past me into the archway.

I looked back once more, to the dock below. Koy would make it back to the beach any minute, and Speck wouldn't wake from his rye-soaked stupor to find his boat gone until morning. Either way, I'd never see him or this island again.

I hoped.

The crew watched me as I pushed off the railing and followed Willa into the narrow passage, the weight of their stares pinned to my back. The handle of the lantern squeaked ahead, and I followed its light down the wooden steps and into the thick smell of pickled fish and over-ripened fruit. The crest of the *Marigold* was burned into the three doors that lined the wall. I lifted a finger as I passed, tracing the outline of a flower inside a wreath of leafed branches. In the center of the bloom lay a tiny, five-pointed star.

As a little girl sailing on my father's trading ship, I knew every trader's crest. But I'd never seen this one until the *Marigold* showed up two years ago on the barrier islands, looking to trade for pyre. Wherever they had come from, they had to be a low-rung crew just beginning to get their route established. But how they'd managed to get a ship and a license from the Trade Council was a question that couldn't have a simple answer.

Willa pushed through an open doorway and hung the lantern on a rusted hook driven into the wall. I ducked inside, where patchwork hammocks swung from low-hanging beams in a small cabin.

"This is where you'll sleep." Willa leaned into one of the posts, her eyes trailing over me until they stopped, and I looked down to see she was eyeing the tip of the scar peeking out beneath my sleeve. "It'll be a few days before we get to Ceros. We have to make a stop in Dern first."

I nodded, keeping my back to the wall.

"Do you need to eat?"

"No," I lied. I'd eaten only a single perch in two days, but I wasn't stupid. She was trying to get me to owe them something.

"Good." She smirked. "Because our stryker's only stocked enough food to feed this crew. When you do need to eat, you'll be expected to work for it."

And there it was—the hook. I knew how this worked because I'd grown up on a ship. I'd known what game I'd have to play since I'd first made the plan to use the *Marigold* to get off Jeval, but I hadn't counted on having nothing to barter with. I would have to keep my head down and do whatever was asked of me to pay the price of getting to Ceros.

But the way the girl looked at me now made me feel unsteady on my feet. I'd already gotten on the wrong side of the crew, and if I didn't figure out a way to fix it, I'd find myself overboard before we crossed the Narrows.

I ducked below the bulkhead and found a hammock only half-hung, one end touching the wet ground. The wood and iron trunks lining the walls were bolted neatly into place, all secured with locks except for one, where the slow drip of water trickled in between the slats overhead. It sat open, a small, rusted chisel inside. Above it, a pair of boots hung by their laces on a crooked nail. Maybe the crew's dredger.

Willa took the lantern from the wall and walked back into the passageway; the gleam of the jeweled dagger tucked into the back of her belt. She climbed the stairs, leaving me in the pitch-black as the sound of footsteps trailed across the deck. I secured the other end of the hammock on an iron hook and climbed in, my weight sinking into the thick, damp quilt.

The hum of the sea hugging the hull was the only sound except for the faint vibration of voices above. I pulled the musty air into my lungs, listening to the groan of the wood and the slosh of water. And suddenly, I was that little girl again, swaying in my hammock on the *Lark*.

I'd been asleep on my father's ship when I heard the sharp ring of the bell echo out into the night. Only a few minutes later, the loud crack of the mast and the howl of an angry wind was followed by screaming. His hands had found me in the dark, his face peering down at me in the little sliver of moonlight coming from the slats above.

The night the *Lark* sank. The night my mother died.

And in a single moment, everything changed.

The next day, he left me behind on Jeval.

I reached into the tiny pocket I'd sewn into the waist of my pants, prying the last of my coppers free. I hadn't given them *every* copper. Those six coins were the very first I'd ever earned, and I'd never spent them. I'd saved them for the most desperate of moments. Now, they were all I had left. But six coppers would only keep me fed and sheltered for a day or so in the city. If we were stopping in Dern, it would be my only chance to try and multiply my coin before we reached Ceros. If I didn't, I'd have to show up on Saint's doorstep empty-handed—something I swore to myself I'd never do.

A board creaked in the passageway, and my hand went straight to my belt, pulling my knife free. I stared into the shapeless, empty dark, waiting for another sound as I tucked the coppers back into the little pocket. But there was only the thrum of the storm creeping toward Jeval. The knock of a door closing as the ship tilted. I clutched the knife to my chest, listening.

Only a few days.

That's how much longer I had to survive. Then, I'd be at my father's door, asking him for what he promised me. What he owed me.

I reached beneath the sleeve of my shirt, finding the thickly roped scar that was carved into my arm. My finger followed it up like a maze of blood-filled veins in a pattern I had memorized. It was my father who'd given it to me, the day he left me on Jeval. I had watched in horror as he dragged the tip of his knife through my flesh without so much as a twitch of his hand. I told myself it was the madness of losing my mother that made him do it. That his mind had been fractured by grief.

But I remembered the soft set of his mouth as he cut me. The way his head tilted to the side as my blood ran over his fingers. I'd done nothing since the last time I saw him but dream of the moment I'd see him again. I'd thought of nothing else. And now that it was so close, my stomach turned, my pulse skipping unevenly. The man who'd taught me to tie knots and read maps wasn't the same man who'd put the knife soaked with my blood back into his belt and sailed away.

Soon, I'd be in Ceros. And I wasn't sure anymore which man I would find.

SEVEN

The sharp ping of a pulley hitting the deck jolted me from sleep. I blinked, rubbing at my eyes as the cabin came into view. The hammock swung back and forth as an empty bottle on the ground rolled over the wood planks, and I sat up, unfolding myself from the fraying fabric.

I braced myself on the wall, moving through the passageway slowly and squinting against the bright sunlight of midday coming down the steps. The crew was already well into their duties when I stepped out onto the deck. I turned in a circle, a lump coming up in my throat as I looked out to sea. In every direction, there was only blue. Only the hard line of the horizon and the wind and the saltwater thick in the air.

I leaned out over the railing, listening to the bilge cut through the water in a familiar whisper. A smile pulled at my lips, igniting the pain of the torn skin, and I reached up, touching the hot, swollen cut.

The feeling of eyes on me made me look up to where Willa sat in a sling high on the foremast with an adze in one hand. The thin, arched blade was set into a wooden handle at a right angle with one blunt end used as a hammer. It was the tool of a ship's bosun—the member of the crew who kept the ship afloat.

"Move."

I jumped, pressing my back against the rail before I looked up to see the young man with shorn hair and smooth obsidian skin standing over me with a case in his hands.

"Out of the way, dredger," he muttered, shoving past me.

"Where are we at on time, Paj?" West stepped into the open breezeway, stopping midstride when he saw me.

"Checking now." The man he called Paj set the case down at his feet, and the sunlight hit the bronze octant inside as he opened it. He was as broad as he was tall, the sleeves of his shirt too short for his long arms.

I looked between him and West, confused until I realized he must be the *Marigold*'s navigator. But he was too young to hold a position like that. Really, they were all too young to be anything other than deckhands. They were boys on the edge of being men.

Paj took the octant from the velvet lining carefully, bringing the eyepiece up and pointing the scope toward the horizon. The sunlight reflected off the little mirrors as he slid the arm forward and adjusted the knobs. After a moment, he stilled, doing the calculations in his head.

West leaned into the doorway, waiting. Behind him, I

could see the corner of a desk and a pair of framed windows behind a neatly made cot. It was the helmsman's quarters.

Paj lowered the octant, looking back at West. "The storm only put us half a day behind. We can make it up if the wind stays strong and Willa keeps the sails together."

"The sails are fine," she snapped, glaring down at us from where she was suspended on the boom.

West gave Paj a sharp nod before he disappeared into his quarters, closing the door behind him.

"Blasted birds!" Willa shouted, covering her head with her arms as an albatross hovered beside the sail. It picked up one of the twisted locks of her hair before she swatted it away.

At the top of the mainmast, the one with the long, dark hair laughed. He was perched in the lines with bare feet, holding a wooden bowl in his hands. The birds were gathered around him, their wings flapping against the wind as they fished out whatever was inside.

He was sowing good fortune for the ship, honoring the dead who had drowned in these waters. My father had always told me that seabirds were the souls of lost traders. To turn them away or not give them a place to land or nest was bad luck. And anyone who dared to sail the Narrows needed every bit of luck they could get.

Boots hit the deck behind me, and I turned to see Willa unbuckling the sling from around her waist. Her hair was twisted like rope in long, bronze strands falling over her shoulders, and in the light, her skin was the color of the tawny sandstone that crumbled over the cliffs of Jeval.

"I'm Fable," I said, reaching out a hand to her.

She only stared at it as she threw the sling over her shoulder. The burn on her face unfolded over her jaw, coming to a perfect point on her cheek. "You think because I'm the only girl on this ship that I want to be your friend?"

I dropped my hand. "No."

"Then get out of my way." She said the words through a bitter smile, waiting for me to move aside.

I took a step toward the mainmast, and she climbed the steps to the quarterdeck without looking back. It was only then that I got a good look at the ship.

The *Marigold* was a lorcha, just small enough to maneuver in the storms that haunted these waters, but with a hull big enough to hold decent inventory for a small trade operation. Its unique sails were what made the ship easy to spot out on the sea—like sheets of white canvas with wooden ribs, their shapes arced a bit like bat's wings. Saint's ship, the *Lark*, had been much bigger with five times as many crew. But the smell of stained wood and salty rope was something that was on every ship.

If I closed my eyes, I could almost imagine I was there again. My mother up in the masts. Saint at the helm. But the memory wasn't painted in the brilliant colors it once had been. Not like my memories of Jeval.

Every day I'd watched the green ridge of the island lifting up from the water in a slant, reaching for the sky before it dropped down at the cliffs. The trees below hid the hovels of the dredgers, but the smoke from their fires lifted up in twisting, white strands. I tried to carve the memory out of my mind. The crystal, teal waters. The way the wind sounded moving through the branches.

I didn't want to remember it.

"Time to pay rent."

I turned back against the wind. The young man who'd been at the top of the mast was suddenly beside me, half of his thick hair unraveling from where it was pulled back. His dark lashes rimmed gray eyes set against a warm ivory complexion. Altogether, he had the coloring of driftwood. He stood with a pile of nets in his arms, the rope crusted white with dry salt.

"Rent? I already paid West."

"That was for passage. If you want to sleep in that hammock, it'll be an extra charge." He winked, his deep voice turning the words up just slightly at the ends. He was trying to hide the accent, but I could hear it. He wasn't born in the Narrows. "And West told me to see to that." His hand lifted, gesturing toward my face.

"So that you can add it to my tab?" I said, sucking the swollen lip between my teeth. "It's fine."

He turned, not waiting for me to follow. "Come on."

I matched his gait, trying to keep up, and I saw him glance down at my bare feet on the hot deck. They were callused from the years walking on the sunbaked beach. Boots were a luxury I hadn't been able to afford, but more than that, they didn't have much use on Jeval.

He led me up the stairs to the quarterdeck, dropping the nets in a heaping pile at my feet. "I assume you know how to mend nets." He didn't wait for me to answer, handing me a white bone needle before he went back to the stack of crab traps.

The truth was that I didn't know anything about nets. I'd only fished with traps and lines on the island because there hadn't been anyone willing to teach me how to make them.

He unclamped the trap at his feet and got to work. I wasn't going to tell him that I'd never used a needle or that entrusting me with the nets would probably mean losing fish. Instead, I sat and acted like I knew exactly what I was doing.

Finding the breaks was easy enough. The fraying, splitting strands of rope were scattered but numerous. I set the needle on the deck beside me and inspected the knots, turning the net over to see every side before I cut away the damaged bits.

"You're the stryker," I said, not really meaning it as a question. The only one who handled the nets and traps on the *Lark* when I was growing up was the crew member responsible for feeding everyone. If West asked him to stitch up my lip, he was probably also entrusted with tending to wounds and sickness.

"I'm Auster." He tossed a piece of broken wood overboard. "Ceros, huh?"

My hands stilled on the net, but he didn't look up from the traps. "That's right," I answered, pulling the threads free.

"You had enough of dredging on Jeval?"

I threaded the twine through the needle and pulled to tighten it. "Sure."

That seemed to be enough for him. He pried the broken latch from the trap and replaced it with a new one as I compared the nets to try and find out how the knots were made. We worked in the long afternoon hours, and it only took me a few tries to figure out how to stretch the net to weave the needle left to right, tightening the new sections. I caught Auster watching my hands more than once, but he said nothing, pretending not to notice each time I pulled the wrong way or missed a loop and had to redo it.

Paj reappeared below, taking the helm with West at his side, and I watched as they bore the ship east. They talked in hushed voices, West's eyes on the horizon, and I studied the sky.

"I thought we were going to Dern," I said, looking to Auster.

His gaze narrowed at me as he looked up from the trap. "If I were you, I wouldn't ask questions you don't need the answers to."

West and Paj talked at the helm for another few minutes, watching the others climb up the masts to adjust the sails. They were changing course.

I worked on the nets until we were losing the daylight and the air turned cool, soothing my hot skin. My back and shoulders ached, my fingers starting to blister, but I finished off the line of knots I was working before I let Auster take them.

He inspected my work carefully before he gave a tight nod and went down to the main deck where Willa and Paj sat together at the prow with bowls of stew. Willa's feet hung over the edge, her boots kicking against the wind, and my stomach turned at the smell of cooked fish.

Night fell over the sea, painting the *Marigold* black except for the white sails stretched against the dark, clouded sky. The stars and moon hid, giving no sign of where the sea ended and the sky began, and I liked the feeling. Like we were floating in the air. The west wind was warm, finding its way onto the ship before it ran back to the wake on the water behind us.

My teeth clenched against the hunger in my belly, but I couldn't afford to spend a single copper, and both Willa and Auster had made it clear that nothing would be given for free. I slipped past them in the dark, stopping before the steps that led below deck. The soft glow of candlelight spilled through the crack in the door to my right, and I watched a shadow move over the floor as a heavy hand landed on my shoulder. I spun, pulling my knife free in one motion to hold it ready at my side. The young man with the spectacles from last night looked down at me, only half-lit by moonlight. "You're Fable."

My grip on the knife loosened.

"I'm Hamish, coin master of the *Marigold*." His reddened cheeks looked as if his skin wasn't suited for the wind and sun of sailing. "You put one finger on anything that doesn't belong to you on this ship, and I will know."

I lifted my chin. Most people in the Narrows were cut from the same tattered cloth, but even the lowest rungs of society had its castoffs. Jeval was the only bit of land between the Narrows and the Unnamed Sea, and it had become a sort of catchall for those who either couldn't outrun their reputations or had too many enemies on the mainland to stay below notice. Among traders, they were known as thieves.

I pulled the sleeve of my shirt down instinctively, making sure my scar was covered. Traders were even more superstitious than Jevalis, and the last thing I needed was for them to start wondering if I was going to draw the eye of sea demons. The first storm we saw could get me thrown overboard.

I could live with the crew not liking me, but if they were *afraid* of me, I was in real trouble.

Hamish reached around me for the door, and it swung open on creaking hinges.

Inside, West was bent over a table of unrolled maps with a cup of something steaming hot in one hand, where the gold ring on one of his fingers caught the light. Hamish stepped into the small room, coming to his side with a rolled parchment and a black feather quill.

"Thank you," West muttered, stilling when his gaze travelled to the door and he spotted me.

"I—" But the words sputtered out, my heart coming up into my throat. I wasn't sure what I'd even meant to say.

West jerked his chin to the door and Hamish obeyed, moving past me without a word and disappearing in the dark breezeway.

"What is it?" West set the cup down on the map, turning the ring on his finger as he stepped in front of the desk. I didn't miss the way he stood in front of the maps so I couldn't see what was on them.

"I wanted to thank you." I stood a little taller.

"For what?"

My brow pulled. "For taking me on."

"You paid for passage," he said flatly.

"I-I know," I stuttered, "but I know you didn't want to—"

"Look," he cut me off. "You don't owe me anything. And I want to be clear"—he met my eyes for a long moment—"I don't owe *you* anything."

"I didn't say—"

"You put me in a bad position by coming to the docks last night. One I didn't ask for." A sharp edge cut into the smooth current of his voice.

I knew what he meant. His crew didn't approve of his decision to give me passage. Now, he'd have to square it with them somehow. "I'm sorry."

"I don't need an apology. I need you off my ship. As soon as we get to Ceros, you're gone."

In the entire time I'd been trading with West, he'd never said as many words. He'd always been cold, his words clipped and his manner impatient. His gaze had always jumped around the docks, never landing on me, but it did now. His eyes met mine for the length of a breath before they dropped to the floor between us.

"I didn't know it would cost you anything," I said, my voice softer than I meant it to be.

"It did. It will." He sighed, dragging one hand over his face. "While you're on this ship, you'll pull your weight. If someone asks you to do something, you do it without question."

I nodded, biting the inside of my cheek as I tried to decide whether to ask him. "Why are we headed north?"

"If you want me to approve our route with you, it'll cost you another fifty coppers." He walked toward me, closing the distance between us. "When we make port in Ceros and you set foot on that dock, I don't want to see you again."

I opened my mouth to speak, but he was already closing the door in my face, the latch rattling into place.

The words stung, and I wasn't sure why. He'd bought my pyre for the last two years, but West and I weren't friends. He was right that he didn't owe me anything, but when I'd run down that dock screaming his name, he'd saved my life. And somehow, I'd known he would.

Something had made him take the copper and go against his crew. Something changed his mind. Really, I didn't care what it was. West didn't want me on the *Marigold,* but the fact was that I was finally on my way to Ceros. That was all that mattered.

EIGHT

My knuckles bled as I wound the heavy ropes into neat stacks at the foot of the foremast. I'd been working since before dawn, stowing the stays as Paj changed them out with new lines. Both the foremast and the mainmast had been strained in the storm on the way to Jeval, and the weakened ropes might not hold if another came. And it would.

We were still sailing north, almost half a day off course on the route to Dern. It had been a number of years since I was on the water, but I still knew how to navigate by starlight, and I'd spent half the night out on the deck, mapping out the sea in my mind. The only two directions to sail from Jeval were north into the Narrows or south to the Unnamed Sea.

I'd never been to the Unnamed Sea, but my mother was born there. Her leathered skin and callused hands made her look as if she'd grown up on a ship, but she'd come to the Narrows on her own when she was no more than my age, finding a place on Saint's crew as a dredger and leaving her past in the Unnamed Sea behind. She would wrap her arms around me as we sat up on the mast with our feet dangling, and she would tell me about Bastian, the port city she called home, and the huge ships that sailed those deep waters.

Once, I asked her if she'd ever go back. If she'd take me there one day. But she only said that she'd been born for a different life, and so had I.

My bare foot slid on the wet deck as the *Marigold* slowed, and I looked up to see Hamish, Willa, and Auster taking up the sails. Paj didn't even look up from his work, tossing another pile of rope onto the deck. It landed in front of me as the door to the helmsman's quarters opened and West came out of the breezeway.

He buttoned his jacket up to his throat, pulling a cap onto his head as he climbed the steps to the quarterdeck. From the look of him, we were headed into port. But we were in the middle of nowhere, hugging the edge of the waters that opened to the Unnamed Sea. Hamish followed on his heels, and as if he could feel my stare, he looked over his shoulder at me, his eyes narrowed in warning.

I dropped my gaze back to the ropes, watching from the corner of my eye as Auster unlocked the anchor and loosed the lines along the railing. Willa and Hamish worked the pulleys to the rowboat secured to the back of the ship and when it was free, West climbed down.

I set the next coil of rope down and leaned over the starboard side to look down the length of the ship. In the distance, a cluster of small coral islands sat atop the clear blue water like a pile of stacked stones. Below, West turned the rowboat about, leaning back and pulling the oars to his chest as it drifted away.

But the little islands were stark and bare, the coral whitewashed by the sun. I watched West disappear behind them. He'd gotten into the boat with nothing, and from the looks of it, there was nothing on the skeleton enclave.

"Eyes on the deck, dredger," Paj muttered, throwing more rope toward me.

I obeyed, taking the lines up and dragging them to the foremast, but Paj's eyes didn't leave me.

He crossed his arms over his chest so that his shirt pulled across the expanse of his shoulders, watching as I carefully wound the rope and knotted its end. "We cast bets, you know."

I shook out my hands as I stood, stretching my fingers and then clenching them. The raw skin stung as it pulled over the bone. "On what?"

"How long it will take you to steal something." He grinned.

I realized then that Paj, too, had an accent that curled his words just slightly. But he was much better at hiding it than Auster.

Willa looked down at us from the quarterdeck as she locked the anchor's crank, Hamish behind her.

"I'm not a thief," I said. "You want to check my belt? Go ahead."

"You wouldn't be stupid enough to keep it in your belt, would you? Dredgers are cheats, but they aren't stupid,"

Auster spoke from behind me, and I turned, pressing myself against the mast.

All four of them stared at me as a silence stretched over the ship, leaving only the sound of the wind sliding over the canvas sails above us. They were baiting me, pulling at my edges to see what I was made of. And I didn't blame them. They had no reason to trust me, and their helmsman had taken me on without asking them.

"I don't care what you've got in your hull or what's written in your ledgers. I just need to get across the Narrows," I said.

"You're lying." Paj took a step forward, standing a whole head taller than me. "Not that you can help it. It's in the Jevali's nature."

"I'm not Jevali," I said. "And I'm not a thief."

Auster threw the last trap over the side and it splashed in the water below. "The last person who stole from us is at the bottom of the sea." His long, raven hair was unbound, falling over his shoulder. He raked it back, tying it as he came down the steps to the deck.

"Look, I'm going to go ahead and give you some coin before you steal it." Paj reached into the pocket of his vest, pulling out a single copper.

Willa leaned against the foremast, watching.

Paj held the copper up between us, pinched between his fingers. "This is what you want, right?"

I gritted my teeth, trying to read him. Wherever this was headed, it wasn't good. And with their helmsman off ship, this crew would take liberties.

He snapped his fingers and the coin flew into the air, over the side, before it plunked into the water below.

"How deep are we, Auster?" Paj didn't look at him as he asked it, his smug gaze still set on me.

Amusement lit on Auster's face as he answered. "I'd say about four hundred and eighty feet. Maybe five hundred."

Hamish's spectacles scrunched up on his nose as he lifted one hand to smooth the combed, sandy hair at his brow. "Guess I was wrong, Paj. Looks like there are some things a dredger won't do for coin."

Willa still stood silently behind them, the look in her eyes different from the others. It was more curiosity than suspicion. As if she could hear me thinking it, her head tilted to the side.

They were trying to put me in my place. Trying to degrade me. Because with traders, everything was a test. Everything was an attempt to measure you.

I met Paj's eyes as I pulled my shirt over my head and dropped it on the deck.

"What are you doing?" His brow pulled as he watched me climb the railing.

I stood against the wind, watching the movement of the water around the coral islands. It pushed up the shelf gently, and if it was as calm beneath the surface as it was above, I could do the dive in just minutes. I'd made deeper descents more times than I could count.

Hamish leaned over the starboard side as I jumped, falling through the air before I plunged into the cold water in a cloud of bubbles. When I broke the surface, all four of the crew were watching from above, Paj's eyes wide.

My chest filled with the warm wind, and I pushed it out in a long hiss over and over until my lungs felt pliable enough to hold the air I needed. I tipped my head back, sipping in just a little more before I dove, kicking toward the seafloor.

The ash-white coral above the water was only the corpse of what lay below, where steep walls of the vibrant reef were filled with life. Bubble coral, spiny sponges, and urchins covered every inch beneath schools of colorful fish, and I watched the airy climb of an octopus scale the shoal as I sank down.

The surface stopped tugging at me once I'd dropped deep enough, and I let myself drop with my arms out around me, falling between beams of sunlight casting through the water.

The *Marigold* shrank to a dark spot far above me, and I watched the silt for the shine of copper, kicking in a circle as I neared the bottom. Challenging me to find a single coin on the seafloor had been an arrogant ploy meant to humiliate me. But these bastard traders didn't know me. Or what I could do.

Copper was a mineral, not a gemstone. But it had a language, like anything else. I stilled, listening for the tinny ring of it. I sifted through the sounds of the reef until a faint resonance made me turn. A flash lit in my peripheral vision, and I blinked, turning to see the sparkle play against the light. But it was too far from the ship in these clear, still waters. The coin should have fallen through the water in only a slightly diagonal path.

I turned myself around, studying the fronds of coral swaying back and forth gently. And it hit me, sinking in the pit of my stomach, just as the pull of the water brushed the bottom of my feet.

A current.

But it was too late. The tide swallowed me, yanking me down and jetting me over the seafloor like the tow of a ship. I kicked, trying to break from its grasp, but it only dragged me faster. The coral raced by and a stream of air slipped from my lips as I screamed, my hands sliding over the bottom and kicking up a trail of dust in my wake.

The *Marigold* pulled farther away from me, and I twisted, searching for something to grab as the current slammed me into the reef.

The coral scraped across my back and over my shoulder, tumbling me over the ridges before I found a hold. The cold water rushed past me, pushing my hair back from my face, and I pulled myself up. My muscles screamed, the weakness deepening in my limbs until my hands were shaking on the holds. My skin was already on fire, where the poison of the coral was seeping into my bloodstream.

I pulled myself along the wall until I was out of the current, and clung to the shelf, trying to force my heartbeat to slow behind my ribs before it ate up all the air inside of me. The undertow had carried me at least a hundred feet and I would need to surface fast.

I kicked up away from the grasp of the tide, but a soft glimmer on the seafloor made me stop, my fingers clutching to the sharp rock. I looked up to the *Marigold* above, cursing, and another bubble of air wriggled up through the water. I wasn't going back up with nothing.

I crawled back down, holding on to the reef until I was back in the current, and inched along until I reached the place I'd seen the flicker of light. The stream pushed against me as I raked an open hand into the sand, and when I brought it back up, the current pulled the grains through my fingers until the coin was sitting in the center of my palm.

The ladder was already unrolled when I broke the surface and I gasped, my chest aching with the feeling of the bones caving in. I pulled myself up the rope rungs and dropped myself over the railing, where the crew was still waiting.

A grin was pulled up the side of Auster's face as my feet hit the deck. I walked straight to Paj, blood rolling down my wet skin from the cuts on my shoulder and dripping onto the deck in a trail.

Hamish muttered something, shaking his head.

"Thought we'd lost you, dredger." Paj smirked from where he stood behind the helm, but the nerves were showing beneath the calm of his face. I didn't know what West would do if he knew what they were up to, but I could see that Paj was wondering.

I stopped before the wheel, opening my hand between us. His mouth dropped open before he uncrossed his arms, standing up straighter. "What the . . ."

My hand tipped, letting the coin fall to the deck with a ping, and I looked up into his eyes without a word. Behind him, Willa's look had turned from curiosity to inquiry, a question playing in her eyes.

I turned on my heel, shoving past Paj to the steps that led below deck, and muffled voices sounded through the passageway as I slammed the door of the cabin closed behind me. Suddenly, every bit of pain in my back awoke, the sting of blood making my stomach turn. I stumbled to the pail in the corner, falling to my knees and shaking with cold before I retched.

Four years on Jeval and this close to Ceros, I almost drowned on a dive for a single copper. But that was one of Saint's rules.

Nothing is free.

He wasn't just talking about food or passage or the clothes on your back. He was talking about respect. Safety. Protection. They were things no one owed you.

And one way or another, you always paid.

NINE

The pain searing under my skin almost made me forget how hungry I was.

I'd been stung by coral many times, so I knew what was coming. Fever would spread and my bones would ache for a few days, but that was better than welcoming more taunting from the *Marigold*'s crew. If I made myself easy prey, taunting could turn into something much more deadly.

I cracked the shell of another crab on the table, the nausea in my belly twisting. As soon as Auster pulled the traps from the water, he'd dropped one at my feet and walked away. I stood in the breezeway, my hands numb from working the spiny shells. But I'd cleaned an infinite number of crabs in my lifetime, and even if it was a job no one wanted, I could do it with my eyes closed.

Hamish went to the bow, peering over the water, and I looked around the corner to see West coming around the coral islands. He'd been gone long enough for the sun to drop halfway down the sky, but the hull still looked empty.

Auster and Paj hoisted the little boat back into place on the stern and secured it. A moment later, West was coming over the side. He unbuttoned his jacket, letting it slide off his shoulders as he came into the breezeway, and he stopped short when he saw me, his gaze hardening as his eyes ran from my face, down my back.

"What happened?" His teeth clenched on the words.

Behind him, Paj reached up, rubbing a hand over his shaved head, the faintest flicker of uneasiness in the set of his shoulders. And I wasn't sure why. If I'd drowned in the current, it wouldn't be West's problem. Or maybe this was a test too.

"Slipped on the jib and fell into the shrouds," I said, turning my back to him.

The feel of his stare crawled over my skin as I dropped another empty shell into the bucket at my feet. He disappeared into his quarters, and I let out a long breath, pinching my eyes closed against the sting creeping up my neck.

When I opened them again, Auster was standing beside the table, setting a bowl down in front of me as I picked up another pair of crab legs.

I eyed the steaming stew, swallowing hard. "I'm not hungry."

"You work, you eat. It's fair," he said, sliding the bowl closer to me.

I looked up, studying his face. There was no hint of a trick in his eyes, but some people were better at hiding them than others. Anyone who looked at me could probably see that I was starving, but I couldn't afford to owe anyone anything else.

"You've cleaned an entire crate of crab. It's a square trade." He picked up one of the pails and walked away, leaving me alone in the breezeway.

My hand tightened around the edge of the worktable as I leaned into it, thinking. The truth was that it didn't matter why he was giving me the food. I needed to eat, especially if I had days of fever ahead of me.

I dropped the mallet and took the bowl into my shaking hands, sipping carefully. The salt and herbs stung the broken skin around my lip, but the broth warmed my insides and I groaned. The taste of it resurrected a string of faded, frayed memories that made the knot in my stomach tighten, and I blinked them away before they could fully take shape. I fished a soft bit of potato out of the stew with dirty fingers, dropping it into my mouth and letting it break in my mouth until it burned my tongue.

My eyes went to the closed door of the helmsman's quarters, and I wondered if West knew Auster was feeding me. He'd been clear he didn't owe me anything. Maybe a bowl of stew for a couple days of work didn't count, like Auster said. Or maybe he pitied me. The thought made me want to not take another bite.

I poured the last of the liquid into my mouth, my stomach already sore from being too full, and got back to work. Once the last of the crab was finished, I went down the steps with another pail in my arms. The creak of the hull was the only sound in the shadowed passageway, where the three doors lined the walls, each one marked with the *Marigold's* crest.

"In here." Auster's voice sounded in the darkness of the cabin, and I looked up to see the flash of his eyes as the lantern swung on the hook. He unfolded himself from his hammock and met me at the door.

The same grin still wrinkled the corners of his eyes as he pulled at the chain that held the keys around his neck, making him even more handsome than he already was. The cut of his body was lean, covered in skin the color of faded wheat, and I'd thought more than once that I'd glimpsed a kindness in Auster's face that I hadn't seen in the others. The sleeves of his shirt were rolled up, revealing a black-inked tattoo on his forearm of an intricate knot. It took a moment to realize that it was two snakes intertwined, each one eating the other's tail. It was a symbol I'd never seen before.

He stopped at the first door, fitting one of the keys into the rusted iron lock that hung from the latch before he kicked it open. I followed him inside, and the cracks of sunlight illuminated a small supply room packed with tarred barrels of water and crates of food. Blue and amber glass jars lined the walls on shelves, and drying, salted meat swung from hooks hanging from the bulkhead. I lifted the bucket up to set it down on the workbench when the pop of floorboards overhead made me look up. I could see movement between them as shadows slid between the cracks. It was the helmsman's quarters.

I stepped closer to the wall, leaning forward to try and catch sight of West.

"That's all." Auster held the door open with one hand, waiting.

The heat burned under my skin as he glanced up to the bulkhead and I realized he'd caught me looking. I gave him a quick nod before I ducked out, and he set the latch into place. He'd fed me, but he wasn't going to take a chance in letting me linger in the supply room or get too comfortable with the lay of the ship. Really, he shouldn't. Being the stryker was a meticulous job, not only because they oversaw inventory and were tasked with filling the ship's supplies at port. He was also the hunter, trapper, and forager among them. I wouldn't trust a hungry dredger below deck either.

Willa was already in her hammock as I came through the door. I let the lid of the open trunk fall closed and sat on top of it, hissing when my back touched the wall.

She pulled the length of her hair over her shoulder, watching me. "What's a Jevali dredger want in the Narrows?"

"I'm wondering the same thing." I bristled as Paj appeared in the passageway, leaning into the doorpost. I hadn't even heard him come down the steps.

I looked between them, the prick of gooseflesh racing over my skin. They were curious and that made me nervous. Maybe I'd made a mistake, playing along with their games and diving for the copper. But if I played my cards right, I might be able to use it to get the information I needed. I just had to give them enough of the truth.

"I'm looking for someone," I said, leaning forward to prop my elbows on my knees.

Willa was the one to take the bait. "Who?"

I pulled the knife from my belt, poising its tip on the trunk beside me. I twirled it until it made a small hole in the wood. "A trader. His name is Saint."

Their eyes cut to each other as Willa sat up in the hammock, her feet swinging to the floor.

"What do you want with Saint?" Paj laughed, a brilliant smile stretching across his face, but the sound of it was uneasy.

That was where my father's rules came into play again. There was only one promise he had ever asked me to make. I roamed the ship as I liked, I explored the villages and docks and did as I pleased. As long as I didn't break that promise, I never fell out of his good graces.

I was to never tell a single soul that I was his daughter. That was it.

I'd never once broken it, and I wasn't going to start now.

"A job." I shrugged.

Willa leered at me. "You want to crew for *Saint*?" But corner of her mouth turned down as she realized I was serious. "As what? A dredger?"

"Why not?"

"Why not?" Paj's voice lifted. "Crewing for Saint is a death wish. Your chances were better on Jeval."

The cabin fell silent, and from the corner of my eye, I could see a flicker of light as Willa turn the dagger in her hand. The handle was set with faceted gems in every color, the intricate silver scrolling up toward the blade.

"How long have you two crewed for West?" I stood and climbed into my hammock carefully, biting my lip as the fabric brushed against the swollen scrapes on my shoulder.

"Since the beginning—two years," Paj answered easily, which surprised me. "When West got the *Marigold,* he took Hamish and Willa on. Me and Paj soon after."

But then I realized why he'd offered the information so readily. It was part of a story. And the only people in the Narrows who needed stories were the ones who had something to hide. Anything given freely was probably a lie.

I sank deeper into the hammock. "You're all so young," I said, though I meant it as a question.

"We were brought up together on different crews," Paj answered. "Waterside strays—all of us."

That bit could be true. At least, partly. But the accent in Paj and Auster's voices weren't from Ceros.

Willa's eyes dropped to her dagger. The stones set into the handle were sapphire and amethyst. Not the rarest of gems, but their sizes made them valuable. Far too valuable to be in the hands of a Waterside stray.

It was the way Saint had taught me to lie too—you always construct a lie from a truth. At least a few of them probably were Waterside strays. Trading crews often took on street kids who lived on Waterside of Ceros, offering food and training in exchange for dangerous labor. Most grew up to crew the ships they'd been brought up on, but I'd never heard of a Waterside stray becoming a helmsman.

Even more unbelievable was the idea that they'd been

able to secure a license to trade. There were five guilds that controlled almost every aspect of life in the Narrows—the Rye Guild, the Shipwrights Guild, the Sailmakers Guild, the Smiths Guild, and the Gem Guild. Each had a master, and the five guild masters sat on the Trade Council. They were the only ones who could grant traders the licenses they needed to do business at every port, and there was no way this crew had been able to get one on their own. Whoever West was, he had at least one powerful friend.

When I said nothing, Paj turned back into the passageway, leaving Willa and me alone. Her eyes were half-closed, and it occurred to me that I hadn't seen her sleep since I'd come onboard. I wasn't sure how any of them were able to, when it seemed as if each of them had three jobs instead of one.

"How long have you been dredging?" Willa asked, her voice growing quiet.

"Forever. My mother started teaching me to dive as soon as I could swim."

Saint always said she was the best dredger in the Narrows, and I believed him. He only took on the best, and the people who crewed his ships never left him. Not when they made more coin than anyone else in the Narrows.

But my mother had another reason.

I'd only ever seen Saint smile once, when I was spying on the two of them in his quarters. My mother took his hands from the maps he was working on and pulled his arms around her small frame. He set his chin on top of her head and smiled, and I remember thinking I'd never seen the spread of his teeth like that before. The frame of wrinkles around his eyes. He looked like a different person.

Saint broke his own rules when he fell in love with my mother. He broke them a hundred times over.

"Is she back on Jeval?"

I blinked, pushing the memory down. "No." I let the single word hang in the air, answering more parts to her question than she'd asked. Before she could ask another, I changed the subject. "So, you're the bosun?"

"That's right."

"Where'd you learn the trade?"

"Here and there."

I wasn't going to press. I didn't want to know any more about any of them than I needed to, and I didn't need them knowing anything about me either. I'd given away all I could afford to by telling them I was looking for Saint.

The best bosuns were usually women, able to climb high quickly and fit into small spaces. I'd always been bewildered, watching them from the main deck on the *Lark*. And there was no shortage of jobs for them, because every ship needed at least one.

The *Marigold* seemed to be getting by on the barest of crews—a helmsman, a coin master, a stryker, a bosun, and a navigator.

"You don't have a dredger," I said, eyeing the boots illuminated by a beam of sunlight on the wall.

Her voice dropped lower. "No. Not anymore."

The gooseflesh returned to my skin, the air in the cabin

feeling suddenly cold as I remembered what Auster said before I jumped the railing.

The last person who stole from us is at the bottom of the sea.

My eyes went back to the trunk against the wall, where the dredger's belt and tools were left behind.

Because he or she didn't need them anymore.

The unsettling silence that seemed to rise from Willa only confirmed it. She wanted me to put it together. She wanted me to know. I peered around the edge of my hammock, and she was still watching me, the dagger glinting in her hand.

TEN

Sunlight spilled through the cracks of the bulkhead above me, and the thick smell of lantern smoke and oil lingered in the cabin. As soon as my eyes opened, the ache in my jaw woke where I'd slammed into Koy's skiff. I pinched my eyes closed, the bone throbbing as I clenched my teeth. It was followed by the burn on my skin that wrapped over my shoulder and down my back.

I sat up slowly and set my feet on the damp floorboards. Willa's hammock was already empty.

Auster pried the lid off of a crate in the supply room as I passed the door, letting it fall on the ground before he started on another. He glanced over his shoulder at me, grunting as he pulled a jar of pickled fish from inside.

The humid wind spilled into the passageway as I climbed the ladder and I lifted a hand, letting it pull through my fingers. Warm but strong. I didn't like the feel of it. Too sharp for the pale, cloudless sky that hung above us, which meant that a storm was most likely brewing past the horizon.

Willa and Paj were already working the sheets, trimming the sails to accommodate the push.

"You're lazy, for a dredger." Her voice fell down on me from where she stood in the nets above. She had one foot tangled in the ropes and the other propped against the mast, the black shine of tar on her fingers.

"How far until Dern?" I watched her climb down to the next sail.

She looked over me, to the west. "We're here."

I turned to see the little port village sprawled over a hill in the distance, where the sea met the shore in a long, rocky wall.

A smile spread across my lips, a small laugh escaping my chest. I hadn't seen Dern in years, but I remembered it clearly—the misshapen cobblestone buildings and the blackened mouths of crooked chimneys. There was always a lady on the dock selling blood oranges and Saint's navigator, Clove, used to buy me one every time we made port.

The burn of tears lit behind my eyes as the memory flooded into the places I'd been so careful to keep damned up. I thought about Saint every day, his face coming to life in my mind as if it hadn't been four years since the last time I'd seen him. But I tried not to think about Clove almost as often as I tried not to think of my mother. What my father lacked in affection, Clove had given to me in spades.

"West . . ." Willa stopped her work, her eyes going wide before she slid down the mast and landed on the deck.

He stepped out of the archway, scanning the docks before his lips pressed into a hard line. "Hamish!"

Willa's face paled, and for a moment, she looked like she was going to be sick.

Hamish ducked out from the helmsman's quarters, finding a place beside West at the railing. He let out a long breath, cursing, before he disappeared back through the door.

I studied the port, looking for whatever it was they saw there among the ships. Six long docks jutted out from the scarps, the narrow bays filled with boats of every size. They all looked to be traders. Some crests I recognized and one or two I didn't, but the ship from the Narrows gave itself away. Its wide, ornate construction and detailed woodwork didn't fit beside the simple ships made in the Narrows.

My heart twisted in my chest when I spotted Saint's crest—a wave curling over a triangle sail, painted on one of the crisp white shrouds of a clipper.

He wouldn't be on it. The ship was too small to be his, and there was no telling how many he had under his command now.

"Open her up!" West shouted over the sound of the wind, his shoulder brushing mine as he passed me.

Auster and Paj jumped from the foremast, and Willa pushed the can of tar into my hands before she went for the ladder that led to the quarterdeck. They unwound the lines, pulling in synchronized movements as West stood and watched one side of the quarterdeck lift up to reveal the cargo hold.

They secured the lines, tying them around iron hooks at the foot of the railing, and Auster and Paj climbed down into the hull where barrels of apples and crates of nets were stacked in the corner. They passed them to each other in a line until they were arranged in rows, ready to be unloaded.

The others said nothing, but I could feel the tension coiling around the ship. Whatever Willa had seen on the docks had set them all on edge as they worked, organizing goods until Hamish emerged from the helmsman's quarters with five small red leather purses in his hands. He tossed them to each of the crew before they secured them to their belts.

West's attention was still fixed on Dern as he lifted the hem of his shirt and tucked his purse into the waist of his trousers.

"What's out there?" I asked, studying his face.

His green eyes flashed as he turned the spokes of the helm, but he didn't answer. I could see him calculating in his mind, measuring the angle of the ship against the dock. He tilted the wheel a fraction more before he was satisfied, and Paj came down from the quarterdeck to take his place.

"Dredger." Auster jerked his chin toward me.

I climbed the steps, and he handed me the hauling lines as he and Willa closed up the storage. Hamish stood below, carefully knotting the end of a rope to a small chest at his feet, and West stepped in front of him, blocking my view. "Strike all sails," he called out, meeting my eyes in a warning.

Whatever Hamish was doing, West didn't want me to see

it. Just like the maps in his quarters and the coral islands to the north. It had taken me less than a day to see that the *Marigold* was more than a trading ship, but the list of questions I had was growing by the minute.

Auster and Willa obeyed the call, running to the mast to take up the downhauls. Behind them, Hamish dropped the length of rope over the stern into the water, and the chest sank into the deep.

If Hamish was the coin master, there was only one thing he'd be hiding before the *Marigold* made port. I wound the rope up tightly, eyeing the village. Whatever or whoever was there, West didn't think his coin was safe.

Auster climbed down to help Willa drop anchor, and we crept toward the dock slowly. As soon as we were close, I split the heaving lines in my hands and swung my arm back and forth, aiming for the post at the end of the dock. I let go with a grunt, watching it unfurl as it floated through the air. It rippled away from the ship until the end was free, and it slapped against the post as the loop slipped over it.

I took up the length in my blistered hands and propped my feet against the railing before I leaned back, wrenching it toward me, hand over hand.

"Nice throw." Willa smirked, taking the rope behind me and pulling. "You wouldn't have made it from that far, Paj!" She taunted.

He looked at me from over the wheel, and I was so surprised to see a smile pulling at his mouth that my feet almost slipped on the oiled wood. The rhythm of crewing a ship was like a melody I'd known my whole life and had only been able to hum to myself for the last four years. In only a few short days, we'd make port in Ceros, and I'd have my chance to finally take my place on Saint's ship the way my mother had. The way I was born to.

West took the lines behind Willa and helped pull us in as two men came running down the dock. They put their hands out, waiting for the *Marigold* to come closer, and when she made it to the edge, they pushed to keep her from scraping.

The crew dropped another anchor and then the loading ramp as Hamish talked to the dock workers below. A rogue wind swept into the cove, and I turned to face it, pulling the damp air deep into my lungs.

The current in the air sent a chill up my spine as I watched the sky turn. Slowly. That was the way of storms in the Narrows—they were clever. It was what made sailing these waters so dangerous. Nearly every ship that lay at the bottom of this sea had been put there by a storm.

Willa and Auster came up out of the passageway with their satchels and coats, and Paj pulled a knitted cap over his head before swinging up and over the railing to climb down the ladder. I lifted myself up to follow, but a hand jerked me back down to the deck.

West stood behind me, one hand hooked into the back of my belt. "You're not leaving the ship."

"What?" I gaped at him, instinctively trying to pull away from his grip. But his hand only tightened, making me hold my breath.

"We'll be back in the morning, then we'll set out for Ceros."

I looked over his shoulder to the village. I needed off the ship if I was going to figure out a way to trade for more coin. "I'm not a prisoner."

"You're cargo. And the only cargo that gets off the ship at this port is the cargo that's staying here." He stared at me, daring me to argue. But we both knew he couldn't make me stay on the ship. Not without tying me to the rafters in the hull. "I don't think you have enough coin left to pay another trader for passage. So, if you don't want to be left on this dock tomorrow, you'll stay put."

When he pushed past me, I caught hold of his sleeve, pulling him back. He bristled, looking down at my hand wrapped around his arm, as if stung.

"What's down there?" I didn't care what mess the *Marigold* had gotten itself into, but if it was going to keep me from getting to Ceros, it was my problem.

His jaw worked, moving beneath his sun-darkened skin. "Get off this ship, and you won't get back on," he said again.

He yanked free of my grip, putting the cold air between us and I finally breathed, the taste of his scent on my tongue. He pulled a cap on over his unruly gold hair before he climbed down, and I watched him press a few coins into the hands of the two men on the dock. They were probably hired to watch the ship. Or me. Maybe both. The crew wouldn't leave the *Marigold* without having eyes on her.

West didn't look back as he followed the others in a single

line down the weathered wood planks leading up the dock to the village. I watched them, my hands wound so tight around the railing that my bones felt like they might crack. I needed to turn my six coppers into at least twelve before we set out from Dern, and if I didn't get off the ship, I'd have no way to do it.

I cursed, the smell of him still thick in my throat.

Getting kicked off the *Marigold* was a risk I would have to take.

ELEVEN

I still had an hour or two until nightfall, and that was plenty of time.

West was either stupid for leaving me on his ship alone, or he had no choice. Judging by the tension that filled the *Marigold*'s crew as we drifted into the harbor, I guessed it was the latter. Whatever West was up to in Dern, he needed his entire crew for it, and he didn't want a Jevali dredger as a witness.

I climbed the mainmast and watched the five of them weave through the narrow streets of the village below, walking in a single file line with Auster leading and West taking up the tail. They were headed to the tavern, where three tilting chimneys rose up from a long, rectangular building that also served as an inn.

It was usually the first stop for traders when they made port, and even as a child, I'd known what happened behind those doors. I'd seen enough of my father's crew disappear into taverns with purses full of coin and leave with empty ones. There were only two things strictly forbidden on a ship because both could get you or your shipmates killed: love and drunkenness. Only on dry land could you find someone to warm your bed or empty a bottle of rye into your belly.

The brilliant glow of firelight spilled onto the street as the door opened and the crew disappeared inside. A long breath hissed out between my lips as I raked the hair back from my face, thinking. They probably wouldn't reemerge until morning, when the merchant's house opened, which meant I had a good ten hours to get in and out of Dern without being noticed.

I climbed down to the deck, finding each cold rung with my bare feet. As soon as night fell, I'd slip into the village and get what I needed. Until then, I would use the time to find out what the *Marigold* was up to in the hopes I'd end up with something even more powerful than coin. There was no currency more valuable in the Narrows than information.

I followed the steps into the passageway and stopped in front of the door to the cargo hold, sliding the smallest of my iron picks from my belt. The lock sprung easily, and I pushed the door open, ducking low beneath the rafters with the lantern out before me.

Hamish's words echoed in my mind.

You put one finger on anything that doesn't belong to you on this ship, and I will know.

I'd have to take my chances.

Only a few beams of waning sunlight cast down from the

quarterdeck above, hitting the cases and cylinder drums that lined the walls. The room was full of them, stamped with different seals I recognized, identifying the ports that were scattered along the inlets of the Narrows. From the looks of their inventory, the *Marigold* did well for themselves. And with only five purses between them, profits had to be good.

What was less clear was how they'd been able to establish trade in this many ports as a new crew, especially a young one. Everyone on the ship couldn't be much older than me, and although it wasn't unusual to see young people crewing trading ships, it was strange not to see a single seasoned sailor among them.

Nets and lengths of newly made rope were piled beside sheets of neatly folded canvas and baskets of green tomatoes. But there were always goods on a ship a coin master didn't want anyone to see. I'd learned that as a child, snooping through the cargo of the *Lark*.

I turned in a circle, studying the stacks around me carefully. Every ship had its hiding places, and this one was no different.

Except that it was.

Something about the *Marigold* and its crew was off. I could guess what happened to their dredger, but why were they running only five crew on a ship that really needed twelve? What was West doing at the coral islands and what in Dern had them rattled?

I hung the lantern on the hook and lifted myself up onto my tiptoes, fitting my hands into the grooves of the beams overhead. My fingers followed each one down the length of the hull, moving slowly until they hit the smooth, cool glass of a bottle wedged between the wood. I worked it free and held it to the light, where the amber liquid was turned green by the color of the blue glass. I uncorked it, giving it a sniff.

Rye.

A sly grin pulled at the cut on my lip before I tipped my head back, taking a long drink. The rye burned in my chest until I coughed, swallowing with my eyes pinched closed. A hundred candlelit memories flashed in my mind as the sharp, sweet scent of the rye exploded in my nose, and I immediately stoppered the bottle, tucking it back into its hiding place, as if the visions might disappear with it.

I jumped down and checked the boards in the walls next, taking the knife from my belt and knocking the ends of each plank until one loosened. It swung up, and I reached inside, my hand finding a cinched linen pouch. The pale yellow gems spilled out into my palm and I tilted my hand toward the hazy light. At first glance, they looked like citrine. But my mother had taught me better than that.

The facets that gathered the faint hue at their crests gave them away—yellow feldspar.

They were good pieces, the light scattering evenly on their faces. It wouldn't be the only gems they had hidden, but they would be easily missed if I took even one. I needed something else. Something less conspicuous.

I dropped the pouch back into its hiding place and lifted the lids of barrel after barrel until one of them held something that shined in the darkness. Brass buckles. I sighed with relief and shoved two of them into the purse at my belt, securing the lid back down and twisting it closed. The last of the dimming light spilled through the slats from the quarterdeck and my eyes lifted, studying the break in the darkness. On the starboard side, there was no light.

The helmsman's quarters.

I climbed the crates of cabbage in the corner and reached up, fitting the tip of my knife between the end of one of the slats and the beam. I pulled the handle down carefully, prying up with my weight until the nail popped. Once both ends were free, I lifted the plank and set it on the stack of ropes beside me. Above, the shutters on the windows in West's quarters were closed.

My knife slid easily beneath the other planks and a few minutes later, I had an opening big enough to fit through. I went back for the lantern before I wedged myself into the narrow opening, my feet dangling over the open hold before I pulled them inside.

A small shadow swung beside my foot as I stood in the middle of the room, and I took a step toward the shuttered window, where a string of adder stones swayed in the bit of wind slipping through the cracks.

I smiled to myself, reaching up to take one of the smooth pebbles between my fingers. In the center, a perfect hole made it look like an eye. Legend said that adder stones brought good luck. They were collected on beaches and strung up as talismans to hide the helmsman from the eye of sea demons.

My father had them hanging in the window of his quarters too, but that hadn't kept the *Lark* from sinking.

Behind me, West's desk was bolted to the floor, a pile of unrolled maps and charts covering its surface. I stepped closer so that I could press my hands to the soft, worn parchment. Its curling edges framed in the precise, delicate ink that mapped the islands, coves, and underwater trenches of the Narrows. Depth notations and landmarks and the geometrical web of straight lines filled the margins in slanted, clumsy handwriting and I wondered if it was West's or Paj's. I went to the next one, studying. At the top edge, Jeval sat like a buoy in the middle of nowhere.

A shining, brass compass unlike any I'd ever seen sat in the very center. I picked it up, setting it into my hand and examining the strange face in the lantern light so that the needle danced in a wavering line.

A white, rough stone sat beside it, the size of my palm.

But it was the hatch I'd made in the floor that pulled at my attention, appearing in the shadowed corner of my vision. I walked back to the opening, looking down into the cargo hold, where one of the planks I'd lifted from the floor stared up at me. On one end, black paint was brushed onto the lacquered surface where it had been tucked beneath the rug.

I turned, eyeing the tasseled edge of the ruby wool tapestry beside my feet and sank down, lifting up its corner. My heart plummeted into my stomach as the lamplight flickered over the shape of a black wave. I pulled the rug back farther, gasping as the rest of the symbol came into view.

The scuffed outline of a crest was painted onto the floor. But it wasn't the *Marigold*'s.

It was Saint's.

My mind raced, trying to make sense of it. Trying to put the pieces into an order I could understand. But the only explanation was one that couldn't be true.

This wasn't West's ship. It was my father's. Or it had been at one time. But the crest on the sails and the prow wasn't his. So, either West was hiding where this ship came from, or he was hiding what it actually was.

A shadow ship.

I'd heard of them before—ships that were controlled by a powerful trading outfit but operated under a different crest to hide their true identity. They carried out tasks that their master didn't want to be associated with, or worse, manipulated trade at ports to tip the scales in their favor. It was a grave offense against the Trade Council and one that would get a ship's license permanently revoked. It didn't surprise me that Saint had a shadow ship. Maybe he had many. But why would he trust a job like that to a bunch of Waterside strays?

That was how they'd gotten their license from the Trade Council—Saint.

The sharp clang of a bell made me jolt, and the heavy compass slipped from my cold fingers. I leapt forward, catching it before it slammed onto the floor, almost knocking the lantern from the table. I sucked in a breath, steadying myself against the desk.

It was the bell that signaled sundown, ringing out over the village as the last of the light disappeared over the horizon.

I replaced the compass in the very center of the desk with trembling hands before I climbed back through the floorboards and secured them back into place. I couldn't replace the nails, but so close to the desk and half-tucked beneath the rug, I hoped it would take a while for anyone to notice.

I came back up onto the main deck and looked out over the village. If I remembered where it was, I could make it to the gambit and back in a little more than an hour.

Below, the two men West had paid were on the dock, bent over a game of cards. I lifted myself over the stern of the *Marigold*, winding my legs into the rope of a fish trap so I could lower myself all the way down without a sound and slip into the still water of the harbor. I filled my lungs with air and sank below the surface, swimming with my hands out before me in the dark, headed for the shore.

I knew that in the Narrows, nothing was what it seemed. Every truth was twisted. Every lie carefully constructed. My instincts had been right about the *Marigold*. It wasn't a trading ship, or at least that wasn't all she was. It was only a matter of time before the crew of Saint's shadow ship found a rope around their necks. And my only chance at making it to Ceros would be gone.

TWELVE

I wove through the crowded street, headed for the bell tower that stood in the center of Dern. On Jeval, there had been little to frame the expanse of sky before it dove into the sea. Here, it was hedged in by the wayward patterns of crude, slanted rooftops, making me feel like I could disappear.

On Jeval, there had been nowhere to hide.

I kept a careful watch around me, turning to scan my surroundings every eight to ten steps to keep track of my path. I remembered more of the village than I thought I would, because not much had changed in the years since I'd last walked its streets. The shapes and the sounds came back to me in another rush of memories. But the last time I was in Dern, I was holding the hand of my father's navigator, Clove. I'd followed after him in the dark with quick, splashing footsteps as he pulled me through the crowds to the shop of the gambit. But I wasn't the sweet little girl who'd once ridden through these streets perched on his shoulders. I'd been whittled into something else now.

The smolder of a pipe illuminated in the dark alley, and a woman watched me through a puff of white mullein smoke. I was already drawing more attention than I wanted to.

I took a sharp turn, noting the red rooftop at the northeast corner to mark where I was. Boots clapping on wet stone sounded behind me, and I pressed myself into the shadow that draped the stone wall with my hand wound tight in my wet braid until they were gone. Most people were headed home with market carts in tow, making their way out of the congested part of the village. But a few were headed up the hill, toward the tavern, and the thought made me nervous. If there weren't any rooms at the inn, the crew might return to the *Marigold*.

The gambit's shop appeared at the end of the next alley, lit by only one dim street lamp. It was no more than a bricked lean-to beside the smooth wall of a windowless building, but it looked exactly the same as I remembered it, down to the framed-out window with one cracked pane. Five uneven steps led up to the green door, where a sign was painted in a chipped, fading blue.

VILLAGE GAMBIT

I stopped, listening for a moment before I stepped one muddy foot into the slice of moonlight that lit the cobblestones. The door swung open, and two women burst forth, laughing as they stumbled down the stairs. I shot back, trying to fit every bit of me into the darkness. They walked right past me without even looking up, and it was only after they were turning the corner that I saw the glitz of something shine around one of their wrists. It glinted like a little flame below the sleeve of her cloak.

If there was a stroke of luck to be had in this village, I'd just found it.

I started down the wall in the opposite direction, picking up my pace to head them off, and when I reached the next alley, I waited, watching for their shadows on the ground with my breath held in my chest. A simple grab, that's all I needed, but it had been a long time since I'd done one and even longer since my late-night lessons with Clove.

Don't hesitate, Fay. Not even for one second.

I could almost hear his rough, thundering voice. I had thought my father would be angry when he found out that Clove was teaching me to pickpocket, but I found out later that Saint was the one who'd asked him to do it. It was my mother who'd disapproved.

As soon as I could hear voices, I stepped out into the path, my eyes up on the rooftops, and I faltered backward, slamming into one of the women and knocking her sideways.

"Oh!" I caught her by the arms before she fell into the mud, and she looked up at me with wide eyes. "Please, let me help you."

She steadied herself against me as I clumsily slipped the bracelet from her small wrist, and I bit down hard on my lip. It was a skill that needed practice, but I'd never had the guts to pickpocket on Jeval. Not when it could get me tied to the reef and left for dead. I looked up, sure that the woman had noticed the feel of my fingers at the clasp, but as soon as her eyes focused on me, she recoiled, her hands balling into fists at her chest and her mouth gaping open. "Don't touch me!"

It took a moment for me to understand. I studied her face and looked down to my bare feet and ragged clothing. Both gave me away as a Jevali dredger, even if I wasn't one by blood, and my busted lip told anyone who looked at me that I'd seen trouble in only the last few days.

The other woman wrapped one arm protectively around her, leading her away with a scowl on her face, and I bowed my head in an apology.

As soon as they were out of sight, I exhaled, trying to slow my erratic pulse. The gold bracelet shined as I turned it over in the light. It was maybe the only time looking like a Jevali would serve me well.

Another shadow moved in front of the window of the gambit's shop before the door latch pinged, and I stilled when a figure appeared in the center of the alley. The light from the shop fell on a lock of golden hair peeking out from under a cap, and I sucked in another breath, my fingers closing over the bracelet.

West. He stood in the middle of the alley, his eyes on the closed door of the gambit's shop. I slid myself down the wall and tucked myself behind the corner, my heart slamming in my chest again.

Before I could even turn to run, the shop door was swinging open and Willa came down the steps, stopping short when she saw him. His face was only half-painted in light, and he slid his hands into his pockets as the door closed behind her.

"How much?" His deep, even voice was sharp enough to cut through bone.

Willa smoothed the look of surprise on her face, coming down the steps to push past him, but he stepped in front of her.

"How much?" he said again.

I slunk back farther, watching them.

Willa turned to face him, squaring her shoulders to his though she was half his size. The lantern light deepened the color of her skin to a dark umber, making her bronze hair almost glow. "Stay out of it, West."

He took the few steps between them and reached for her wrist, unwinding her arms and turning her around. She yelped as he lifted the hem of her shirt, checking her belt, and he stilled. The jewel-rimmed dagger she carried at her back was missing.

He pulled his knife from his own belt and started for the steps of the gambit, but she lunged forward, hooking her hands into his arm and pulling him back. "West, don't," she rasped, her eyes pleading. "Please, don't."

The knife was clutched so tightly in his hand that the light bounced off the blade as it shook. "How much did he give you for the dagger?"

"Twenty coppers." Her voice was suddenly missing the anger I'd heard in her words only moments before. She sounded like a child.

West raked a hand over his face, sighing. "If you need something, you ask *me*, Willa."

Her eyes were shining as she looked up at him, and even in the dark, I could see West's jaw clenched tight. It suddenly dawned on me that there must be something between them. They didn't spend much time together on the ship, but I could see its shadow in the way they looked at each other now. They were more than shipmates, and the realization made me bite the inside of my cheek. I was almost . . . angry, but the feeling was immediately replaced by humiliation. I didn't like that I cared one way or the other.

"I owe you enough," she whispered. Her cheek shined with a rolling tear and she reached up to wipe it away, careful to avoid the burn that was branded on her skin.

"I told you I'd take care of it."

She stared at the muddy ground between them, her chin dipping down as if she was trying to breathe through the tears.

"When are you going to start trusting me, Willa?"

Her eyes snapped up then, filled with fire. "When you stop treating me like the Waterside stray you used to steal food for."

He stepped back, as if the distance would ease the weight of her words. But it didn't. They hung between them like the stench of a rotting corpse. Something never forgotten.

So Willa was telling the truth when she said they were Waterside strays. And she and West had known each other long before the *Marigold*.

"I'm sorry." She sighed, softening. Her hand reached out

for him, but he stepped to the side, making way for her as he slid his knife back into his belt.

She looked at him for a long moment before she started back down the alleyway. It wasn't until she was out of sight that West turned again, and when his eyes lifted, I froze. He was looking right at me, his gaze like a focused ray of light, illuminating my hiding place.

I looked over my shoulder, but there was nothing. I was completely swallowed by the dark.

"Get out here." He spoke so low that I could barely hear him over the sounds of the soft thunder above us. *"Now."*

I hesitated before stepping out from the shadow and onto the cobblestone path. A cold drop of rain hit my cheek as his eyes ran over me slowly, the tension still wound tight around the set of his shoulders.

"What are you doing out here?"

"I told you"—I met his gaze—"I didn't pay for a prison cell. I paid for passage."

His gaze raked over me until it stopped on my hand. The gold bracelet was tangled in my fingers, sparkling in the lamplight. "You know what would happen if a passenger I brought to this village was caught stealing?"

I did know. He'd be fined for it. His license to trade in Dern's merchant house could even get docked, depending on the number of black marks on his record. As helmsman, he was responsible for every soul that he brought into port.

I glared at him, dropping the bracelet into my pocket. "I gave you all my copper. I can't go into Ceros with nothing."

West shrugged. "Then you can spend the next six months here in Dern, scraping together the coin you'll need to pay another trader to take you on."

My eyes widened. He was serious.

"You've lost your passage on the *Marigold*," he said, his eyes falling to my dirty feet. "Unless you want to make a new deal."

"What?" I hardly recognized the sound of my own voice, pulled thin by the silence.

"Passage to Ceros and thirty coppers."

"Thirty coppers?" My eyes narrowed in suspicion. "For what?"

For just a moment, a look lit in his eyes that I had never seen on him before. The hint of some frailty beneath all of that hard-edged stone. But it disappeared as quickly as it had surfaced.

"I need a favor."

THIRTEEN

The rain began to fall as I waited in the alley, the mist that fell over Dern pushing through the streets like the spirit of a long-dead river.

West told me to wait before disappearing down the street, and when he finally returned, he was carrying a bundle in his arms that I couldn't make out in the dark. He shoved the heap into my hands as he reached me, and I stepped back into the moonlight, looking down at it. It was a pair of boots and a jacket.

"No one is going to trade with you, let alone speak to you, looking like that."

I could feel the flush dance over my face. The boots weren't new, but they may as well have been. Their leather was polished, the hooks all shining. I stared at them, suddenly feeling embarrassed.

"Put them on."

I obeyed, pulling the boots on each foot and tying up

the laces as West watched the alley around us. He pulled a handkerchief from his back pocket, leaning out to where the rainwater was falling from the corner of the rooftop above and soaking it.

He handed it to me, and when I didn't move, he sighed. "Your face."

"Oh." The heat came up in my cheeks again as I took the cloth, wiping across my forehead and down my neck in long strokes.

"You should have let Auster stitch that up," he said, tipping his chin toward the cut on my lip.

"What's one more scar?" I muttered, irritated.

He looked as if he might say something, his lips parting just enough for me to see the edge of his teeth. But he pressed them together without a word, holding the jacket open for me. I slid my arms in before he buckled the clasps one at a time.

"Don't go straight for the dagger, look around a little first. Ask a few questions." He pulled the hood up over my head, brushing off the shoulders of the jacket with his hands.

"What do I trade?"

He slipped the ring from his finger, pressing it into my palm.

I lifted it before me so that the gold glowed, a string of notches winding all the way around its surface. "What if it's not enough?"

"You'll figure something out," he said gruffly. "Don't mention my name, or Willa's. If he asks who you are, just say you're a dredger on a small ship making port for the night."

"All right." I held my hand out to him.

He looked at it. "What?"

"Thirty-five coppers."

"I said thirty."

I shrugged. "We're negotiating."

He gave me a long, incredulous look as he dug into his pocket and fished the coin purse out.

I studied him as he counted them into my hands, resisting the smile that was tugging at my mouth.

But when I looked up into his face, his brow was pulled, his eyes more tired than maybe I'd ever seen them. He was anxious.

The dagger may have belonged to Willa, but it clearly meant something to West too.

I dumped the copper into my pocket and turned on my heel, walking out into the alley and straight for the gambit's shop. The rain hit my hood in heavy drops, and I climbed the steps, knocking twice on the rusted green door.

Footsteps struck the floor inside before it opened and a bald man with a long, dark beard stood in the doorway. I pulled my knife from its sheath slowly as I ducked inside, and the door closed behind me, the bell jingling. He didn't even bother to look at me, making his way back to a stool in the corner of the shop where a lantern was lit over a mounted magnifying glass. Beside it, a pipe was still smoking, filling the little shop with the sweet, spicy smell of mullein.

Candles fixed into old, grimy rye bottles were set on almost every surface, their light flickering off every shiny thing tucked into corners, on shelves, laid out on tables. Raw stones, polished jewelry, gold-plated cartographer tools. Little things that had once meant something to someone, somewhere. But for people like me, very little held more value than a roof or a meal. I'd given anything that had ever meant anything to me for both.

I picked up a comb set with a row of rare seashells like the ones Fret sold at the barrier islands, inspecting it. A matching hand mirror sat beside it, where my reflection looked back at me, and I stilled when I saw my lip. West was right, it needed to be stitched. The swollen skin was reddened around the edges, the bruising almost to my chin.

I moved to the next table before I could spend another moment looking at myself. I didn't want to see what or who might look back at me in that mirror or how different she was from the one who used to live inside these bones.

"What's this?" I picked up a bronze statue of a naked woman wrapped in a ship's sail.

The gambit looked up from his magnifying glass, the pipe clenched in his teeth. He glanced at the statue without answering and then went back to work. "You either came in for somethin' or you didn't."

I set it down, making my way to his worktable. My eyes searched the glass cabinets behind him, where shelf after shelf of knives were laid out. But I didn't see the dagger.

A flash illuminated in the corner of the shop, and I turned toward the single beam of moonlight reaching through the murky window. It landed on a small wooden chest with a tarnished brass lock. Inside, the dagger lay in a narrow, velvet-lined box.

The gambit's eyebrows rose when he saw what I was looking at.

My fingers caught the edge of the lid and I lifted the glass.

I felt him behind me before I heard him, and I dropped my hand, stepping back. His face was turned up in a question, studying me as his arm reached over my head. He picked the box up and set it down on the worktable between us.

"Just bought this off a trader," his gruff voice turned up in a sudden friendliness.

"Can I?" But I didn't wait for his permission. I opened the glass and picked it up, leaning into the window. It was even more valuable than I'd realized. The blue and violet stones were set in swirling patterns, sparkling so the light rolled like waves over their facets. Their unique voices danced between my fingers like the notes of a song. If I closed my eyes, I could pick them out one by one.

"How much?"

The man leaned back on his stool so his shoulders were pressed against the wall, puffing at his pipe until the smoke was billowing again. "Make me an offer," he said.

I looked at him from the side of my gaze, calculating. He'd want more than what he'd paid Willa to make a profit. I wasn't sure what the ring was worth, but it would be smarter to use the coin West had given me and keep the ring for trade in Ceros. "Twenty-five coppers."

He laughed, a rattling cough catching in his throat. "Get out of here." He reached for the dagger, but I clutched it to my chest when I saw the glint in his eye. That was my first mistake.

"Thirty." I tried again.

"That's Bastian made." He lifted his chin, looking down his nose at me.

The great port city in the Unnamed Sea was known for its gemstone creations. Nothing as intricate as the dagger was made in the Narrows because anyone truly skilled with stones went to Bastian, where the Gem Guild was powerful and paid well. There was no shortage of apprenticeships and plenty of work.

It was also where my mother had learned everything she knew about gems. Everything she'd taught me.

My life had depended on bartering, and I'd already broken the most important rule of negotiation. He could see that I'd give him everything for it if I had to. If I didn't, West would leave me in Dern, and I'd be right back where I was on Jeval.

"Thirty coppers and a gold ring." I wanted to bite my own tongue off as I pulled West's ring from my pocket and set it on the counter before him.

It was already more than he'd ever get from someone else, but I could see by the way his mouth twitched that he wasn't finished with me yet.

A wicked smile curled on his lips as he waited.

"And these." I clenched my teeth and fetched the gold

bracelet I'd pinched and the two brass buckles from my other pocket, dropping them on the table. "If you throw in a dredging mallet." Mine was still sitting at the bottom of the reef.

"Deal." He plucked a mallet from the tray of tools behind him and waited for me to count thirty coppers before he handed it to me handle first.

If I didn't have the bracelet to trade in Ceros, at least I could dredge.

I looked out the window, trying to find West's shape in the dark. I couldn't see him, but I felt him watching.

He'd made the same mistake I had, showing me that he cared about the dagger. And he didn't just want it. He *needed* it for some reason. If I knew what that reason was, I might be able to find just a little leverage.

"You know anything about that trader you bought it from? The dagger."

He dropped the coppers into a can behind him and pointed to a handwritten sign beside the window.

NO QUESTIONS

I glared at him. No one wanted to trade with a gambit who would talk about where the things in his shop came from. I wasn't the first dishonest customer he'd had in a single day, and I wouldn't be the last either.

He gave me the mallet and dismissed me with a wave of his hand.

When West saw me coming, he emerged from behind a cart down the alley, waiting with his hands in his pockets.

I pulled the dagger free, holding it out to him, and the relief wasn't hidden on his face.

He took it, giving me a nod. "Thank you."

"It wasn't a favor," I reminded him. He'd paid me thirty-five coppers and passage to Ceros to get the dagger back, and I'd done it. Even if I only had a few of the coppers left, it was still more than I had before we got to Dern.

I followed him through the village streets, back toward the three leaning chimneys of the tavern. The heat of fire pushed through the door as we entered, and I looked for the crew, but there were only faces I didn't know huddled around tables with glasses of rye. West wound between them, leaning into the counter beside the fire until a skinny woman with a pile of hair wrapped up in a red cloth on top of her head stopped in front of us. "West."

"Supper. And a room." He dropped three coppers on the counter, and she tucked them into her apron, smiling up at me knowingly.

I blushed when I realized what she was thinking. "No," I said, lifting a hand, "we're not—"

The woman winked at me, but West didn't bother correcting her and I wondered if it was because I wasn't the first girl he'd brought into the tavern and disappeared up the stairs with. That same uneasiness I'd felt as I watched West and Willa in the alley churned in my stomach.

He set a hand on the counter, leaning into it, and I eyed the pale line of skin encircling his finger. "The ring. Was it important to you?"

His hand curled into a fist, and he shoved it back into his pocket as he turned toward the stairs, ignoring the question. "Good night."

I watched him climb the steps and a crack of light spilled down the hallway as he opened and closed a door.

"Come on, then." The woman behind the counter looked disappointed, stepping past me with a ring of keys dangling from her hand. She unlocked the door beside West's, where the candle had already been blown out. "Here we are."

A small bed and washing basin sat against one wall of the tiny room and a chair against the other. I stepped inside.

"I'll be back with somethin' for you to eat." She smiled, backing out of the room and closing the door softly.

I went to the window and looked out over the rooftops to the harbor, where the ships were only barely visible in the dark. When I could no longer hear the woman's footsteps in the hallway, I looked over my shoulder at the wood plank wall that divided my room and West's. No light came through the cracks, and I took a step closer, crossing my arms and pressing my forehead into the wall.

In one night, I'd almost lost my passage across the Narrows, made and lost enough coin to get me by in Ceros, and unearthed the single most powerful weapon I'd had since leaving Jeval—the truth about what the *Marigold* was.

If West was running a shadow ship, it was likely the most dangerous place in the Narrows I could be. I'd chosen wrong when I fled to the barrier islands with Koy on my heels. Any trader would have taken my coin, but I'd run to the *Marigold*.

FOURTEEN

Morning came with a hard knock at the door, and I rolled to my feet, opening it with one eye open.

Willa stood with her twisted locks pulled back from her face, amusement playing in the smirk on her full lips. "And how exactly did you swing this?" She looked around the room.

I splashed water from the basin on my face, pressing my palms to my hot skin. The fever had set in, making me feel light-headed.

Willa watched as I pulled the boots on one after the other. "I guess West changed his mind."

"Uh-huh." She eyed the jacket draped over the back of the chair.

I followed her down the steps into the tavern, where everyone but Hamish was already finishing their breakfasts. Two pots of tea and chipped, clay plates filled with hunks of cheese and small loaves of fresh bread were laid out in the middle of the table. West didn't look up at me, his eyes trained on Hamish's ledgers that were open between them.

West hadn't told me to keep quiet about last night, but I didn't think he'd told Willa about it either. I guessed she wouldn't be happy with either of us if she knew what we did, and I didn't need her as an enemy.

I took the open seat beside Paj and filled an empty teacup, studying the pages of the ledger from the corner of my eye.

But I wasn't fooling Paj. He closed the book, leaning on the table with his gaze set hard on me. "I thought we agreed the dredger would stay on the ship."

"We did," West said, picking up his cup. His face was drawn and tired, his wavy hair tucked behind his ears. He set his elbows on the table and sipped, meeting my eyes. "We also agreed that she was to make it across the Narrows in one piece."

I swallowed the hot tea, and it burned in my throat. Silence fell on the table and the crew shot glances at one another before they looked at me. My cheeks flushed hot under the weight of West's stare.

So, he did know what happened at the coral islands. Or at least, he had a hunch. And he wanted them to know it.

It wouldn't be the first time traders misbehaved out from under the watch of their helmsman, but this crew was different. They knew their places, and the rivalry I'd seen on other ships didn't seem to exist on the *Marigold*.

West looked to each of them as he took another sip, and

I could see by the way they dropped their gazes that the message had gotten across.

Paj muttered something under his breath that I couldn't hear, and Auster set two fingers on his arm to silence him before he dropped it. My lips stilled on the rim of my cup, watching Auster set the hand into his lap. Because it wasn't the cool brush of a shipmate in an unspoken message. He'd touched him . . . softly.

I pretended not to notice, slathering a thick layer of butter from the dish onto a piece of bread and taking a bite. Maybe West and Willa weren't the only ones on the *Marigold* who were more than shipmates.

We ate in silence until the morning bell at the docks rang out in the distance, signaling the opening of the merchant's house. The crew stood in unison, chairs scraping as they buttoned up their jackets, and I drained my cup of tea before I followed them to the heavy wooden doors.

West led the way, walking ahead of the others with long strides through the foggy streets of Dern. His blond hair looked even lighter in the morning mist, the twisting strands peeking out from under the cap pulled low over his eyes.

We weren't the only ones moving to the east end of the village. From every direction, it seemed, bodies were funneling toward the merchant's house that sat at the corner of the docks. It looked exactly the same as the last time I'd seen it, though I was never allowed inside. I'd only ever waited in the harbor while my father's crew traded.

We ducked under the low doorframe and into the smoky

light of the warehouse. It was already packed with hucksters and merchants, each with their own stall made of scrap wood and torn canvas. A sharp whistle rang out, and West's head turned toward it, searching the rows for Hamish. He waved us over, and we followed West, pushing through the warm bodies to the other side of the wide room.

"Saltblood bastards," Willa muttered, glaring as a trader in a velvet-trimmed coat crossed our path.

The crews from the Unnamed Sea were easy to pick out, the same way their ships were. Neat, trimmed hair, scrubbed skin, and fine clothes. There was an easiness about them that looked as if they'd never had to steal, cheat, or lie to get by. It was the reason people thought Saltbloods were too soft for life in the Narrows.

The goods the crew had unloaded from the *Marigold* were all laid out, and Hamish's jacket bulged at his hips, where coin purses dangled from his belt. West gave him the ledgers and they exchanged a few quick words before we headed to the southeast corner of the merchant's house.

A hand found the sleeve of my jacket, pulling me past the others, and West leaned down, speaking under his breath. "Stay close to me."

Merchants shouted over one another, their hands in the air, but West walked past them until he reached a man who looked as if he was waiting for us.

"You're a day late," he grumbled, his eyes wandering over us until they landed on Hamish.

"Storm got us in late to our last port," West answered and

I studied him. His mouth hadn't even twitched as he spoke the lie. They hadn't been late to Jeval. They were never late. But we had taken a detour by going to the coral islands.

West held one hand out in front of him and Hamish pulled a small coin pouch from his jacket, setting it into West's palm. "Two hundred and sixty-five coppers." West held the purse out to the man.

The merchant's face was stone. "That's it?"

West leaned into the table, ready to argue. "The cider doesn't sell at other ports as well as it does here. You know that."

"Or you're pocketing my profit." The man glared at Hamish, tapping his merchant's ring against the table. It was set with the striped tiger's eye of the Rye Guild.

West leveled his gaze at the man, and the room suddenly seemed louder around us. "You don't trust us to sell for you, hire someone else." He turned to walk away, pushing back through the crowd.

"Wait." The man sighed. "Two crates to the *Marigold*," he muttered to another man standing behind him. "But don't think that what you did in Sowan isn't gettin' round. Rumors have been pouring in the last three days."

West stilled, the cool façade of his face wavering for just a moment. "I don't know what you're talking about."

Paj and Willa met eyes behind West's back, and Paj took a step closer to him, his hand resting on his belt, beside his knife.

The man leaned in, his voice lowering. "We stick together

here in Dern. You try to pull something like that here, and you'll wish it was the sea demons who got their hands on you."

West's eyes lifted slowly. "Like I said, I don't know what you're talking about."

The merchant smiled, pulling back a spread of burlap to reveal the crates of cider, and West gave a nod in approval. The man's attention travelled over to Willa, and he seemed to pause when he saw the burn that streaked up and out of her collar. "Heard you met some trouble, Willa."

Her face was stone, but the slightest flinch ignited in her shoulders.

"Two weeks." West held out his hand, clearly changing the subject.

"Two weeks." The man shook it, and we moved down the aisle without another word.

I looked back over my shoulder, where the merchant's narrowed eyes were still watching us. There were goods in the ship's cargo hold stamped with the seal of Sowan's merchant's house, so I knew the *Marigold* had been there. And whatever they'd done had followed them to Dern. If they were a shadow ship, there was no telling what it was.

I tried to keep up, staying on my feet when someone shoved into me and not losing more than a foot between me and West. If I did, I would be taken with the crowd back the other way. He haggled with another merchant, and I watched beyond the rise of the stall, where Auster was bartering with a gem trader. One of the red leather purses Hamish had given out was clutched in his fist.

Behind me, Willa argued with a small woman just down the aisle, four sparkling gems that looked to be amethyst in her hand. Another one of the red leather purses sat on the table before her.

West caught Auster's eyes over my head, jerking his chin toward Willa. "She better not leave your sight."

Auster nodded, moving closer to her, and I looked around us. There was a lot of coin in this room and a lot of bodies. It would only take a second to lose a purse at your hip. In fact, there were probably people in Dern who made their living that way inside this merchant's house.

My hand went to my own belt, where the few coppers I had were tucked into the little pocket I'd sewn. Paj watched around us, his eyes scanning in every direction as we moved from stall to stall, and I bumped into West as he suddenly stopped in front of me. His attention was on a man who stood along the back wall, leaning into the frame of a greased window.

"Stay here," West muttered before he disappeared into the crowd. When he reached the man, he pulled the cap from his head, running one hand through his hair as they talked in hushed whispers.

"Who is that?" I watched the way they turned their backs to the room.

Paj didn't answer, but he looked as curious as I was, his eyes pinned on West.

Willa rejoined us with a sack of fish hooks slung over her back, Auster on her heels. "Where is he?" She looked around us.

"Price?" Paj gestured to the fish hooks, and I watched,

paying close attention to the way he stepped in front of her to block the view to the window. He was distracting her. Covering for West, even if he didn't know why. And now that I thought about it, they all seemed to do that.

Willa pulled a piece of paper from her pocket, handing it over, and shoved her empty red purse into her jacket. It was then that I understood what they were doing. It wasn't coin in those purses; it was gems. Just a little in each one. Every crew member was splitting off one at a time and trading the small amounts to different merchants.

Trading a few pieces of pyre from Jeval was one thing. But you needed a special permit from the Trade Council to actually run a gem trade, and I guessed they didn't have one. There weren't many in the Narrows who did, because the powerful gem merchants in Bastian controlled the trade.

It was the perfect way for an illegitimate operation to hide beneath the guise of trading large amounts of anything *but* gems. Just a little here and there to avoid notice. A few stones wasn't going to turn heads. But this looked rehearsed. Planned. They probably did this at every single port, and there were probably a lot more purses hidden in the hull than the one I'd found.

If they were Saint's shadow ship, they'd hold a permit to trade gems because he would have made sure of it. But they didn't, and that could only mean one thing—they were running side trade and pocketing on Saint's ledgers.

It was genius. And also, enormously stupid.

West pushed back through the crowd without a word,

and we moved to the next stall, where an old man sat before a tray of gemstones and melted-down metals. The onyx in his merchant's ring said he was a gem merchant. The guild required ten years of apprenticeship for that ring, and even then, it wasn't guaranteed. The guilds were as cutthroat as the traders. If a sailmaker or shipbuilder or gem dealer was caught conducting business without one of those rings, it was a crime punishable by death.

The bronze scale that sat in front of the man caught the bright light from the window as he dropped three raw emerald stones into one side. "West." He nodded in greeting. "Pyre?"

So, this was where he offloaded the pyre. And if I was right about what they were up to, he probably traded the pieces for just a few gems instead of coin. Enough not to draw any notice on the ledgers. It was probably the only trade with a gem merchant he'd make in the open.

West pulled a pouch from his jacket, handing it over, and the man dumped my pieces of pyre onto the cloth folded neatly on the table. "Where are you getting these stones? The past few months you've sold me better pyre than I've seen from any trader in two years."

I smirked, watching him pick up the largest one and hold it against the light.

"If you bring more next month, I might have a better price. There's a jeweler here who's been making some new pieces with them."

"That's the last of it. We won't be stopping in Jeval anymore," Hamish answered.

I looked up at him, confused. When I'd traded with West on the barrier islands, he hadn't said anything about it being his last time in Jeval. In fact, he'd offered to pay the next time he came.

Beside me, Willa, Auster, and Paj looked surprised too. The only person who appeared to know exactly what was going on in this crew was West. Everyone else seemed to have only broken pieces of information.

It was intentional. It was what a good helmsman would do—what Saint would do. I wondered if any of them knew about the crest painted under the rug in West's quarters or if that was a secret too.

"That's a shame." The man huffed, pulling at his white beard. "I'd say about thirty-two coppers' worth."

"What?" I whispered. "You only paid me ten."

"We trade to profit, Fable." A bit of sly amusement changed the sound of West's voice as he spoke.

"How did the quartz do in Sowan?" The merchant tucked his hands into his vest, leaning back in his chair.

"It did well. One hundred and twelve coppers for the lot." Hamish handed him another pouch. "What have you got for the pyre?"

"I've got emeralds here that need selling. They'd do well in Sowan too, I think." He nodded to the stones on the scale.

I leaned forward, studying the gems in the bronze tray. Before I'd even thought about it, I picked one up, holding it in the palm of my hand. Something about them wasn't right.

"How much?" West looked at them carefully.

I bit down on my lip, holding the stone between two fingers. The vibration of emerald was low and soft. It moved like a gentle current. But this was different. I held it up to the light, my eyes narrowing, and the man studied me, a scowl on his face.

I cleared my throat, and West looked down at me.

"What is it?" The merchant was annoyed, leaning on the table to look up at me.

"They're—" I looked between them, unsure of how to say it. "They're—"

"What?" West snapped, growing impatient.

"They're fakes," I whispered.

The man stood suddenly, rattling everything on the table. "What exactly are you accusing me of, dredger?" His face reddened, his eyes blazing.

"Nothing, I—" I looked back at West. But he was staring at the emerald in my hand. "I'm not accusing you of anything. Only—" The man glared at me. "May I?" I stepped forward, lifting the tray from the scale and holding it up to the light. I tipped it so that they rolled. "There." I pointed to one of the stones. "It's not emerald."

The man leaned over me, pulling the chain of a ruby-studded monocle from his vest and setting it against his eye. "Of course it is."

"No, it's not."

"West." Paj's low voice rumbled at my back.

I pointed to the hair-thin line in the center of the stone. "The inclusion catches the light. If it were emerald, it wouldn't do that. You'd see right through it. My guess is that it's forsterite. They're not valuable, but they look a lot like emeralds if they're heated to a high enough temperature. They're even found in the same bedrock." I pointed to the white-crusted edges.

It was only a subtle difference, but one that would cost a purse of coin. Whoever had made them knew exactly what they were doing.

The man's mouth dropped open, and the monocle fell from his eye as he stood back, staring at me. It swung from the gold chain above the scale. "I—I believe she's right." He took the tray from my hands, dumping the stones out onto the table.

"They're not all bad," I said, sorting through them quickly. I picked out five forsterite stones among the emeralds and pushed them to one side, away from the others.

"Whoa," Willa whispered, her face beside mine.

"Those Bastian bastards!" the man growled, his bony fist coming down on the table hard.

I flinched, and West stepped in front of me, his back at my face. "We'll take the amber instead." He pointed to the stones in the next tray. "Whatever you've got."

The merchant was flustered, his eyes still drifting to the emeralds and back up to me. But West was suddenly in a hurry, taking the purse without even checking the stones and immediately leading us to the door we'd come in through. We pushed through the crowd until the sunlight hit my face, and I pulled the cool, salty air into my lungs, glad to be out of the stifling heat of the warehouse.

But as soon as we were through the door, West turned on me. "What the hell do you think you're doing?"

I stopped, almost slamming into him. "What?"

His teeth clenched, his eyes boring down into mine. "Auster, make sure everything gets on the ship. Paj, be ready to push off by nightfall."

"We aren't supposed to leave until morning. I've still got supplies to get." Auster looked between us.

"Then I suggest you hurry," he ground out.

"What did I do?" I said, looking between them. "I don't understand."

West stared down into my face, the red creeping up his neck from the open collar of his shirt. "You should have stayed on Jeval."

FIFTEEN

Whatever favor I'd earned from West and his crew was gone.

He and Paj walked ahead of us as we made our way down the dock, where the *Marigold* was anchored. I looked back to the merchant's house, and Hamish caught my eyes.

"Turn around. You've drawn enough attention," he said.

"He's right," Willa snapped, walking in step with me at my side. The length of her open jacket blew back behind her, and she pulled up the collar against the wind. "Turn around again and I'll lock you in the cargo hold until we get to Ceros."

But her steps faltered as she looked past me to the ship anchored at the next dock. A man in a black coat and long, dark hair streaked with silver smiled at Willa from where he leaned against the post.

"West!" he called out, waving a hand in the air.

West stopped short, every hard edge coming into the

angles of his body all at once. He stood straighter, and Paj took a step closer to him. "Zola."

I studied the man, trying to place him. I remembered the name.

"When did you take on a Jevali dredger?" He looked at me, his smile spreading wider.

West stepped off the main dock onto the walkway, and Paj followed, his fingers going to the handle of the knife in his belt.

Zola pulled the scarf from where it was wrapped over his face. His pale skin was reddened and windblown, his eyes a stormy gray. Above him, the faces of a crew peered down from the railing of a large ship. The crest on the bow was painted in white—a crescent moon encircled by three stalks of rye. It was one I recognized.

Zola wasn't just any trader. When I'd sailed with my father, he was the largest operation in the Narrows. But in those days, he'd worn the trimmed coats and shined boots that marked the traders from the Unnamed Sea. From the look of him now, he'd come down in the world since then.

West held a hand out to him despite the tension in his shoulders pulling beneath his jacket.

Zola stared down at it for a moment before he took it. "Any chance you've seen my stryker?"

West cocked his head to the side in a question.

"Come on, West." Zola's eyes jumped back to Willa and her hands clenched into fists at her sides.

"Can't keep track of your own crew?" she spat.

Zola laughed. "I wouldn't want you Waterside strays to get yourself into more trouble than you can handle."

"Crane's probably drunk under someone's skirts at the tavern." West lifted his chin toward the village. "Or maybe he's gotten himself in more trouble than *he* can handle."

The smile melted from Zola's ruddy face, then. He looked at West for a long moment before his eyes cut to me. "You any good? We're lookin' for a dredger on the *Luna*."

West stepped to the side, blocking Zola's view of me. "She's not ours. She's a passenger. That's it."

Zola didn't seem satisfied with that answer, his gaze suspicious, but he dropped it anyway. "You're looking well, Willa."

A few laughs sounded overhead, and Willa paled beside me.

"Let me know if you see Crane. You know how hard it is to find a decent stryker." Zola smiled.

West turned on his heel without another word, and Zola's eyes moved from me to Willa and back again. His stare burned into my back as we walked, making our way down the ship bays to the *Marigold*. The rope ladder was unrolled down the side of the hull, and West climbed first, followed by Paj. When they disappeared over the railing, I turned back to Willa.

"What happened to your face?" I asked, looking her in the eye.

"What happened to your arm?" she shot back, glowering at me.

My hand went to my sleeve, pulling it down by the cuff. I'd been careful to keep it covered, but she must have seen it.

She stared at me until I took hold of the ladder, fitting my feet onto the ropes. The wind pushed back my hood as I swung over the railing, where West was already waiting, his eyes on the deck. He turned into the archway, clearly expecting me to follow him into the helmsman's quarters.

When I hesitated, his voice sounded behind the door. "Get in here!"

I hesitated before I pushed it open and stepped inside. The shutters had been unlatched, filling the cabin with light, and he sat on the edge of the desk beside the white stone. "Close the door."

I obeyed, leaning into it until the latch clicked into place.

"What was that?" He leveled his eyes at me.

"What?"

"With the gems."

I shrugged. "I was doing you a favor. They were fakes."

"I don't need any favors." He stood, walking toward me. "We don't get involved in other traders' business, Fable. Not ever. Right now, that gem dealer is going to whoever sold him those stones. He'll tell them about the Jevali dredger on my ship that spotted fake emeralds that even *he* didn't catch."

I stared at him, unable to speak as the blood drained from my face. Because he was right. I'd made myself vulnerable without even realizing it.

"How did you do it?" He looked down at me. "How did you know they weren't emeralds?"

If I told him the answer to that question, I risked him knowing who I was. There were only a handful of people who could do what my mother could do. The art of a gem sage was something you were born to, not just something you apprenticed for. It was a lifelong study, something that couldn't be taught.

It was the reason Saint had taken my mother onto his crew. The specialized skill was passed through few lineages, kept secret by most sages after the gem trade expanded and it became dangerous to practice. My mother had been teaching me, the way her father taught her, before she drowned on the *Lark*.

But something in the way West looked at me made me realize that he knew the answer to his own question.

"You don't understand how any of this works. Being responsible for you is going to get me killed," West muttered.

"He doesn't know what I can do."

"It doesn't matter. He's wondering if you can. That's enough."

I bristled, embarrassed. "I didn't think," I admitted.

"No, you didn't. Just like you didn't think when you snuck off the ship after I told you not to."

"If I hadn't gone into the village, you wouldn't have gotten that dagger back."

Even I knew it was a stupid thing to say. Implying that West had needed me at the gambit shop was only going to make him angry.

I fished three coppers from my belt. "Here." I dropped them on the desk beside him. "For the jacket and boots."

He looked down at the coins. "What?"

"I'll pay for them like I paid for passage."

"You didn't ask for the boots and jacket. And I'm not asking for you to pay for them."

"I don't need any favors," I repeated his own words back to him. "And I'm not going to owe you anything."

"Fable . . ." He sighed, rubbing his hands over his face, but whatever he was going to say, he thought better of it.

Outside, the rumble of thunder echoed in the distance. Through the open window, I could see the dark clouds knitting together against the blue sky.

"We should wait," I said, my voice dropping lower. "That storm is going to be nasty."

"We don't really have a choice, thanks to you. I need to get you off my ship before the rumors start spreading on those docks and catch up to us in Ceros."

"Like the rumors that followed you here from Sowan? Don't want anyone paying too close attention, right?" I let my head tip to one side. "You're just a small trading outfit."

That made him look up, his hands tightening on the edge of the desk. "You don't know what you're talking about."

"Maybe not." I shrugged. "Believe me, I want off this ship as badly as you want me off."

He stood up from the desk, taking a step toward me. "I know who you're looking for."

My hands found each other at my back, my fingers tangling. "So?"

"You want to start over in Ceros? Fine. But Saint is

dangerous." His voice softened, his face suddenly looking tired. "Whatever you want from him, you won't get it."

I stared up into his face, trying to put together the few pieces of information I had. West was a Waterside stray turned helmsman running a shadow ship for my father. But his loyalty was to himself and his crew if he was running side trade. He wouldn't risk Saint's wrath otherwise. And even if it had nothing to do with me, I was still curious. I still wanted to know.

I dragged the toe of my boot over the edge of the rug, rolling it back to reveal Saint's crest on the floor. "Looks like *you* got what you wanted from him."

West stared down at the crest, not a hint of surprise on his face.

"How many ships like this one exist?"

He didn't take his eyes from mine, and a long, uncomfortable silence stretched out between us. The room grew small with it and for a moment, I regretted saying it. I didn't want West as an enemy. I opened my mouth to speak, but a knock sounded at my back and the door opened.

Hamish's face poked into the room. "Auster's back."

West didn't look at me before he followed him out. "Make ready!" he called from the archway.

Boots pounded on the deck, and Auster appeared at the railing. Paj dropped from the foot of the sail above us and landed hard, going for the lines.

"Raise anchor!" West's voice rang out again, and everyone moved together, winding around each other in a memorized pattern.

Willa and Hamish turned the crank on the starboard side, grunting as the anchor lifted up out of the water. Seaweed dangled from its curves, dripping as it lifted, and she climbed up onto the railing and guided it onto the deck. I caught its end as they lowered it into place and fastened the latch without being asked to. If West wasn't going to let me pay for the jacket and boots, I needed to work them off before we got to Ceros.

"Shove off." West took the helm into his hands and the ship turned, drifting away from the dock. "Raise the main sail, Willa."

She climbed the mainmast, reaching up to untie the lines and slid back down as they unrolled. "You sure about that storm, West?" She watched the flicker of lightning flashing behind the distant clouds.

West's jaw clenched as he looked at his boots, thinking. The wind pushed his sun-bleached hair across his forehead as he lifted a hand into the air, letting the wind blow through his fingers. "You really want to wait?"

She looked over the harbor, her gaze setting on Zola's ship, the *Luna*. "No," she answered.

"Then let's go."

I climbed the mainmast as Willa went up the foremast, helping her with the sails, and Hamish finished tying down the second anchor below. I pulled the lines hand over hand, watching the sheets spread against the gray sky. When they were in place, I jumped down to help the others.

West's eyes were still on the horizon.

He knew how to measure the clouds against the surface of the water and calculate the pull of the wind. Any decent helmsman would. He could see what I saw—that it would blow in fast and dark, churning up the water and forcing the ship closer to shore than it should be. It wouldn't last long, though. And the *Marigold* was small. If she was in deep enough water, the southwest winds wouldn't push her too far.

As soon as I thought it, West tilted the helm, adjusting it just slightly.

Auster climbed down to the dock to release the heaving lines, and as soon as he was on the ladder, we were drifting into the cove. The wind caught the sails, pushing us out quickly, and Paj found a place beside West.

"How long?" I asked, watching the coastline pull away.

"Two days," Paj answered.

I wrapped my arm around the shrouds bolted into the deck and leaned into them, closing my eyes as the wind picked up. When the faint whisper of someone's eyes brushed my skin, I looked back to the village, where a figure stood at the end of the dock. The length of Zola's black coat blew around him in the wind, his gaze taut as he watched us sail away.

SIXTEEN

I could feel the seafloor pull away from us as we made our way into deeper water. A silence had fallen over the *Marigold,* everyone busy with securing the new inventory from Dern below deck before the winds hit.

Hamish and West worked over ledgers by lantern light while Auster and Paj sorted crates and barrels, organizing what would come off the ship in Ceros and what would be taken on to Sowan.

Willa was perched at the top of the mainmast, leaning back into her sling and keeping an eye on the storm creeping toward us. I climbed the pegs, finding a place to sit in the riggings beside her. My bare feet dangled out in the air, and I watched the lightning in the distance, tangling like tree roots. From that high, it looked like we were sailing through the clouds, the thick mist hugging around the ship and hiding the water.

"Looks like it might be bad," she said, softly.

But by the look of the sky, we both knew what was

coming. It would be violent, but it would be swift. "I think so."

Willa was quiet for a long time before she spoke again. "Where'd you learn how to do that? With the gems."

I propped myself against the mast, trying to read her. She looked genuinely curious. "I'm a dredger."

"I've never seen a dredger spot a fake like that."

"I'm just good with gems." I shrugged.

She laughed, giving up. "I'd keep that to myself if I were you."

I smiled. "That's what West said."

"Well, he's right." She picked at the rope beneath her with the tip of her finger. "How'd you wind up out there? On Jeval?"

An ache lit in the center of my chest. "What do you mean?"

She raised an eyebrow.

"I don't know. How do any of us end up where we are?"

Another strike of lightning lit the black sky, a little closer this time. "Whatever you had to do to survive," she spoke quietly, "it will be worse in the Narrows. Harder."

"I know that."

"I don't think you do." She sighed.

"You think I should have stayed on Jeval."

"I don't know. But you'll find out soon enough."

A loud knock sounded below, and Willa sat up, hooking an arm into the lines so she could lean forward. West was standing at the base of the mainmast, looking up at her. A long chisel was clutched in his hand and behind him, Paj and Auster were carrying a large crate down from the quarterdeck.

As soon as she saw his face, Willa stood on the boom. "What's wrong?" she shouted.

But he didn't answer. He looked at her for another long moment as they set the crate down behind him.

"What is he doing?" I tilted forward, trying to see.

We both watched as he fit the end of the chisel beneath the edge of the lid, prying it up. The wood popped, and Willa pulled the hair back from her face, squinting. West freed the other end, and the chisel hit the deck with a loud ping as he dragged the lid toward him.

Willa gasped, almost losing her balance in the ropes as she pressed a shaking hand to her open mouth.

Below, the crisp, white moonlight fell on the open crate, where a man with wide eyes peered up at us from a bed of muddy straw.

"What the—" I breathed.

But Willa was already sliding down the mast, trying to find the pegs in the dark. I landed on the deck beside her. She was frozen, every muscle tensed, the bright gleam of tears in her eyes.

The man grunted, writhing in the crate before us and pulling at the wires that were wound tightly around his wrists and ankles. His mouth was stuffed with tarred cloth, muffling the noises trapped in his throat, where Zola's crest was tattooed into his skin—a crescent moon framed by stalks of rye.

It was the man Zola was looking for. Crane. It had to be.

Willa cried into her fists before she finally looked up at West, her cheeks wet. The others stood silent, as if waiting for her to say something. The sea calmed around us, the quiet that hit right before a storm conjuring an eerie silence as the man looked up to Willa with pleading eyes.

She drew in a deep breath, her hands unclenching before she gave a quick nod, pulling the adze from her belt. Auster and Paj took hold of the lid, securing it back into place and the man's muted screams disappeared as Willa took a nail from the purse at her belt.

"What are you doing?" I whispered.

But I already knew.

She set the nail at the corner, slamming the adze down to drive it into the wood with one hit before she pulled out another. She did the same at each corner, and when she was finished, West, Hamish, Paj, and Auster each picked up a side of the crate, lifting it from the deck like pallbearers.

"No." My lips formed the word but no sound came. "West, you can't just . . ."

He wasn't listening. None of them were.

The man screamed once more as he was raised up and over the side of the ship. At the same moment, every finger slipped from the crate and they let it go. It fell through the air, splashing into the dark water below, and I ran to the railing, peering over as it sank into the black.

The shaking in my hands crept up my arms, and I wrapped them around me, clutching the fabric of my shirt into my fists. When I turned back to the others, Willa's fingers were on the burn reaching across her cheek, her stare blank.

I'd guessed that Zola had something to do with the

burn on her face. And I knew that every action demanded a reaction in the Narrows. A few times, I'd seen verdicts like this carried out on my father's ship. Once, I'd crept onto the deck in the dead of night and saw him cut the hand off a thief with the same knife he used to cut his meat at supper. But I had forgotten what it felt like. I'd forgotten what the sound of a grown man screaming sounded like.

That's what West had been doing at the merchant's house. Whoever he'd been talking to was probably delivering on an order to find the man who'd hurt Willa. When he told her that he'd take care of it at the gambit's, this is what he meant.

She walked across the deck, stopping before West and lifting up onto her toes to kiss him on the cheek as more tears streamed down her face. It wasn't the kind of kiss that lovers shared, but there were a hundred secrets in the way that they looked at each other. A hundred stories.

His hand went to the back of his shirt and he pulled her dagger free, holding it between them. She wiped her face with the back of her arm before she took it, turning it over in the moonlight so the gems twinkled.

"Thank you," she said.

They stood in silence as the wind picked back up, and West watched her slide the dagger back into her own belt. I stood at the railing, every bit of warmth draining from my body. Below us, a man was sinking into the deep. But Willa tied the length of her bronze hair back with a strand of leather, as if they hadn't just committed murder. As if the whisper of death wasn't still lingering on the ship.

That was the way of life in the Narrows. And for the first time, I thought that maybe Saint had been right.

You weren't made for this world, Fable.

A roaring wind came over the starboard side, making me shiver, and I looked up to see the lightning was right over us now.

"Secure the decks!" West shouted, climbing the stairs.

And everyone went back to work. Willa climbed up the mainmast, and Paj and Auster scrambled to finish tying down the cargo. I looked for something to do. A task that would pull the vision of the sinking crate from the front of my mind. I flew down the steps in the passageway, closing the trunks in the cabin and checking the doors.

When I came back up the steps, West didn't look at me, standing there in the flashing light. But he could feel me. It was in the way he turned just slightly away, his eyes on the deck where my feet were planted. Maybe he was ashamed of what he'd done. Or ashamed of not being ashamed. Maybe he imagined that I thought him a monster. And he would be right.

I looked up into the blinding flash of lightning overhead.

He was. We all were. And now this storm was going to make us pay for it.

SEVENTEEN

I tried not to watch it.

I fixed my gaze on the ropes, ignoring the growl of the wind and the swell of the waves. But as the chill bled into the air, my heart began to sprint. Cold rain poured from the sky, filling the deck with water. It raced down the stairs to the passageway in a flood.

My eyes flitted up to the snapping sails, and I swallowed hard, keeping my head down.

"West!" Paj was on the mainmast, one arm hooked into the lines and leaning out to look behind us.

He was watching the clouds. They looked like a rising plume of black smoke, their edges curling under. I let out a long breath, waiting for West to call out the order before I moved an inch. Any second, he was going to realize what this storm was.

"Reef the jibs!" West's voice was drowned in the sound of thunder.

I didn't wait for Auster to make it down the ladder from

the quarterdeck. I climbed the foremast, reaching for the lines just as the first gale slammed into the ship. The *Marigold* heeled, and my boot slipped from the peg, sending me dangling over the deck thirty feet below.

In the distance, West stood at the helm, bracing against the spray.

I held my breath, kicking through the air as the boat tilted farther and the dark blue of the sea came beneath me. When West saw me, his eyes went wide, his mouth moving around words I couldn't hear. They were lost in the roar of wind.

I pulled myself up, hooking my arm into the ropes just as the ship righted, sending me crashing into the mast. As soon as my boots found the pegs, I reached for the lines, bound tightly around the cleats. My fingers pulled at the wet knots until the skin at my knuckles broke, but they were too tight.

The next gale pricked the surface of the water as it rolled toward us, and I jerked against the rope, cursing. With the next tug, the knot finally unraveled, and the loosened line lurched forward, pulling me from the mast. I swung out into the air and the sail pulled up as I fell, slowing just as I landed on the deck hard. The rope slipped through my fingers, burning against my palms, and the sail dropped open.

"Paj!" West shouted over the sound of the water as the next gale hit us, and the *Marigold* heeled again, sending Auster sliding across the deck.

"Got it!" Paj took his place at the helm and turned us north, away from shore. We were already being pushed toward the shallows.

West ran for the mainmast. "Get the storm sails up now!"

I looked up. He knew the storm sails could be the wrong call. In a few minutes, we might need to drop sails altogether and take our chances on the swells. But by then, they would be too full to get closed.

Willa and Auster climbed the masts in lockstep and in the next full wind, the storm sails flew open, jolting the ship forward. The water underfoot swept me toward the portside railing, and West caught me as I passed him, his hands taking hold of my wrists and pulling me back up to my feet.

"Get below deck!" he shouted, pushing me toward the open archway.

Over the stern, I could see the clouds rolling over the sea toward us. Hungry.

I closed my eyes and drew the humid air into my chest. I'd spent my childhood in the face of storms just like her, many of them angrier than this one. It was the reason only the most daring traders sailed the Narrows. And even though I could feel her power in every bone, every muscle, there was something deep inside of me that opened its eyes from sleep when I felt it. It was terrifying, but familiar. It was as beautiful as it was deadly.

Silence fell over the ship for the length of a breath as the others saw it. Every head turned to West, who stood at the bow, his eyes ahead as the quiet rumble of wind rushed toward us.

"Brace!" West called out and everyone ran for the nearest anchored thing to hold on to.

I threw myself at the nearest iron cleat, wrapping my arms around the railing before the ship tipped. The crates in the breezeway broke free and slid into the water, cracking into pieces as they hit the waves. To the west, the faintest shadow of the shoreline was visible. We were too close. Way too close.

Auster shouted overhead, where he was still clinging to the foremast. The ship tilted before it snapped right, and he went flying, his arms and legs flailing as he soared toward the sea.

"No!" Paj's raw scream tore through the raging wind, and we all watched as Auster hit the water and disappeared.

Paj didn't hesitate. Not even for a second. He picked up the end of the rope lying on the deck.

"Don't!" West shouted, running toward him.

But it was too late. Paj threw himself toward the railing and jumped. West slid through the water on the deck, catching the length of rope before it rippled over the side, and I fell to my knees behind him, anchoring it as Paj's weight pulled against us. West watched over the rail, searching the water.

A sick, nauseating silence fell over the ship, the wind stalling for just a moment, and I pinched my eyes closed until West was shouting. "There! Pull!"

I couldn't see, but I leaned all the way back and towed the ropes behind him, my palms shredding against the fibers as we hauled it in. And suddenly, a hand appeared on the railing. I screamed, pulling as hard as I could, and Paj's head came into view, his mouth wide open as he gulped in the air. Willa and Hamish dragged him over, and when he hit the deck, Auster was clutched in his arms, vomiting seawater.

Paj's face broke and he cried into Auster's wet hair, holding him so tight that his fingers looked as if they might tear the seams of Auster's shirt open.

"You stupid bastard!" Auster choked.

The moment was cut short by the sharp, metallic ping that echoed through the ship.

"Bowanchor!" Hamish leaned over the starboard side, looking down.

It had freed itself from where it was secured on the hull, dropping into the water, the line pulled taut. West cursed as he went to the helm and steered us into the wind. The storm was almost on top of us now. There was nothing to do but let it hit us and hope we didn't run aground.

West held his hand out, reaching for me. "Get below deck. Now!"

The waves reached higher and the rain fell harder, dumping into the ship. It blew in sideways, the drops like bits of glass on my skin. I shook my head, searching the deck for Willa.

"Get below or I'm dropping you at the next island and you can swim to Ceros!" West took hold of my face with his hands, meeting my eyes.

A look like thunder after a lightning strike lit on his face. Fear wound around every inch of his body and squeezed, and the feel of his hands on me sent a chill up my spine. There was something knowing in the way he looked at me. Something that pulled at the knots in the net of lies we'd both told.

Behind us, the worst of the storm was seconds from hitting the ship. It was strong, but the *Marigold* would be fine as long as she didn't hit the reef. As long as she didn't . . .

"Fable!" he shouted again.

The ship tilted, and he let go, sending me sliding across the deck toward the archway. I caught hold of the post and swung myself down the stairs with a spray of water, hitting the floor flat on my back. Willa appeared in the opening above me before she slammed the hatch closed, leaving me in the dark.

I stumbled to my feet, sloshing in the deepening water. The ship groaned around me as I huddled into the corner of the cabin, wrapping my arms around my knees and drawing them to my chest. The muffled sound of the crew shouting and the knock of boots were washed out by the roar of the storm hitting the boat and the last bit of light coming through the slats flickered out.

She's saying something.

My mother's words found me, there in the black.

I pinched my eyes closed, her face coming into perfect view. One long, dark red braid over her shoulder. Pale gray eyes the color of morning fog and the sea-dragon necklace around her neck as she looked up into the clouds above us. Isolde loved the storms.

That night, the bell rang out and my father came for me, pulling me from my hammock bleary-eyed and confused. And when he put me in the rowboat, I screamed for my mother until my throat was raw. The *Lark* was already half-sunk, disappearing in the water behind us.

My mother called it touching the soul of the storm. When she came upon us like that, she was taking us into her heart and letting us see her. She was saying something. And only then would we know what lay within her.

Only then would we know who she was.

EIGHTEEN

*S*he's saying something.

I didn't open my eyes until the first slice of sunlight cut through the darkness, casting down to the green water trapped in the cabin. The storm had barreled over the *Marigold* quickly, but it had taken hours for the winds to stop tossing the ship. We hadn't capsized and hadn't run aground, and that was really all any crew could ask for.

Hoarse voices sounded outside, but I stayed curled up in the dark for another few minutes. The water sloshed around me, carrying the contents of the toppled trunks like little boats around the cabin. A small box of mullein, a quill, a corked empty rye bottle. It would take days to get all this water from the hull and the sour smell would only get worse.

Sailing the Narrows meant braving the storms. Once, I asked Saint if he was ever scared when the dark clouds came for the *Lark*. He was a big man, towering over me from where he stood at the helm. When he looked down at me, his face was shrouded in the white smoke from his pipe.

I've seen worse things than a storm, Fay, he'd answered.

The *Lark* was the only home I'd ever known before Jeval, but in the years before I was born, Saint had lost four other ships to the sea demons' wrath. As a child, the thought made tears well up in my eyes, imagining those beautiful, grand ships trapped in the cold deep. The first time I ever saw one for myself was diving in Tempest Snare with my mother, where the *Lark* now slept.

I pulled myself to my feet slowly, every muscle and bone sore from being thrown from the lines. Dried blood crusted my hands, my palms stinging where the skin had torn against the ropes, and I hit the hatch with my fist. The light touched my face as it lifted above me. Hamish crouched over the top step, and my eyes adjusted to the brightness slowly. The sandy hair that was usually combed back was stuck to his forehead, his spectacles fogged. Behind him, the heat of late morning was making the moisture on the deck steam like a pot of water.

Paj tipped his chin up at me, smirking. "Looks like our bad luck charm survived."

I came up the steps, my boots heavy with water. All around us, the sea was calm, smoothed out in a clear, deep blue.

West stood portside, a length of rope belayed across his back. A deep gash was cut into the thick muscle of his forearm, and another grazed across his temple. The blood was dried in trailing lines down the side of his face.

I peered over the side of the ship to see Willa sitting back in her sling, biting down on the blade of a knife with her teeth. She propped her feet on the hull, working on the breach where the iron clasps that held the bowanchor had been. The rings had ripped through the wood in the force of the waves.

She pulled the adze from her belt and pounded a cone of raw wood into each hole. It would stop water from filling the hull until we got to Ceros, but there would be more work to do while it was docked.

Auster was suspended beside her, pulling at the rope that secured the loose anchor, but it wasn't moving. Paj watched him over the railing with his jaw clenched, and I remembered the way he'd jumped into the black water. How he'd held Auster in his arms, his face twisted as he cried into Auster's hair. I'd been right about the two of them. It had been clear as glass in the moment they landed on the deck.

Paj loved Auster, and from the look on his face as he peered up at him, Auster loved Paj.

Never, under any circumstances, reveal who or what matters to you.

It was the reason Saint had made me promise to never tell a soul that I was his daughter.

I looked up to a flap of the topsail dangling from the foremast, where the wind had ripped it through. In the breezeway, the riggings that kept supplies in place had also broken free. The *Marigold* would be anchored at least a week for these repairs.

Auster climbed the rope ladder and jumped back onto the deck, dripping seawater. "Must be a reef. I can't see down that far."

West was studying the surface below. "How deep?"

"Two hundred feet maybe? I'm not sure."

I took hold of the rope and gave it a tug. "I can get it."

But West kept his back to me. "No."

"Why not? It's only two hundred feet."

"It's the least she could do." Auster glared at me, but humor illuminated his steely eyes. "Bad luck and all."

"What are you talking about?"

"We took a vote this morning." Willa squinted against the sunlight. A patch of red bloomed beneath the tawny skin of her cheek, where she'd likely been hit by the railing or sliding cargo. "It's unanimous. You're bad luck, dredger."

I laughed, letting go of the rope. "Can we hold a new vote if I free the anchor?"

West's eyes went to my bloodied hands. "We'll wait for low tide. It'll free itself when the ship lowers."

Below, Willa looked up at him before she shot her eyes to me. "We're already behind schedule."

West leaned out, inspecting her work. "How long?"

"Not long."

"And the sail?"

"I'll take care of it." Paj pushed off the side, heading below deck.

I followed after him, snatching a lantern from the archway and striking the flame as I went down the stairs. I got down onto my knees in the cabin, searching with my hands in the water until I found it—my belt. There was no reason not to let me dive, just like there was no reason to make me stay on the ship in Dern or go below deck in the storm. But if I freed the anchor, we could call whatever West had done for me square. There'd be no debt, and I'd have the crew as witnesses.

I could only find three of my tools, but I guessed it was enough for whatever was keeping the anchor lodged. I fastened the belt around my hips and tightened the buckle, coming back up the steps. West was on the quarterdeck, helping Hamish secure the last of the crates.

I kicked off my boots and looked into the water, where the rope disappeared beside the hull.

"What are you doing?" Auster leaned into the railing beside me.

"I'll pull when it's free," I said lowly, stepping up. "Then you can bring it up."

Auster looked at me from the corner of his eye before he nodded discreetly. I climbed to the outside of the boat and stood, balancing on the rail.

"Fable," Hamish warned from the quarterdeck.

A smirk pulled at Willa's mouth.

West turned, looking over his shoulder, and I met his eyes just as I let go. The sight of him disappeared as I fell, plunging into the water feetfirst. My body sank, and I let the cold wrap around me, the salt stinging my eyes.

I broke the surface to the sound of West's rough voice. "Fable!"

I ignored him, turning away from the boat and pulling the air deep into my belly until it filled me up to my throat. I let it out in a long, measured exhale as West shouted again. "Fable!"

Two more breaths, and I dove. The cloudy blue stretched out in every direction, the sediment still settling from the churn of the storm. I kept one finger on the rope to follow it into the void, and the current pushed my hair back as I descended. I smiled, looking around me to the vast emptiness. I'd dove almost every day since I was a child. The water was more of a home than Jeval ever was.

The truth was, I liked being a dredger. In fact, I loved it.

I followed a group of parrotfish down, their violet edges rippling as they twisted and turned. The pressure pushed in around me, and I let out a stream of air as the shoal came into view below. The black rock stretched out across the white-sand seafloor in a wandering fissure. My feet landed on the ridge lightly, where the anchor was caught beneath the shelf. Far above me, the *Marigold* was no more than a dark spot on the surface.

I braced myself on the rock, my palms stinging, and kicked at the anchor with my heel. When it didn't free, I pulled the chisel and mallet from my belt and got to work on the edge, crumbling the rock with every tap. Little black pieces sank to the seafloor, a dusty cloud coming up around me, and when I had a large enough crack, I set my feet on the ridge and pushed against the rope as hard as I could. The burn for air awoke softly in my chest, my fingers tingling.

It groaned before the rock gave way and the anchor snapped up, loosening the tension of the rope. I pulled in sharp jerks until the line began to move, fitting my feet onto the arms of the anchor and watching the glittering light above grow and stretch as I slowly came closer. Fish swarmed beneath the *Marigold*, twisted in the ribbons of seaweed trailing from the barnacles and mussels that covered the hull. I let the last of my air out just before I reached the surface and filled my lungs again with a gasp as I came up. West was still leaning over the side, his lips pressed into a hard line. As soon as he saw me, he disappeared.

Auster and Paj worked the crank, lifting the anchor up out of the water, and I reached for the ladder as they heaved it onto the deck. Willa was finishing the plug in the hull with a layer of tar, and she smiled to herself, shaking her head.

"What?" I stopped on the ladder beside her, catching my breath.

"I can't decide if I like you or if I think you're stupid." She laughed.

I smiled, climbing up until I was over the rail and my feet hit the hot deck.

West was already climbing up the mainmast, that same tension running up his spine that was always there when he was angry. He wasn't used to being disobeyed, and I wasn't used to being told what to do.

He fit his hands and feet onto the iron rungs until he was balancing against the foot of the sail. His hands worked at the ropes, his knife in his teeth and his hair blowing across his face.

He was right—the sooner I was off this ship, the better. But I was going to walk off the *Marigold* not owing anything.

NINETEEN

Willa was the only one in her hammock when I came into the cabin after dark. My trunk was still flooded, but I opened the lid and dropped my belt inside anyway. Above, footsteps creaked in West's quarters and candlelight leaked through the cracks. He hadn't looked at me since I dove for the anchor, and maybe he wouldn't until I was off the ship. Maybe that was best.

I climbed into my hammock, pulling a sail into my lap as we swung over the green water that filled the cabin. The tear reached diagonally across the canvas and I studied it, measuring the length of thread I would need.

"I've had it since I was five years old," Willa said, and I looked up to see her holding her dagger out before her. She turned it over in her tar-stained hands. "I took it from a drunk man on Waterside who passed out in the middle of the street. Just took it right out of his belt."

That wasn't what I expected her to say.

"It's not special, really. It's just the only thing of value I have. I tried to sell it to the gambit in Dern, but West got it back for me somehow."

I kept my eyes on the sail. "Why?"

"Because he has a really bad habit of making other people his problem."

I pulled the needle toward me, sliding the thread through the fabric, and when I looked up, I could see what she meant. She wasn't just talking about the dagger. She was talking about me. "Is that why you're crewing on his ship?"

She half laughed. "Yes."

"But Paj said you've been on the crew since the beginning."

"We were on crews together growing up." She stared up at the ceiling, the look of a memory flashing in her eyes. "When West got the *Marigold*, he wanted people he could trust."

I tied off the thread, lifting the sail before me to make sure the stitch was straight. "And how did a Waterside stray become the helmsman of a ship like this?"

She shrugged. "He's West. He knows how to get what he wants."

"Is that what you want? To be a trader in the Narrows?"

"What I want is not to die alone," she said, her voice suddenly small. "I didn't really choose this life. It's just the only one I have."

My hand stilled on the canvas.

"As long as I'm on this crew, I won't be alone. I think that's a pretty good place to be when death comes knocking."

I wasn't sure what to say. It was sad and familiar. Much

too familiar. She'd spoken aloud the one and only silent wish I had ever dared to make. And that gave it too much flesh and bone. It made it feel like a delicate, fragile thing. Something too easy to kill in this kind of life. "What happened to the *Marigold*'s dredger?"

"What?"

"The dredger who was on this crew. What happened to them?"

Her eyes went to the trunk against the bulkhead that had been empty when I came onto the ship. "He stole from us," she said simply.

"But what *happened* to him?"

"It wasn't like Crane, if that's what you mean. We cut his throat before we threw him in." The calm in her voice was unnerving.

"And the burn?"

"Yeah, that was Crane. Well, it was Zola, really." She reached up, touching the smooth, pink skin at her jaw. "It was a few weeks ago, in Ceros."

I wanted to say I was sorry for what happened to her. But I knew how I'd feel if someone said that to me. In some ways, being pitied was worse than being hurt. "Why'd he do it?"

"We've been making too much coin for his taste. He's warned us a few times, and we didn't listen. So, he decided to make a move."

That was the way traders worked. Warnings followed by grand, public punishments. Whatever kept those beneath them in check.

"What are you going to do in Ceros?"

I looked at the sail in my hands, folding it neatly into a rectangle. "I told you. I'm going to find Saint and ask for a position on one of his crews."

"No, I mean what are you going to do when he says no?"

My eyes shot up, my teeth clenching.

"Supper's up." Auster came into the cabin before I could answer her, pulling his jacket off and hanging it on the hook. "It's not much, but it's edible."

Willa rolled out of the hammock and ducked into the passageway, and I followed, climbing the steps behind her. The main and the foremast sails were bowed in the wind, and the black water rushed under the *Marigold*. We were making good time, but there was no way for them to get back on schedule. They'd lost inventory in the storm, and now they'd take even more losses in trade.

I climbed the foremast and started rigging the mended sail, securing it to the mast. It caught the wind above me as I untied the lines and pulled. The night sky was black and empty, stars cast across it in swirling sprays. There was no moon, leaving the deck of the ship dark below. I leaned into the mast, letting my weight fall into the ropes, and tipped my head back, feeling the wind rush around me.

Below, the crew was eating on the quarterdeck, hunched over bowls of porridge. Everyone except for West. He stood at the helm, almost invisible in the dark. His hands gripped the handles, the shadow of his face sharp as he looked ahead.

I tried to imagine him as a little boy—a Waterside stray.

So many traders got their start that way, plucked up from the dirty streets by a crew and worked to the bone. Many found their ends on the sea, but a few rose up the ranks to take valuable positions on important ships, sailing across the Narrows and some, even into the Unnamed Sea.

When we made our stops in Ceros on Saint's trading routes, I would watch the children on Waterside, wishing I had playmates like them. I had no idea they were starving or that most of them had no families.

Once the sail I'd repaired was stretched out beside the others, I lowered myself down the mast. West watched me walk toward him, bristling only enough for me to barely see that he was still angry.

"I don't like not being of use," I said, stepping in front of him so he had to look at me.

"You're not a part of this crew." The words stung, though I wasn't sure why. "You're a passenger."

"I've already paid you. If I get myself killed before we get to Ceros, you've still got my coin."

His eyes shifted then, running over me. There was more behind what he was saying, but I could see by the look on his face that he wasn't going to give me anything else. There were a lot of demons on this ship, and West seemed to have the most of all.

"Is Saint's outpost still in the Pinch?" I leaned into the post beside him.

"Yes."

"Willa thinks he won't take me on."

"She's right."

I watched his hand slide down the handle to catch the spoke of the helm. "He took *you* on."

"And it cost me."

"What do you mean?"

He put the words together before he said them aloud. "Nothing comes free, Fable. We both know that surviving means sometimes doing things that haunt you."

The words made me feel even more unsteady. Because he was talking about the man in the crate. But what was there to say? The man was dead. It was done. As horrified as I was by it, I understood it. And that single thought truly scared me.

"What else have you done that haunts you?" I asked, knowing he wouldn't answer.

There was an ocean of lies dragging behind this ship. They'd killed their dredger and another helmsman's stryker. Whatever they'd done in Sowan was spreading in rumors across the Narrows. And if that wasn't enough, they were running side trade under the nose of their own employer. Saint.

No matter how much he may have changed in the time since I last saw him, my father was still my father. He wouldn't hesitate to do worse to West than the crew of the *Marigold* had done to Crane. I didn't want to see that happen.

I was scared for West.

I'd only ever bartered with him at the barrier islands when he came to Jeval, but it was his coin that had kept me fed, and in the two years since I first met him, he'd never failed to show. He'd saved my life more times than I could count, even if he hadn't meant to.

When I got off the *Marigold* in Ceros, I'd probably never see him again. And I didn't want to worry about what became of him.

"I don't care what you've done. When I showed up on the docks at the barrier islands, you didn't have to help me."

"Yes, I did," he said, his face unreadable.

The words worked their way beneath my skin. They snatched the air from my chest. And just as I was about to ask why, his eyes lifted, focusing on something in the distance. I turned, following his gaze to the horizon, where the soft orange glow of light was just coming into view.

Ceros.

And there, in the twinkling lantern light, was the only future I had waiting for me.

TWENTY

Dawn broke as we entered the harbor. I stood at the bow as Auster tied off the last bandage, watching the city come closer. For four years, I'd dreamed of the moment I would reach Ceros, and now that it was here, all I could think about was the moment I would see my father's face. Wondering what he'd say. What he'd do.

The stone buildings crowded into one another, sprawling down the hill that led to the water. The early light reflected off the square window glass as the sun rose behind me, making the city look like it was studded with diamonds. And suspended above it all, an intricate grid of rope bridges hung, already filled with people making their way across the city.

"Keep them clean." Auster waited for me to nod in answer before he picked up the pail at his feet and climbed the mast.

I looked down at my scraped hands, now wrapped in white linen strips. The fever and the swelling along the cuts on my shoulders had begun to fade and my lip was beginning to heal. In the end, I'd have more than one scar to remember the journey across the Narrows by.

Auster's shadow danced on the deck as he balanced in the lines with the seabirds overhead, their wings stretched against the wind. He threw a perch into the air and one caught it in its mouth as another landed on his shoulder. I couldn't help wondering if what my father had always said about the birds was true. If it was, maybe one of them was Crane.

The crew readied the *Marigold* to dock, and by the look of the other ships in the harbor, I could see that we weren't the only ones who'd come through the storm. Split masts, torn sails, and scraped hulls marked several other vessels down the line. The dock crews would make good coin for the next week, their livelihoods often dependent on the faithful storms that plagued the Narrows.

More than half of the ships in the harbor bore Saint's crest, and I wasn't the least bit surprised. Even after losing the *Lark*, his trade had grown in the years since I last saw him. My mother had always admired that about him, the refusal to be beaten and his hunger for more. There was no telling how many ships were under his command now.

Willa crouched beside the main anchor and I took hold of the line, lifting it as she untied the knot. "What if Zola finds out what happened to Crane?"

"He knows."

My hand tightened on the rope. It wasn't only West I was worried about. "What will he do?"

She shrugged. "Zola's got bigger problems."

"Bigger than one of his crew getting murdered?"

"He got into some trouble with a big gem trader from Bastian who crippled his operation years ago. He can't so much as swim in the waters of the Unnamed Sea without getting his throat cut, and with Saint taking control of the trade in the Narrows, he's desperate. That's why he's had his eye on us. He can't expand his trade route, so he needs to stay on top. He knows he can't touch Saint, but he can keep smaller crews from coming up."

The trade war between the Unnamed Sea and the Narrows was older than my father. The Narrows had always controlled the production and trade of rye, but Bastian controlled the gems. Both were needed to put coin in the pockets of the guild masters.

It was a world poised on the tip of a knife.

"What gem trader?" I asked.

"The only one that matters. The Trade Council has been holding out against giving Holland license to trade in the Narrows, but it's only a matter of time. There will be nowhere for Zola to hide then."

Holland had been legend long before I was born. She was the head of a Bastian empire that ruled the gem trade, and Saint's operation was a drop in the bucket compared to the power she held over the guilds. If the Trade Council ever gave her license to trade in our ports, it would wipe out every Narrows-based operation, including my father's.

Below, fishermen were already bringing in their first

catches, and the smell of seaweed was thick in the air. Auster and Willa threw the heaving lines to the men on the dock, and they pulled us in slowly as the harbor master walked toward us, a stack of parchment under his arm.

"*Marigold!*" he shouted, stopping at the end of the platform.

"Get West, will you?" Willa said, going for the anchor's crank.

I looked over her shoulder to the closed door of the helmsman's quarters. West and Hamish had been out of sight since before dawn, and I wondered if they were getting the ledgers in order for Saint. The hit on their books from the storm would come with consequences, and my father wasn't an understanding man.

I knocked on the door and stepped back, pulling in a deep breath to put together some sort of goodbye. There'd be no more early mornings on the cliffs of Jeval, watching for the *Marigold*'s sails on the horizon. No more ferries on Speck's boat with pyre heavy on my belt, and never again would I see West waiting at the end of the dock for me. My stomach wavered, making me feel sick. I didn't like the idea of never seeing him again. And I didn't like that I felt that way.

Footsteps sounded before the door creaked, but it was Hamish who appeared when it opened. Behind him, stacks of copper were spread over the desk, the maps rolled up tight.

"What is it?" West's voice sounded behind me, and I turned to see him standing beneath the archway.

"Oh, I thought you were . . ." I looked behind him into

the dark passage that led below deck. "The harbor master's asking for you."

He nodded, coming up the last step, and I realized he was holding my belt and jacket. He pushed them into my arms as he moved past me.

I looked down at the stitched leather of the shoulder seams, biting down on my bottom lip. He hadn't been kidding when he said he wanted me off the ship as soon as we pulled into port. I wished it didn't sting, but it did. I was standing in the breezeway with my heart in my throat, trying to figure out how to say goodbye, and West couldn't wait to be rid of me.

I slipped the belt around my waist and fastened it, the red blooming beneath my skin. My hand found the post of the archway, and I ran my fingers up the oiled wood one more time, looking out over the ship. Even bruised from the storm, the *Marigold* was still beautiful. And in a way, I would miss her.

Men called out below as Hamish unrolled the ladder. He reached into his jacket and handed me a folded parchment. "A map. It's a big city."

"Thank you." I took it, smiling at the rare kindness.

"Be careful out there." Willa perched her hands on her hips. The sun caught the burn on her face, making it look bloodred, but the skin was healing. And now that Crane was at the bottom of the sea, I wondered if the part that couldn't be seen would begin to mend too.

"I will."

Her mouth twisted up. "Somehow, I don't believe you."

Paj offered me his hand, and I took it. He squeezed once. "Good luck, dredger."

"Thanks."

Behind him, Auster gave me one of his easy smiles.

"Fable." West walked across the deck, the wind pulling his shirt around the shape of him as he stopped before me.

"Thank you," I said, holding a hand out between us. Whatever his reasons, he'd taken a risk in letting me come onto the *Marigold*. If I was never going to see him again, I wanted him to know that I understood that much.

He didn't take it. He shifted on his feet before me, his gaze trailing everywhere except my face. "Keep the jacket buttoned up and keep your knife where you can reach it. Don't trade your tools, not even to eat. And don't sleep on the street." He lifted my hood into place as I pulled the jacket closed and fastened the buttons up to my neck. "Don't draw attention to yourself. It's better to be no one than to be someone in this city."

He thought better of whatever else he was going to say, closing his mouth and swallowing hard. I lifted my hand again, waiting for him to take it, and this time, he did. His fingers wrapped around my wrist and mine around his as I looked up into his face. "Thank you, West." My voice was small.

He didn't move. It looked as if he wasn't even breathing. I tried to let go, but his grip tightened, holding me in place. The pulse at my wrist quickened as he pulled my hand toward him and the scar carved into my forearm peeked out from beneath my sleeve.

"I mean it, Fable," he breathed. "Be careful."

His fingers unwound from my arm, and I stepped back to put more space between us, my heart pounding in my chest. I dropped my eyes to the deck and lifted myself over the rail, onto the rungs. He watched me climb down, the ladder swinging, and as soon as my boots landed on the crowded dock, something crashed into my side. I flew forward, catching myself on the hull of the ship with my hands to keep from falling into the water.

"Watch it!" A broad-shouldered man barreled past me with a crate of fish on his shoulder, not even looking back.

I pushed into the crowd, pulling the sleeve of my jacket down to be sure my arm was covered. The docks were alive with the business of the port, at least six times the size of Dern's harbor. I wove in and out of the pockets of people, and when I reached the main walkway that led up into the city, I looked back one last time to the *Marigold*. She sat in one of the last bays, her warm golden wood the color of honey. On the quarterdeck, West stood with his arms crossed, looking out at me.

I met his eyes one last time, hoping that even if I hadn't said it, he knew.

I did owe him. I owed him everything.

He watched me for another moment before he finally turned, disappearing from the deck of the ship, and I breathed past the sting in my eyes.

I walked into the river of hucksters, swirling around one another up the ramp that led into Ceros's Waterside. Crews that had just docked were already on their way up the hill where temporary companions and bottles of rye awaited them in the city's taverns.

Saint's outpost was nestled in the Pinch, a pitiful hollow where no respectable person lived or did business. Most everyone who did call it home survived off his patronage, which meant Saint collected a lot of favors. It was one of the reasons he'd been able to build all he had. He knew how to make people depend on him.

Another shoulder shoved into me, throwing me back, and I hit a post, stumbling. But the thought hissed like a faint whisper, my eyes following the polished boots beneath the length of a sapphire blue coat.

I looked up and the chaos of the dock halted, everything slowing with the stalled beat of my heart. The breath burned in my chest, my mind racing through a flood of memories that rushed in, drowning me.

The man looked over his shoulder as he passed me, the set of his angled jaw tight.

It was him. It was Saint.

The trader who'd built an empire. The father who'd left me behind. The man who'd loved my mother with the fury of a thousand merciless storms.

He blinked, his eyes sparkling beneath his hat for just a moment before his gaze fell back to the dock.

And as if I'd only imagined it, he kept walking.

TWENTY-ONE

He'd seen me.

He'd seen me and he knew exactly who I was. It was in the clench of his fist as he looked back over his shoulder. In the tick of his jaw when his eyes met mine. He'd recognized me.

Saint knew I'd made it to Ceros and he knew why. Just like I knew why he'd kept walking. I'd never broken the promise I'd made him. Not a single person in the Narrows knew that I was his daughter except for Clove, and Saint wouldn't acknowledge me out in the open like that. He wouldn't risk anyone wondering who I was.

He disappeared in the crowd of dock workers, his steps steady as he made his way to the large ship pulling into the bay. His crest was painted onto the sail at its bow.

I pulled my hood up tighter, my breath hitching in my chest. My throat burned, tears pricking behind my eyes. Because he looked the same. How was that possible? He was the exact same handsome, rugged man he was the last time I saw him.

The bell rang out, marking the opening of the merchant's house, and I turned in a circle, steadying myself on the post with one hand. Saint would meet with the helmsmen of his arriving ships before he went back to his post at the Pinch. When he got there, I'd be waiting for him.

I climbed the steps up from the harbor and stood at the scrolling iron entry to Waterside. It was the worst of Ceros's slums, a filthy stretch of burrows that ran the length of the shore past the harbor. Beyond that, the city was a maze. Streets and alleyways wound like tight knots, people spilling out of every window and doorway. The largest port city in the Narrows, it was a bustling hub of trade and enterprise, but it was nothing compared to the opulence of the cities that lay in the Unnamed Sea.

I pulled the map Hamish had given me from my satchel and unfolded it against the mud wall in the alley. If the harbor was behind me, then the Pinch was northeast. It wasn't easy to get to, and maybe that was one of the reasons my father had chosen it for his post. No one expected a wealthy trader to hole up in the most squalid corner of the city.

I lifted myself up onto my toes, trying to spot the nearest ladder to the bridges. Beyond the next market, I could see shadowed figures scaling up over the rise of rooftops. I folded the map and shoved it into my jacket, slipping into the main street. People crowded between the buildings, coming to and from the market with baskets of potatoes and bushels of grain.

The mouth of the street spilled out into the square, where brightly colored canvas canopies and awnings cast a pink shade over the market. The dusty air was filled with the scent of roasting meats, and the vendor stalls snaked in wayward lines, their tables and carts stacked with fruits and fish and bolts of cloth in every color.

I shoved through, watching the bridges to keep track of where I was going. My belt and my coin purse were tucked safely inside my shirt, where no one could get to them without cutting through my jacket. But my hand instinctively reached between the buttons to find the handle of my knife.

A short woman with a huge silver fish slung over her shoulders pushed through the market, carving a path, and I followed her, sticking close until we were on the other side. I found the line to the ladder, and when it was my turn, I climbed the ropes. The cool wind blowing over the city hit me as I rose higher, the thick odor of the streets cleared away. I pulled the fresh air into my lungs, leaning into the netted wall of the bridge as people moved past. The wood planks bounced under my feet, slightly swinging, and I hooked my fingers into the ropes and looked out over Ceros. The rising brick walls and tattered roofs reached up from every inch of the city, the system of bridges weaving in between them all.

To the east, I could see the Pinch. It was the lowest part of the rolling landscape and the most densely populated. The crumbling structures were stacked on top of one another like teetering blocks.

"Miss?" A little girl stopped, pulling at the hem of my jacket. She held up a small square of white silk with a ship embroidered in blue thread. "Coin?" Her pale blue eyes looked almost white in the bright sunlight.

I stared down at it, the wrinkled cloth spread across her dirty hands. The ship was a large trader, with four masts and more than a dozen sails.

"Sorry." I shook my head, moving past her.

I started across the bridge, keeping to one side and watching carefully. There was a time when I had the route to the Pinch memorized, but the bridges were confusing, and it was easy to end up in the opposite direction if you weren't careful. I took a turn, going east until I found one that ran north. The late morning sun bore down, reflecting where the harbor crept out over the water. I couldn't even tell which ship was the *Marigold* from here.

In the distance, the bells in the tower rang out, signaling the close of the market, and a moment later, a flood of people were climbing the ladders in a steady stream. I stepped onto a bridge that tilted up before it dropped back down again, and I could already smell it. The stink of the Pinch was something that burned in your nostrils and didn't leave for days. And for those who lived there, it was something that became a part of them.

The streets below turned muddy and dark as the bridge slanted all the way down and came to a dead end. The ladder that dropped to the ground was covered in the same muck. I pulled the collar of my shirt up out of my jacket to cover my nose and held my breath as I climbed down. The shadows of the buildings cloaked most of the Pinch in shade, despite the time of day. The sound of wild dogs barking and babies crying echoed through the narrow street, and I pulled my map out again, trying to get my bearings.

It looked the same as it did four years ago, except there was more of everything—mud, people, refuse. And with the walls of buildings pulling up around you, you could hardly see the sky overhead.

I followed the alley that broke off from the main pathway. It twisted through buildings so narrow that I had to turn sideways in places to get through. Eyes peered down at me from windows above, where wet clothes flapped on lines. The familiar broken archway reached over the roofs in the distance. The rusted iron was a garland of the same triangular sails that adorned Saint's crest. I made my way toward it as the sun dropped, the temperature falling with it.

The alley widened again, opening up to a circle of wooden doors. All green but one—a brilliant blue with a bronze knocker depicting the face of a sea demon. Its wide eyes looked down at me, its tongue unrolled.

Saint's post.

More eyes peered down from above, probably people my father had paid to keep watch. But I knew how to get in. I'd done it a hundred times. I unclasped my jacket and took it off, tucking the length of it into my belt before I fit my fingers into the crevices of the smooth white clay wall. My hands were bigger than they were the last time I'd climbed

173

it, but the cracks and holds were the same. I lifted myself up, using the door knocker as a foothold, and when the edge of the little window was within reach, I leapt for it, catching the rim with my fingertips and swinging over the drop.

My elbow hooked into the lip of wood, and I fished the chisel from my belt. The edge slid in easily, and I shimmied it up to lift the latch. It was a small window, and I had to wedge myself in, dropping my belt inside and shifting my hips until I'd squeezed through. I landed on the tile hard, groaning against the sharp pain that exploded in my ribs, and pushed myself back up to my feet.

The room was dark, only the light from the small open window coming inside in an angled beam. I searched for a lantern, feeling along the shelves until the toe of my boot ran into the leg of a desk and my fingers found a candle. I struck a match and held the lantern up before me, the lump coming back up in my throat.

Maps. Charts. Lists. Diagrams.

A bronze scope with his name engraved on its side.

Saint.

It was all the same. Just the same, like him. As if the last four years hadn't happened and no time had passed at all. He was still here, still sailing, still trading and bartering and building ships.

Like I never existed.

TWENTY-TWO

Four years ago

That night, the sharp sound of the bell rang out, and my father came for me, pulling me from my hammock, bleary-eyed and confused.

I didn't know what was happening until the hatch flew open before us, and the lightning struck so close to the ship that it blinded me, the sound erupting painfully in my ears. Black spots drowned out every bit of light in my vision, and I blinked furiously, trying to clear it.

Saint tucked me into his jacket as well as I could fit and then he barreled out into the roaring wind, the rain spinning, not falling in any one direction.

I'd never seen rain like that before.

"Mama!" I shouted, looking over my father's shoulder for her, but there was almost no one on deck. And when I looked up to the tangle of clouds above us, I screamed. The mainmast of the *Lark* had snapped in two.

I knew what that meant. There was no coming back from a broken mast.

We were abandoning ship.

I clawed out of Saint's jacket, slipping from his grasp and hitting the deck so hard it knocked the breath from my lungs.

"Fable!" A wave crashed over the starboard side, sweeping him off his feet, and I ran for the hatch.

"Mama!" I screamed, but I couldn't even hear my own voice. There was only the howl of the wind. The growl of the ship.

Arms wrapped around me, dragging my weight to the back, and another face appeared before me. Clove. Saint threw me in his direction, and I slid over the flooded deck until I slammed into him.

He didn't wait. Clove climbed up onto the railing with me in his arms and jumped into the wind. We fell into the darkness, hitting the water with the sound of a thunderclap, and suddenly, everything was quiet. The raging storm was replaced with the deep hum of the sea. Beneath the surface, motionless bodies churned in the black water, the masts and prows of long-dead ships illuminated below us as the lightning struck again and again.

When we came back up, I choked, clinging to Clove with shaking hands.

Saint was suddenly beside us. "Swim!" he shouted.

Another ear-splitting crack sounded like a cannon shot, and I turned in the water. The *Lark*'s hull was splitting in two. Right down the middle.

"Swim, Fable!" I'd never heard my father's voice sound like that. I'd never seen his face broken into pieces with fear.

I cut through the water, swimming as fast as I could against the suck of the sinking ship pulling it down with it. Saint stayed with me, coming up over the crest of every wave at my side. We swam until I couldn't feel my arms or my legs and my stomach was half full of seawater. When the orange light of a lantern flickered ahead, I started to sink. Clove's hand took hold of my shirt, and he pulled me along with him until I was floating on the water in his wake. When I opened my eyes again, one of my father's deckhands was lifting me into a small boat.

"Mama . . ." I cried, watching the bow of the *Lark* sink in the distance. "Mama, mama, mama . . ."

Saint didn't speak a word when he climbed in after me. He didn't look back. Not even once.

We didn't raise the small sail until the next morning, when the gales had hushed and the sea fell into sleep. I sat at the stern, filling buckets of water until the hull of the rowboat was empty. Saint's eyes stayed on the horizon. It was only then I noticed that the man who'd pulled me from the water was injured, his pale face betraying his fate. It took him only hours to die, and just moments after he took his last breath, Saint dumped him over the side.

We pushed up onto the smooth beach of Jeval the next morning. I'd never been to the pyre-rich island, but my mother had dredged its reefs. I lay on the sand, the waves crawling up to touch my bare feet, and while Clove went to find food and water, my father took the knife from his belt.

"Do you trust me?" he asked, looking me straight in the eye with a calm that terrified me.

I nodded, and he took hold of my hand with his rough fingers, turning it over until the soft skin of my forearm was between us. I didn't know what he was going to do until the tip of the knife had already drawn blood.

I tried to pull away, but a firm look from him made me still under his touch. I buried my face into my knees and tried not to scream as he cut into me, engraving smooth, curving lines that reached from my elbow to my wrist. When he was finished, he carried me out into the water and cleaned it, bandaging the wound carefully with torn pieces of his shirt.

Clove returned with a bucket of shellfish he'd bartered for down the beach, and we made a fire, eating the meager supper in silence. My stomach roiled against the pain throbbing in my arm, my heart aching with the loss of my mother. And we didn't speak of her. In fact, I would never speak of her again in those years on Jeval.

I didn't ask what had happened. If she were alive, Saint would have never left her behind.

We slept there on the beach, and when the sun came up, Clove readied the rowboat. But when I waded out into the water behind him, my father set a heavy hand on my shoulder and told me I wasn't coming with them. His lips moved around the words as he looked down into my face, his expression as unreadable as ever. But I couldn't understand him. He said it three times before the bits finally came together in my mind and my hands started to shake at my sides.

"Why?" I croaked, trying not to sound pathetic. My father hated it when people were pathetic.

"Because you weren't made for this world, Fable." For a moment, I thought I saw the glimmer of tears in his eyes. The edge of emotion in his voice. But when I blinked, the mask that was the father I knew had returned.

"Saint . . ." I didn't want to beg. "Don't leave me here." I looked to the boat, where Clove was waiting. But he didn't look at me, the set of his shoulders like the cut of stone.

"You make me a promise and I'll make one to you."

I nodded eagerly, thinking he'd changed his mind.

"Survive. Get yourself off this island. And the next time I see you, I'll give you what's yours."

I looked up into his face. "And if I never see you again?"

But he only turned, his hand slipping through my fingers as he walked away.

I didn't dare cry as he got back into the boat. I didn't make a single sound. The tears streamed down my face in hot rivulets, disappearing into my shirt. My heart twisted up on itself and threatened to stop, every part of me screaming on the inside.

And when the little triangle sail disappeared over the horizon, I was alone.

TWENTY-THREE

I sank back into the tufted leather chair behind my father's desk, drinking in the warm scent of his pipe smoke. It was soaked into every bit of the room, sweet and spicy and so familiar that it made my chest ache.

Traces of my mother were everywhere.

A compass that belonged to her on the windowsill. Dredger tools spilling from a small chest on the floor. Beside the door, a fraying turquoise silk scarf hung from a rusty nail. If I closed my eyes, I would still be able to see it wrapped around her shoulders, her long braid swinging down her back as she walked.

So, I didn't close my eyes.

I lit the candles as the sun fell and went to the window, looking out over the Pinch. Eyes still watched from dark windows, and I wondered if any of those faces were ones I'd recognize. If any of them would recognize me as the little girl who used to walk these streets on Saint's heels.

I glanced over my shoulder to the gilded mirror on the wall. The silver had begun to boil behind the glass, making everything in its reflection look like it was underwater.

In its center, there I was.

I stilled. Because I didn't know the girl in the reflection. And also, I did.

I looked like *her*. So much like her, in shape and color and angle of jaw.

The years had changed me. I was taller, of course, but there was a curve to my hips I hadn't realized was there. The freckles that once sprinkled over my nose were now too numerous to count, many of them melting together. My auburn hair was darker, the colors shifting with the turn of light. There was something I didn't like about seeing myself like that. It was unnerving.

I reached up, touching my face and letting my fingertips trail the shape of my bones. My hand froze when I felt it— like a deep current rushing inside of me.

Isolde.

I could feel her, as if she stood in the room beside me. As if the warmth of her was dancing over my skin. Something flashed on the shelf against the wall, and I squinted, my eyes focusing on the pale green glow.

Inside an open wooden box was something I recognized. Something I never thought I'd see again.

A sharp pain awoke behind my ribs, hot tears springing up into my eyes. It couldn't be.

The simple pendant sat inside the box, the silver chain

spilling over the side. A green abalone sea dragon. Worth nothing, really. Except that it was *hers*.

My mother's necklace had dangled over me every single night as she kissed me. It pulled around her throat when we dove the reefs. She was wearing it the night she died.

So, how was it here?

I picked it up carefully, as if it might turn to smoke and disappear.

Voices trailed in through the glass-pane windows, and my fingers closed over the necklace as I looked out.

Saint's blue coat glowed in the dim light, the only bright thing in the dismal street. People moved out of his way as he walked, his silent presence almost seeming to leave a trail behind him. He'd always been that way.

The tremble in my bones returned and I shoved my hand into the pocket of my jacket. The necklace tangled in my slick fingers as I sank back into the chair. I sat up straight, squaring my shoulders to the door.

His boots stopped outside, and he waited a short moment before he fit his key into the lock. I tried to slow my racing heart, but beads of sweat were already gathering at my brow. I bit down on my bottom lip to keep it from quivering.

The door swung open, letting the cool air in, and the man I'd never been allowed to call my father stood before me, his ice-blue eyes sharpening in the candlelight.

I stilled, unable to even draw breath. "I'm—"

"Fable." The deep grind of his voice filled the quiet room. He *had* recognized me. I knew he had.

Saint closed the door behind him and walked to the desk, leaning into it with both of his hands as he looked down into my face. I tried to blink back the tears threatening to come up into my eyes, but it was no use. I waited for him to speak, my thoughts racing with what he might say. What he might do. But he only stared at me.

"I bartered for passage on one of your ships," I said, the sound of my voice like a stranger.

"The *Marigold*."

I nodded. "That's right."

The floorboards creaked beneath his feet as he stood and went to the shelf, picking up his pipe and filling it with mullein leaves.

"Where's Clove?" My father's navigator was never far from Saint, and I wondered what he'd say when he saw me.

"Gone."

"Gone?"

He hunched over the flame, puffing until the leaves smoldered.

But that couldn't be right. Clove and Saint had crewed together since before I was born. There was no way he'd moved on from my father's ship. Unless . . .

I wiped a stray tear from the corner of my eye when I realized what he meant. Clove was dead. And if Clove was dead, Saint was alone. The thought made me feel like I was back under that dark water, the flash of lightning silent above me.

"I saw your ships in Dern and down in the harbor." I sniffed, changing the subject. "How many are there now?"

He sat in the chair before me. "Twenty-eight."

My eyes widened. I'd thought maybe twenty. But almost thirty ships sailing under your crest was something more than a trading outfit. If he had that many ships, then he wasn't the rising trader I'd known four years ago. He was the at the top of that ladder now.

"You did it," I whispered, a smile pulling at my lips.

"I did what?"

"You opened your route to the Unnamed Sea."

He drew in a mouth full of smoke, and it rippled out through his lips slowly.

"Just like Isolde—"

"Don't say her name." He stiffened, his eyes narrowing.

I tilted my head, trying to read him. But Saint was a fortress. An abyss with no end. Very few things put him on edge, and I hadn't suspected my mother's name would be one of them.

It wasn't the greeting I'd expected. He wasn't a warm man, and I didn't need an embrace or a display of emotion, but he hadn't even asked me what happened after he left me on Jeval. How I'd survived. How I got to Ceros.

"I've come for what you promised me," I said, the anger bleeding out into the words.

The lines around his eyes carved deeper as he surveyed me for a long moment. He bit down on the pipe and stood again, sending the chair scraping over the floor, and went back to the shelf. He picked up stacks of dusty books by the armful, setting them on the desk. "Your inheritance," he said.

I leaned forward. "My what?"

He pulled a thickly rolled parchment from the back of the shelf and dropped it onto the desk in front of me. I picked it up slowly, a tingle running over my skin. He watched me unroll it, and the candlelight spilled over a faded map. It was Tempest Snare.

"I don't understand."

Saint pulled a single copper from his jacket pocket and set it on a point in the upper right section of the map. "The *Lark*."

The sting on my skin grew, traveling over the whole of me until I was buzzing with the heat of a storm. "What?"

He set the tip of his finger onto the coin. "She's there. And she's yours."

I looked up at him through my eyelashes.

"I saved her for you."

"You never went back?"

"Once." He cleared his throat and my fingers tightened around the necklace in my pocket. That's how he had it. He'd gone back. For Isolde. "But I left the cargo."

"There was a fortune in the hull of that ship . . ." My voice trailed off.

"There are only three people who survived that night." For a moment, it looked like the flash of memory pained him. "Only three people who knew where the *Lark* went down."

Me, Saint, and Clove.

"It belongs to you," he said.

I stood, moving around the corner of the desk and wrapped

my arms around him. I pressed my face into his shoulder and he stood erect, the tension widening throughout him. But I didn't care. I'd spent every day of the last four years trying to get back to him. And I'd spent every day wondering if he'd keep his promise to me.

He had.

The *Lark* slept in Tempest Snare with my mother, waiting for me. For *us*.

There was enough coin and gems there to do whatever I wanted. After four years of scraping every single day, I would want for nothing.

I let him go, wiping my eyes. "When do we go?"

But his face changed then, the slant leaving his eyes. "We're not."

I stared at him.

"I left that ship at the bottom of the sea for you. If you want it, then go get it."

"But I thought . . ." The words broke off. "You said you would give me what's mine."

"And I have."

"I thought you meant a *place* here." My voice strained. "I came back to be with you. To crew for you."

"Crew for me?"

"I'm a good dredger and an even better gem sage. I'm not as good as Isolde was, but—"

"Don't . . . say . . . her *name*," his voice clipped.

"I don't understand," I breathed.

"I never should have let your mother step foot on my ship.

I'm not making the same mistake twice." He stood, walking to the window. I watched the muscles in his neck tense as his jaw clenched.

"You're turning me out? Just like that?"

"I just gave you your future!" He flung a hand at the map.

I picked it up, throwing it across the desk. It hit him and fell to the floor. "I don't want the *Lark*. I want to crew under your crest."

"No."

Hot tears rolled down my face, the panicked breath in my chest coming faster. "You have no idea what I had to do to get here."

"And now you know how to stay alive in this world." He lifted his chin.

"What does that mean?"

"The best thing I could have done for you is to leave you on Jeval."

"You mean the best thing you could have done for *you*. I was starving. I was terrified!" I glared at him, my teeth gritted. He expected me to be grateful for the hell he'd put me through, so he could take credit for who I was. "I lost my mother and my home. And then you dumped me on the nearest rock to fend for myself."

"Fend for yourself?" He spoke quietly, bitter and sharp. "Who do you think kept you fed? Who do you think put the coin you used to get passage in your pocket?" His voice rose.

I stared at him, confused.

"What do you think the *Marigold* is, Fable?"

"I know what a shadow ship is. It's the decoy you use to manipulate trade and gather information. I'm not stupid. West is probably saddled under a debt to you that he'll never be able to pay."

"Very smart." He looked pleased.

"What does that have to do with me?"

"You think West would have shown up in Jeval if I hadn't sent him there? You think he would have paid you for pyre if I hadn't ordered him to?"

My eyes widened, my mouth dropping open. I reached out with a shaking hand to the desk, bracing myself against the words. "What are you saying?"

"I took care of you."

A sob broke from my chest before it turned into a bitter laugh. Of course. West knew exactly who I was. This whole time. And when he sailed into the barrier islands two years ago looking to buy pyre, he was really just looking for me. That's why he didn't want me on his ship. That's why he couldn't let anything happen to me.

I was the most expensive cargo he'd ever taken across the Narrows.

I stared at the ground, trying to keep the room from spinning. Everything was sideways. Everything was wrong.

"You don't see it yet. Maybe you never will. But I did what was best for both of us. You kept your promise and I kept mine." He picked the map back up, rolling it tightly. "Now it's time to go your own way, Fable."

Another cry slipped from my lips, and I covered my face

with my hands, humiliated. I'd crossed the Narrows for a man who'd probably never even loved me. For a dream that would never come true. And in that moment, I had no idea why I'd ever believed it could.

"You're strong and you're sharp. You'll figure it out."

"If you're not coming with me, then this map is useless." I stared at it, my body feeling suddenly heavy. "Even if I find a way to get there, I'll never be able to navigate Tempest Snare without you. You're the only one who knows the way through those reefs."

His hand reached out for me and I flinched, stepping back. But he followed, snatching up my arm and pushing the sleeve of my shirt up to my elbow. In the flickering light, the raised, pearly skin of my scar glimmered between us.

"There." He pointed to the upper right corner, at the tip of the longest thread of the scar.

A sick, sinking feeling pulled in the pit of my stomach as I put it together. As if I were seeing it for the first time, the pattern came to life, taking shape before my eyes.

It was a map.

That proud, stubborn bastard had carved a map to the *Lark* into my skin. It was the intricate path through the graveyard where two hundred years of sunken ships were laid to rest.

I wrenched my arm away, my face on fire.

"You have everything you need to build your own life."

He meant a life away from him. This wasn't an inheritance. It wasn't even a gift. It was a bribe to stay away. "Fine," I choked.

"I'll go my own way. And if you think I'll owe you anything . . ."

"You're my daughter, Fable."

I looked him in the eye, my voice seething with every drop of hatred that boiled within me. "I'm *Isolde's* daughter."

The ironclad set of his mouth faltered then, just barely, and I knew the words had hurt. But I meant them. I'd been a fool for believing that Saint would welcome me back to the Narrows. That he'd be happy to see me.

He was the same cruel, cold tyrant he'd always been.

And I hated him more than I'd ever hated anything in my life.

I took the map, walking straight past him. My reflection in the gilded mirror flashed like a ghost as I passed, and when I opened the door, the foul smell of the Pinch rushed inside. I stepped into the muck, tucking the map into my jacket.

And this time, I left Saint behind.

TWENTY-FOUR

I walked the bridges in the dark.

The salt-soaked wind blew in from the sea, and I ran one hand along the knotted rope walls, following them in whatever direction they took me. I didn't care where. There was no place to go anyway.

People with skirt hems and boots painted in mud passed me, and lanterns flickered to life below as darkness swallowed Ceros one rooftop at a time. When the bridge finally came to a dead end, I found myself alone above a pocket of the city that was tucked behind Waterside. I climbed down the ladder, and my boots splashed in the muck as the last bit of orange light found its way through the crooked streets.

"You should get inside, girl," a woman with a crimson shawl draped over her head called out to me from a cracked window.

I pulled the hood of my jacket up and kept walking.

The city was a tangle of narrow paths, buildings covering every inch of it. My mother used to say that Ceros was like the coral on the reefs, except for the noise. Living things were stuck into every crack and crevice, but underwater, there was only a deep silence that vibrated in your bones. She'd never loved this city like Saint did. The sea was where she belonged.

I pulled the necklace from my pocket and held it up so the pendant dangled in the moonlight.

I hadn't meant to take it. Not really. But with every poisonous word that dropped from Saint's lips, my fingers had wound tighter into its chain. Until it felt like it didn't belong to him anymore.

I clasped the necklace around my neck and pulled at the chain with my fingers until it bit against my skin. If Isolde hadn't drowned with the *Lark,* maybe we'd be walking these streets together now. We'd wander the bridges while my father inspected ledgers at his post and met with merchants at the harbor. We'd buy roasted plums at the market and find a place to watch the sun go down over the rise of land, the juice of the warm fruit sticky on our hands.

The vision was too painful to hold in my mind, like boiling water filling my skull.

"Hi there." A man stepped into the alley, blocking my path. His eyes glinted in the lantern light, his lips spreading over missing teeth.

I looked up at him, reaching for the knife in my belt without a word.

"Where are you going?" He took a step toward me, and I slid the blade free.

"Let me pass."

He leaned in closer, stumbling forward as he reached clumsily for my belt. Before he could right himself, I swiped up in one clean motion, catching the edge of his ear with the knife.

He threw himself backward, the drink suddenly clearing from his eyes, and I followed, taking three quick steps until his back was against the wall. I lifted the blade, setting it at the hollow of his throat and pressing down just enough to draw a single drop of blood.

He froze, straightening, and I looked him in the eye, daring him to make a move. I wanted a reason to hurt him. I wanted an excuse to lean forward until the edge of the steel sunk into his skin. It was the only thing that seemed like it may dull the sharp pain inside me. Cool the raging heat that still burned on my face.

He stepped to the side slowly, moving around me, and a string of curses trailed off into the dark as he disappeared. I stood, staring into the brick wall until the sound of glass breaking made me turn. At the end the alley, a window with one dangling shutter was lit. When the wind picked up the familiar sour scent of spilled rye, I exhaled, heading straight for the door.

I ducked into a dimly lit tavern where every bit of space was filled with people, the grime of Ceros on their skin and on their clothes. Traders. Dock workers. Ship repair crews.

They were stuffed into every corner, small green glasses clutched in their hands, and the peppered smell of unwashed bodies filled the small room.

There was only one stool free at the counter between two towering men, and I lifted up on the toes of my boots and slid onto it. The barkeep tipped his chin up at me, and I reached into my belt to fish out a copper.

My hand stilled as I took the weight of the purse into my hand. It was heavier. Fuller.

I pulled at the strings, opening it, and looked inside. There were well over twenty coppers that hadn't been there the day before. I felt down the length of my belt, trying to make sense of it until the realization hit me like the burn of a flame.

West.

The vision of him standing in the breezeway that morning resurfaced. He had filled the purse. That's why he had my belt when he came up from the cabin.

"Well?" the barkeep huffed, his hand held out before me. I dropped a copper into his palm, cinching the purse closed before anyone could get a look at it.

I crossed my arms on the counter and laid my head down, staring at my boots.

West had known who I was all along. And he knew exactly what would happen when I went to Saint. He was looking out for me, like he had been for the last two years, buying my pyre on the barrier islands. Even if he'd done it under Saint's order, he'd done it. But the extra copper in my purse didn't bring me relief. It was only a reminder that none of the copper had ever been mine in the first place.

The glasses sloshed as the barkeep slammed them down before me, and he moved to the next hand raised in the air. The emerald-green glasses sparkled like jewels as I picked the first one up, breathing in the peaty smell of the rye before I took a small sip.

The scent reminded me of Saint. A little green glass sat on his desk every night in the hazy smoke of the helmsman's quarters on the *Lark,* even though there wasn't supposed to be any rye on the ship.

I wanted to hate him. I wanted to curse him.

But in the minutes that had passed since I'd walked out his door, I'd been plagued with the truth that I didn't only hate him. I didn't know anything about where he'd come from, but I knew it was something he didn't like to talk about. He'd built his trade from nothing, ship by ship, and even if he'd left me and betrayed me, there was still a small part of me that loved him. And I knew why. It was Isolde.

My mother had loved Saint with a love that could set fire to the sea.

It was a truth that made it hard to wish him dead. But after three glasses of rye, I thought, anything was possible.

I tilted my head back, swallowing the whole of the glass down, and pinched my eyes closed as it burned in my throat. It travelled all the way down to my stomach, making me feel instantly lighter. The warmth of it spilled into the weight of my legs, and I leaned into the counter.

The only soul left in the Narrows that I could run to was Clove, but he was gone, like my mother. The thought hung heavy inside of me, more tears filling my eyes. In all the time I'd spent on Jeval, I'd never felt as alone as I did now.

"Dredger," a deep voice sounded at my back, and I picked up the second glass, turning on the stool.

Zola stood, leaning into the wooden beam beside the bar, a smile on his face. His cap was gone, revealing a head of long black hair streaked with silver.

"I thought that was you."

I stared at him wordlessly before throwing my head back and draining the glass.

He set his sharp eyes on the man beside me, who immediately stood, leaving his stool open. Zola took it, setting a copper on the bar.

"What are you doing in a tavern alone at night in the most dangerous city in the Narrows?" He looked as if the idea amused him.

The barkeep set three rye glasses down before him slowly, taking extra care not to spill, and I glared at him.

"None of your business."

"Where's your crew?" He leaned in closer.

"They're not my crew."

He half laughed. "Probably for the best. Don't think the *Marigold* will be on its feet much longer. Neither will its helmsman."

I turned my last rye glass in a circle on the bar top. "What's that supposed to mean?"

Zola shrugged, staring into his glass. "Only that West knows how to get himself into trouble. And eventually, it's going to catch up with him." He picked up a glass and shot it back. "I heard something about a dredger in Dern no one had ever seen before, spotting gem fakes. That you?"

"No."

He set his elbows up on the bar, folding his fingers together. "You're a good liar. Anyone ever tell you that?"

My eyes slid to meet his. Koy had said the same thing right before he tried to kill me.

"Not a bad trait in the Narrows. You can dredge, you're good with gems, and you know how to lie. You looking for a place on a crew or not?"

"Not *your* crew." I turned to face him.

"Why not?"

"I know what you did to Willa."

His eyes glinted, the grin on his face spreading even wider. "I don't think I have to tell you what it takes to survive in the Narrows."

"I don't care what your reasons are. I'm not interested."

He surveyed me as I swallowed my last shot of rye, and when I looked up again, the expression on his face had changed. His eyes narrowed in thought, his head tilting to one side.

"What?"

He blinked, as if for a moment he'd forgotten where he was. "You remind me of someone." The words were almost too low to hear. He took his last two shots in a row and dropped another copper down, signaling the barkeep.

The sounds of the room quieted as my heart slowed with the race of rye in my veins. Everything was stretched. The light was softer.

Zola's voice deepened as he stood. "You be careful out there, dredger."

Three more rye glasses landed on the counter, and I looked over my shoulder. Zola was gone, his stool empty beside me. The day I'd first met him in Dern, he said that Crane was his stryker, but Zola's ship, the *Luna*, was much bigger than the *Marigold*. He ran a much larger crew. Did he know the man I'd watched West and the others kill, or was it just a face he'd barely recognize, sent out on a dirty errand? And what else had that man done on Zola's order?

I finished the next glass and rubbed my face with the heels of my hands. That night on the *Lark*, the years on Jeval, the days on the *Marigold*. They came marching toward me in the candlelight of the tavern like a screaming mob. I wanted to close my eyes and not open them again until winter was bearing down on the Narrows.

I set the second glass down and pulled up the sleeve of my jacket, laying my arm out before me. The scar Saint had carved into my arm looked like the angry web of river inlets. Smooth, raised paths snaked down to my wrist, and I traced them with my finger, stopping on the farthest tip, near my wrist.

Where the *Lark* lay in the deep.

"Fable?"

I yanked my sleeve back down and cradled my arm to

198

me, looking up to see Willa. The vision of her tipped and swayed, and I suddenly felt like I was falling off the stool. I clamped my hands down on the edge of the counter to hold myself in place.

"What are you doing here?" She sat beside me, leaning forward to look at my face.

I picked up the last glass and drained it, slamming it down.

"How many of those have you had?"

I closed my eyes, breathing through the nausea creeping up my throat. "What do you care?"

"All right," she said, standing. "Come on."

She took my hand, but I pulled free, almost falling. Her arms caught me, sitting me back up, and then I was standing. Moving. Weaving through the crowded room as it spun around us. When I stumbled, slamming into the wall, Willa ducked down, throwing me over her shoulder.

"Stop!" I slurred, my arms dangling. But she didn't listen. We climbed dark stairs, and the jingle of keys made my eyes pop open. In the next breath, I was lying in a bed.

"Stupid," Willa muttered.

"What?" I croaked.

"I told you I was trying to figure out if I liked you or if you were stupid."

The words jumbled into one blaring sound in my head. A metal pail landed next to the bed, and Willa rolled me onto my side, opening my mouth.

"What are you—"

Her finger went down my throat, and I kicked, trying to pull free. But I was already vomiting. Willa lifted the bucket to my face and hit me on the back with the flat of her palm.

"What are you doing?" I coughed, shoving her away.

"You'll thank me tomorrow when only half of that poison is still in your veins." She laughed, standing.

"How'd you find me?"

"I've been following you for hours. Figured I should make you call it a night before you passed out on the counter."

"You're *following* me?" I pushed her away again.

"Believe me, it's not what I wanted to spend my night doing." She glared at me.

"Then why are you here?"

"Orders." She looked down at me, waiting for the words to settle into something that made sense. When they finally did, I realized she was talking about West. He was still doing his job—keeping me alive. "What happened with Saint?"

I rolled onto my back and fixed my eyes on the rafters, trying to make the spinning stop. "Exactly what you said would happen," I muttered.

"Oh, I see." She crossed her arms, leaning into the wall. "So, you think you're the only girl in the Narrows whose dreams didn't come true?"

"Go away," I groaned.

"You want something in this life?" She came to stand over me. "You take it, Fable."

"What are you talking about?"

"You want to crew on a trading ship."

It wasn't just that I wanted to crew. I wanted to crew for my father. But I couldn't tell her that without breaking my promise to Saint.

"You know the *Marigold* doesn't have a dredger," she said evenly.

"So?"

She sighed. *"So?"*

I blinked, thinking. But everything was too fuzzy. Too clouded.

"You want something in this life, you take it," she said again, louder. "For a girl who lived on Jeval, I'm not sure why I need to tell you that."

"West will never take me on."

"I told you. He has a habit of making other people his problem."

She was right. I didn't have a chance with a single helmsman down on the docks. No one was going to take on a Jevali dredger they didn't know unless I showed them what I could do with the gems. That was a risk I couldn't take. Gem sages found themselves the prey of rival traders and the pawns of gem guilds often enough that it had become just one more thing that could get you killed.

But if I was going to get to the *Lark*, I did need a ship. "He told you to follow me?"

The hardness that always constructed Willa's face wasn't there as she sat back down on the bed beside me, and I wondered if she'd had a few glasses of rye herself. "Make him take you on."

I still wasn't sure what exactly the *Marigold* was up to, but it couldn't be any worse than the crooked work Saint did. Or maybe it was. In only a few days, I'd found that West's crew was trying to outrun more than one enemy. If I was going to take that on, I needed to know exactly what I was dealing with.

"What happened with the merchant in Sowan?" I took a chance in asking it.

Willa stared out the window, her voice hollow as she answered. "West did a bad thing to a good man because he had to. And now, he gets to live with it."

TWENTY-FIVE

Everything hurt.

The light beaming into the room pierced like a knife through my skull. I peeked one eye open, swallowing the urge to throw up again. Beside the bed, the pail I'd emptied my stomach into throughout the night was gone. The window had been cracked open, letting the sea air drift inside, and I sat up slowly. The room wasn't spinning anymore.

A basin of water sat on a stand in the corner, and I washed my face, rinsing my mouth as best I could before I rebraided my hair. The strands caught the morning light, making the hue of red look almost violet. My belt sat on the floor beside the bed, and I picked up the coin purse, throwing it into the air and then catching it. If Willa was telling the truth and West had ordered her to follow me, there might be a chance I could get him to take me on.

The tavern was already awake below. The clang of teacups and the vibration of voices carried up the stairs and under the door, and I took each step carefully, my head pounding. As soon as I appeared, Willa lifted a hand from a bench in the corner and a wide smile erupted on her face. She bit her lip to keep from laughing.

Paj, Auster, and Hamish were hunched over plates of bread and dishes of butter, greeting me with full mouths.

"Look what the rye washed up." Auster tore a piece of bread from the loaf and held it out to me. I shook my head, finding a place to sit beside Paj. But Auster pushed it toward me. "Trust me, you need to get something in your stomach."

Willa set a teacup down before me and filled it with steaming black tea. When a plate clattered on a table behind us, I winced, the pain in my head exploding. I put my face into my hands and tried to breathe through it.

Auster dropped two lumps of sugar into the cup. The hair was pulled up off his shoulders, his face washed clean. "So, what happened to your plan to crew for Saint?"

"It didn't . . . work out," I mumbled.

He laughed. "I could have told you it wouldn't."

"I *did* tell you it wouldn't," Willa echoed.

And she'd been right. Even though I was his daughter, Saint was still Saint.

"What are you going to do?" Paj watched me from the top of his cup.

I picked at the edge of the bandage wrapped around my hand nervously. It was a crew that was better than most, even if they were small and steeped in trouble. I hadn't once had one of their blades at my throat, except for the night I'd climbed the ladder to their ship. They looked out for one another and they traded smart, even if they traded risky. There was an empty hammock in the belly of the *Marigold*, and really, there was nowhere else to go.

I met Willa's eyes, taking a deep breath. "Where's West?"

"Hasn't come down yet." Her eyes drifted to the stairs.

I took a cautious sip of my tea. If I asked them to take me on without West there, maybe I'd have a better chance of stacking the vote. But I'd make an enemy of West when he found out. It was better to wait.

"Probably headed out early." Hamish took his leather book from his jacket and set it onto the table. "All right, Willa, you and Auster are on galley supplies. Just fill the grain barrel and we'll eat lean."

"What?" Auster looked offended.

Hamish sighed. "We need to cut as many corners as we can until Sowan if we're going to pay for the losses and the repairs."

Auster shook his head. "I hate porridge."

"Well, that's all you're going to be eating until the next time we're in Ceros. Maybe longer." Hamish eyed him. "Paj, we need to replace those damaged riggings, but don't go to that bastard on Waterside again. His prices are too high, and after this storm, there's bartering to be done, with so many ships looking for repairs."

"And the hull?" Willa leaned on her elbows. "We need to get back on the water as soon as possible."

"The crew we hired worked through the night, so they should be finishing up the most urgent repairs this morning.

Let's get to the docks and check on them first. West is probably already down there, and I can give you exact numbers for the riggings."

"All right." Paj slathered a thick layer of jam onto another slice of bread with the back of his spoon.

Hamish made a few more marks on the page before he slapped the book closed and stood. The others followed, and I stared up at them. They pulled their caps and jackets on, sipping down the last of their tea. Auster stuffed his pockets with the remaining bread on the table, and Paj took the leftover bits from the empty table beside us.

"Come on, dredger." Willa tipped her chin toward the door.

I hesitated, looking to the others for an objection, but there was none. The four of them stood, waiting in the cool morning light pooling in from the window. I pressed my lips together to keep from smiling and then gulped down my tea, following them out into the alley.

"He'll never agree." I spoke low, so only Willa could hear me.

"Then you better make a good case if you want him outvoted."

She was right. I didn't need West to agree. I just needed a majority of votes. There was nothing he would be able to do about it if the crew wanted to take me on. He'd be forced to comply.

She winked before she pushed ahead, leaving me at the back of the line.

Overhead, the bridges were already full of people. We

wove through the streets, cutting through tight passages and around sharp corners until we were spit out onto the cobblestone paths of Waterside. The wind hit us like a wall as we stepped down onto the street, and the sea reached out before us, behind an endless line of ships bobbing in bays. Barefoot children swarmed around us, their faces streaked with soot and dirt, their hands open.

Waterside strays. Like West.

I couldn't imagine him, sun-bleached hair and golden skin, begging for food on street corners and digging through refuse in alleyways. I didn't want to.

Paj pulled the bread from his pockets and tore it into pieces, passing them out, but Auster lifted his into the air. A swarm of seabirds appeared a moment later, plucking the pieces from his hands as he walked.

Willa stopped short in front of me, and I slammed into her as a strangled gasp tore from her throat. A prick ran up and over every inch of my skin, and I looked around us, searching the docks for whatever she saw. Paj's hand reached back, finding Auster's, and Hamish stopped, every face tilted up to the sky in the distance.

"No." The whispered word broke in Willa's mouth.

I stepped past her, the sting on my skin turning to a devouring fire as my eyes found it.

The *Marigold*.

Her masts reached up against the blue sky, the sails unfurled and slashed. Every single one—sliced white canvas flapping in the wind.

Paj and Auster took off running, their boots slapping on the wet stone, and Hamish pressed the back of his fist to his mouth.

"What—who—?" I stammered.

But Willa was already turning in a circle, her gaze running down the line of ships docked around us until she saw the crest she was looking for. The *Luna*.

"Zola . . ." she growled.

We ran after Auster and Paj, pushing through the crowd of people who were already gathered around the ship, staring. The two men Hamish had paid to keep watch were lying on the dock in pools of their own sticky blood, their wide, empty eyes turned up to the sky.

"West!" Willa called out, climbing up the ladder as fast as her feet would take her. I followed, my palms burning on the ropes. But Auster and Paj were already waiting on the deck.

"He's not here," Paj said, his eyes still pinned to the ravaged sails.

The look on his face mirrored the ones down on the dock. It was a death sentence. The cost of an entirely new set of sails would empty the coffers and the time it took to repair them would put them even further behind on their route. They'd lose even more coin than what they'd lost in inventory in the storm. For a wealthy trader with many ships, it would be a hit. For a crew like the *Marigold*, it would sink their entire outfit.

Hamish's cheeks flushed a deep shade of red as he fidgeted with his book, his thumb skimming the pages back and forth. There was no way to calculate, argue, or sidestep out of this one. Zola had gone in for the kill, swift and precise.

Willa went to the railing, her face afire. Three bays over, Zola was standing on the deck of the *Luna,* his gaze cast upon us.

"I'm going to kill him. I'm going to cut him open and break his bones with my bare hands while he's still alive and breathing," she whispered, tears rolling down her cheeks.

"He told me," I said, remembering Zola in the haze of the night before.

"What?" Hamish and the others came to stand beside us.

"Last night, he told me the *Marigold* wouldn't be sailing much longer."

Willa gritted her teeth, the blood draining from her face.

And that wasn't all he'd said.

Don't think the Marigold *will be on its feet much longer. Neither will its helmsman.*

The wind suddenly turned cold, twisting and turning around us on the empty deck until I was wrapping my arms around myself.

Neither will its helmsman . . .

The same thought seemed to bleed into all of them in the same moment, their faces shifting almost in unison.

Willa's eyes suddenly went wide, filled with terror. "Where the hell is West?"

TWENTY-SIX

W ho saw it?" Paj took the harbor master by the jacket, slamming him into the post in the center of the crowd. Voices erupted all around us, every eye on the *Marigold*.

"Who?" Paj roared.

The man wrenched free, straightening the collar of his shirt. "I told you, the sun came up and the sails were slashed. No one saw anything."

If they had, they'd never say it. There was a code in the Narrows among traders that no one ever broke. If you saw something, you kept it to yourself. No one wanted this kind of trouble, and that was what Zola was counting on. If he was reported to the Trade Council, he could lose his license for slashing another ship's sails. But no one was going to say a word.

The harbor master flung a hand to the two bodies on the ground. "You'd better find that helmsman of yours. I don't need your coin bad enough to have this mess on my dock."

He turned on his heel, taking off down the walkway, and the crowd slowly dispersed around us.

"Let's go." Willa pushed through us, leading the way back to Waterside. We walked in a single line, and Auster and Paj watched the shadows of doorways and windows as we passed.

My heartbeat ticked up in my chest, trying to remember if I'd seen West in the blur of the tavern the night before. I hadn't. Or maybe I had. I only remembered Willa. Zola. The man in the alley I'd drawn my knife on.

Paj pushed open the door to the tavern, and we went straight up the wooden steps, into the dark hallway. Willa didn't knock, pushing into the door with her shoulder until the lock busted and it flung open before us.

The room was clean, the gray wool blanket smoothed neatly over the bed. My stomach dropped.

West hadn't slept here last night.

"Who was the last to see him?" Willa's voice turned weak. Frailty looked so strange on her. It looked strange on all of them. They were scared. "*Think*. Who was the last to see him?"

"Last night. He had supper and . . ." Auster ran a hand through his unraveling dark hair, thinking. "I don't know if I saw him go up the stairs."

"He didn't." Hamish nodded toward the small table in the corner where an unlit candle still sat in the chamberstick. He'd probably never even stepped foot into the room.

Willa paced before the window, her fingers tapping the buttons on her jacket.

"Hamish, go to Saint. See if he's heard anything. Maybe he went to the Pinch last night. Paj and Auster, check every tavern between here and each corner of the city. Fable and I will go to the gambit after we talk to the barkeep."

They were down the stairs a moment later, and as soon as they were out of sight, Willa let out a long breath, the tears welling up in her eyes.

"What are you thinking?" I watched her face carefully. The fury that had been there on the docks was gone now, only the fear left.

"I'm thinking I'll burn this city to the ground until I find him."

She pushed past me, and I followed her down the stairs, straight for the counter, where the barkeep was stacking clean green glasses in neat rows. Willa took a bottle of rye from where it sat before him, and he looked up, watching her from the top of his gaze.

"What is it, Willa?"

Every bit of the feebleness she'd had upstairs was instantly gone, replaced by the hard, cold face of a trader. "Did you see West last night?" She uncorked the bottle, taking a long drink.

The barkeep leaned on the counter, looking between the two of us. "No, why?"

"Hear any talk about him?" There was an eerie calm to her voice, the look in her eye almost dead.

"I don't deal in gossip." He picked up another glass, ignoring her.

"You do now." She held the bottle out before her and turned it upside down. The rye spilled out onto the counter, pouring over the edge onto the stools and pooling at our feet.

"What the—" He reached over the counter, but she already had another bottle in hand, dropping it onto the wood floor. It shattered around us, and I knew what she was going to do before she did it. She turned on her heel and walked past him to were three candles were burning inside a glass lantern on the wall. She took it from the hook, holding it before her.

"Willa . . ." His hands went up before him, his wide eyes trained on the lantern.

It hovered over the puddle of rye at Willa's feet. We all knew what would happen if she dropped it. The tavern would light up like kindling. It would burn to the ground and spread to every building this one touched so fast that there wouldn't be a thing anyone could do about it. A fire in a city like this was a guaranteed death for us all.

She'd meant it—burning the city to the ground.

"Did you hear any talk about West last night?" she repeated slowly, the wax from the candle dripping onto the glass casting of the lantern.

"Maybe!" He took a step closer, his hands now shaking. "Maybe a coin master from one of the trading ships."

"Who?"

"I don't know. I swear. He only asked if the crew of the *Marigold* was staying here."

"And what did you say?" Her head tilted to one side.

"I said you were. That's all. Nothing else." He gulped. "I swear, I don't know anything else."

"I thought you don't deal in gossip." Willa stared into the white-hot flame. "If I don't find West by sundown, I'm coming back. And before I set this tavern on fire, I'll stake your body to that counter."

He nodded frantically, the glisten of sweat beading at his hairline. She was terrifying, her beautiful face marred with the scar of the hot blade. She opened the door of the lantern and blew out the candle before she dropped it on the ground and it broke into pieces, scattering over the floorboards.

"Come on." She opened the door, filling the tavern with daylight, and we stepped out onto the street.

I followed her back toward the harbor. We slipped into the same alleys that we'd walked only that morning, but this time with quick steps. Our boots splashed in the mud, and we pushed through the bodies crowded between the buildings until the cool scent of the sea found us, cutting the stench of the city. Willa led us away from the docks, where the hovels of Waterside were clumped together in a maze of leaning, rotting structures.

"I thought we were going to the gambit," I said, trying to keep up.

She didn't answer, cutting left and right without even looking around her. She knew exactly where she was going.

When she stopped before an empty doorframe, she slid her knife back into her belt, taking a deep breath before she turned to face me. "Can I trust you?"

"Yes," I said, surprising myself with how quickly I'd answered. I hadn't even taken a moment to think about it.

"This stays between you and me." She met my eyes for a moment before she ducked inside. *"Only* you and me."

The squalor of the city was even worse in the dark, cramped room. It was bare, with hardly any furniture, and the walls empty. The air was stifled, making it hard to breathe. Only a small wooden chair sat beside the window, where a basin and a small fire bin made up something resembling a kitchen.

"Mama?"

I froze, my boot hovering over the next step.

"Hmmm?" a high-pitched voice answered.

My eyes adjusted slowly, and the thin, sticklike form of a woman appeared in the shadowed corner. A violet shawl was draped over her bony shoulders, a smear of red painted over her thin lips.

Willa sank down beside her, reaching for her hand, and the woman took it. "Willa." She smiled, blinking slowly.

I'd seen a hundred women like her on Waterside in my lifetime. Poor, hungry. Selling themselves to traders who were docked for the night and ending up with swollen bellies. That's why Waterside was full of children.

"Mama, was West here? Last night?" Willa spoke softly.

I looked around the room for any sign of him, my eyes landing on a basket of turnips that sat in the corner beside a jar of pickled fish and an unopened tin of tea. Maybe he'd made Willa's mother his problem too.

"Mm-hmm." The woman nodded, but she looked tired.

"When? When did he come?"

"Last night. I told you." She pulled her hand from Willa's, leaning into the wall and closing her eyes.

Willa stood, her gaze moving back and forth across the floor in thought.

"Why would he come here?" I whispered.

Willa's face reddened, and she turned away from me, pulling a quilt where it hung from a nail in the wall and spreading it over the woman.

"He's too thin, Willa. He needs to eat," she mumbled.

"I know, Mama."

"You need to make sure he eats."

"I will, Mama," she whispered. "Go to sleep."

Willa stepped around me, and I stared at the woman for another moment as her face grew heavy. Her small cot was old, the frame barely holding together, and the little shack was empty except for the food.

I followed Willa outside, but she stood in the alley, unmoving.

I waited for her to look at me. "What was he doing here?"

She shifted on her feet, her hands sliding into her pockets. "He looks after her."

"Why?"

"Because no one else will."

It hit me, then, the look on her face giving her away. "Is he . . . is West your brother?"

She didn't blink. She didn't breathe.

Never, under any circumstances, reveal what or who matters to you.

"Do the others know?" I whispered.

She dropped her eyes. They'd kept it a secret even from their own crew.

"You tell a soul and I'll kill you," she said, suddenly desperate. "I won't want to, but I will."

I nodded once. I understood this kind of secret. It was the kind of information that could take everything from you.

Willa stilled, looking over my shoulder, and I turned to see a small, barefoot boy swimming in men's clothes standing in the path ahead. He wrung his hands nervously as he glanced over his shoulder and looked back to Willa.

As if they'd shared some secret exchange, he suddenly took off, and Willa followed, running after him. We followed the twisting trail, the boy disappearing around turns ahead of us until we came around the corner of a hovel, and he stopped, jumping up onto the edge of a crumbling rooftop, perched like a bird. He pointed to a stack of toppled crates before he lifted himself up and over the wall, and then he was gone.

We stepped into the spot of light that painted the wet ground, and I sucked in a sharp breath as Willa tore through the crates, throwing them to the ground. She froze, sinking down as an open hand fell into the sunlight.

West.

TWENTY-SEVEN

I stripped the bed of its blankets as Auster and Paj carried West up the stairs of the tavern, the physician on their heels. They lowered him down and the candlelight caught his face. He was beaten badly, his face swollen and bloody, but there was no way to see how bad it was.

The physician set his bag on the floor and rolled up the sleeves of his shirt before he got to work.

"Water, cloth . . ." he mumbled, "better get some rye too."

Paj gave a tight nod and disappeared out the door.

"What happened?" Willa leaned over West, one hand lightly touching the open cut at his brow.

He winced, sucking in a breath as the physician pressed along his ribs with his fingertips. "Zola," he answered. It was probably the only account he would give. "We shouldn't have left the ship. Not after Dern."

Willa's eyes slid to meet mine. He hadn't spoken a word

about the *Marigold*, but he must have known what happened to the sails.

Paj returned with the supplies, and West reached for the rye before Auster had even uncorked it, guzzling it down and draining the small bottle. He lay back, his chest rising and falling as he winced against the pain.

And as if he'd only just seen me, he suddenly looked up, his eyes meeting mine. "What are you doing here?"

I tried to smile, but it was weak. "Scraping you up out of alleyways." I didn't like seeing him covered in blood. The sight made an ache curl tight in my stomach.

Before my face betrayed me, I ducked into the hallway to watch as the physician worked by candlelight into the night.

The floor was littered with used bandages and muddy footprints, and West groaned every time the physician's hands touched him, cursing. When he leaned in again, West shoved him back, sending the physician almost flying from his stool.

Auster laughed beside me, wiping at the smear of West's blood painted across the tattoo of knotted snakes on his arm, but it was half-hearted. The crew had hardly been more than ten feet from West since we brought him up the stairs of the inn, and the quiet worry was carved into each of their faces.

West sat up, swinging his legs over the side of the bed and leaning forward on his elbows so the physician could stitch up the gash on the back of his shoulder. The skin that stretched over his back and arms looked even more golden in the warm light, but it was bruised black and blue like blots of ink on cloth.

"How old were you when Saint took you on?" I whispered, stepping closer to Willa.

She let out a long breath, staring at her boots as if she was trying to decide whether to answer. "He didn't."

"Then how'd you end up on the *Marigold*?"

"That stupid bastard." She jerked her chin toward West. "A trader took him on as a Waterside stray when he was nine years old, and a year later, he came back for me. Snuck me onto the ship in the middle of the night, and the next morning, when we were out at sea, he pretended to discover me as a stowaway." She smiled sadly. "He convinced the helmsman to keep me on because I was small and could climb the masts faster than anyone else."

That was what Willa had meant when she said that she hadn't chosen this life. West had chosen it for her. "And he agreed?"

She shrugged. "He didn't throw me over. He said I'd learn to survive or I didn't belong on the sea."

"Do you ever wish he hadn't brought you onto the ship?" I whispered.

"Every day," she answered without hesitation. "But he didn't want to leave me in Waterside. And now I don't want to leave him on the *Marigold*."

It was the curse that shackled anyone who loved anyone in the Narrows. Through the crack in the door, I could see

West pinching his eyes closed as the physician snipped the length of thread he was stitching with.

"What's with you and Saint, anyway?" Willa leaned in closer to me, lowering her voice.

I straightened. "What do you mean?"

"I mean, why cross the Narrows to crew for a man like that? You couldn't have honestly thought he'd take you on."

I stared at her, my teeth clenched. "I—"

The physician pushed through the door with his bag clutched to his chest and went down the stairs grumbling, his white shirt now stained with fresh blood. Through the door, West had one hand pressed to his side as he drained another bottle of rye.

"Get in here." His gravelly voice drifted out into the hallway.

The crew filed into the cramped room, all looking to West. He was mostly cleaned up, but he was covered in stitches and the bruising was only getting worse. If he'd been left in the maze of Waterside another day or two, he might have taken his last breaths there.

"Tell me." He touched the corner of his swollen lip with his knuckle.

Hamish took a deep breath before he said, "The sails aren't salvageable. If we patch them, they'll give in at the first storm we see. And with the inventory losses, we don't have enough coin to get back on the water."

West's gaze drifted past us as he thought. "What if we borrow until Sowan?"

Hamish shook his head. "No one will lend that much."

"Let me see." He held out his hand, and Hamish set his book into it.

We stood silently as West flipped through the pages, his finger dragging over the numbers. When he finally closed it, he sighed. "I'll go to Saint."

"No." Willa's hands dropped to her sides suddenly. "You already owe."

"So, I'll extend."

"*No*, West," she said again.

"You want to go back to crewing on whatever crew will take you?" he snapped.

Her eyes narrowed. "No. But at least this way, you can give him back the ship. Call it square."

"And lose the *Marigold*?" He glared up at her incredulously.

"It's better than selling the only bit of your soul you have left. It's a debt you'll never come out from under."

West looked to the others. "What do you think?"

Hamish was the first to answer. "I think Willa's right. But so are you. Saint is the only way out of this."

Auster and Paj nodded in agreement, avoiding Willa's fierce gaze.

West growled as he stood, his hand returning to the dark spread of blue on his ribs.

Willa reached out to steady him. "Where are you going?"

"To the Pinch. We'll borrow from Saint and find another way out of this mess."

"I, uh . . . I don't think you need to go to the Pinch to

talk to Saint," Auster said, his eyes going wide as he leaned into the frame of the window.

I went to stand behind him, peering over his shoulder into the street. A figure in the rich blue of a fine coat was aglow in the darkening light, a sea of people like parting waters before him.

Saint.

"Get her out of here." West ran a hand through his wild hair, tucking it behind his ears.

Willa took hold of my arm, shoving me across the room.

"Wait!" I pushed against her, but Paj took my other arm, pulling me back into the hallway.

"You want to make this worse?" Willa spat. She opened the door of the next room and pushed me inside.

"Is that even possible?" I wrenched free of her, and Paj closed the door, leaving us alone in the dark.

Willa lit the candle on the table, and I listened to the hum of the tavern quiet just before heavy footsteps pounded up the stairs.

"Move!" Saint's booming voice bellowed in the hallway, followed by the door slamming on its hinges.

Willa and I pressed our ears to the thin wood-plank wall between our room and West's, and an uncomfortable silence fell, making the sound of my heartbeat ring in my ears.

"Is this what you call being a helmsman?" Saint spoke calmly, but coldly.

I moved down the wall with light steps until I found a crack where the light was spilling through. My mouth twisted to one side as West came into view. He stood tall before the window, his chin lifted despite the pain he had to be in. He looked Saint in the eye, unmoving.

"We made a deal when I gave you the *Marigold*."

"You didn't give me the *Marigold*," West interrupted.

"What?"

"You didn't *give* me the *Marigold*," he repeated.

Saint stared at him. "I gave you an opportunity—the chance to be the helmsman of your own crew and grow your own trade. Instead, my ship is down in the harbor with slashed sails, and your crew is dragging you out of Waterside half-dead."

"Zola—"

"I don't want to talk about Zola. I want to talk about *you*." Saint's voice rose. "You have a problem with another trader, you handle it."

"Yes, sir."

"Get back on the water and find a way to fix those ledgers."

West's gaze dropped to the floor. "I can't."

Saint stilled. "What?"

"I don't have the coin for new sails. Not after the storm."

Saint's eyes turned to slits, his nostrils flaring. "Are you telling me you're dead in the water?"

West gave a single nod.

"And you want me to get you new sails?"

"You can add it to my debt."

"No," Willa whispered beside me.

A second later, Saint echoed the word. "No."

West looked up, clearly surprised by his answer.

"You don't bring your mess to my door, and you don't use my coin to clean it up. If you can't fix this, you have no business sailing that ship."

The muscles in West's jaw clenched, but he bit back the fury that was jumping under his skin.

"I have business you're getting in the way of." The hem of his coat circled his boots as he turned, but he stopped, his hand on the latch of the door. "And if I find out a single soul knows about the cargo you brought back from Jeval, you'll be finding the pieces of your crew all over this city."

West's hands tightened on his belt. "That's what this is about? *Her?*"

The feeling of fire writhed in my chest, and I realized suddenly that I was holding my breath.

"So, this is a punishment." West took a step toward Saint.

"Call it what you want. Your job is to do what I tell you to. You don't make a move without my permission. If you don't like those arrangements, there are a hundred men down on those docks who will take your place."

"If I hadn't taken her off Jeval, she'd be tied to the reef right now, her bones picked clean."

"Fable can take care of herself." Saint's voice deepened.

Willa's face turned toward me, her eyes wide.

"Then why have I been bleeding coin going to that island every two weeks for the last two years? If something happened to her, we both know whose throat would be cut. I saved both our lives by bringing her here."

My father gritted his teeth, the full brunt of his anger filling the silence. "I don't want to see your face again until you've cleaned this up. If you don't, it won't be Zola coming for you. It will be me. And I won't leave you breathing."

The door slammed again, shaking the walls, and Saint's footsteps moved back down the stairs. I went to the window and watched him step out into the alley. He buttoned the top of his jacket methodically before he slipped into the darkness without looking back.

Willa crossed her arms, eyeing me. "Is there something you want to tell us?"

"Yeah." I sighed. "We need to talk."

TWENTY-EIGHT

West stood at the window as we came through the door, his eyes on the street.

"West . . ." Willa lifted a hand toward him, but he moved from her reach.

"He's not going to lend us the coin. We can use the stake."

They all went silent, their gazes pinned on him.

"We can't," Auster said. "We agreed we would never use it."

"We swore," Paj murmured behind him.

A thin silence fell between us and for the first time, I could see the faintest of cracks in the wall of this crew. "What's the stake?" I asked.

"It's the coin we've been pocketing from a side trade we've been running. It's for . . . after." To my surprise, Hamish was the one to answer. Maybe because it didn't matter anymore.

"After?"

He pulled the spectacles from his face, letting them dangle from his fingers. "After we've bought out from Saint."

"Only if we all agree," West amended. "There's enough to buy sails and cover our losses from the storm. We can get back on the sea and make the coin back." He was trying to sound sure. "I can hire a ship to take me to the coral islands tomorrow."

Of course. The coral islands were a cache.

Every crew had them. It was foolish to keep everything you had in one place when ships could sink and city posts could be raided while you were out to sea. Any crew with half a brain had more than one cache to spread out their coin.

"It's taken us two years to save that much," Willa said.

West shrugged. "It's our only choice."

But that wasn't true. And if I was going to make a play for a place on the crew, now was my best chance. I reached into the opening of my jacket, finding the sea dragon with my fingertips, my stomach dropping as I opened my mouth.

"It's not the only choice," I said, meeting West's eyes.

Silence fell over the room again, and my skin flushed hot as their eyes landed on me. There was no going back once I said it.

"What?" Hamish looked suspicious.

"I have another way out of this," I said, standing up straighter. "If you want it."

He pushed the spectacles back into place. "What do you mean?"

"Take me on as the *Marigold*'s dredger and I'll get your sails," I said, the words running together in a single breath.

"No." West's answer was heavy on his lips.

228

But Willa was curious. "And how exactly are you going to do that?"

"Does it matter? I can get you the sails. Take me on as your dredger, and I'll get you enough copper to buy yourself out from under Saint in one trade."

Auster stood up off the wall. "What are you talking about?"

"That's the deal." My attention was still trained on West.

"No," he said again, this time with a flash of anger.

Willa looked between us. "Why not? If she has a way to—"

"There's no one better for this crew. I'm a skilled dredger," I added.

"No!"

I recoiled, stepping back. The others looked to one another, confused.

Willa gaped at him. "We don't have a dredger. She says she'll front the cost of sails and buy us out from Saint. And you say *no*?"

"That's right. We're not taking her on."

"Why not?" Willa pushed.

I gave West one last chance, letting the silence fall again. The secret burned in my throat like the rye I'd drowned in only the night before. It was something I'd never said aloud. Something I swore I'd never do. But Saint had broken his promise to me. He'd left me the *Lark,* but he hadn't given me what was mine. Not what he owed me.

Now, I would break my promise to him.

"Don't," West whispered, reading my thoughts.

"Saint is my father."

The tension in the room pulled tighter and a chill ran over my skin. It was something I could never unsay.

"What the—" Willa gasped.

"That's why West had the *Marigold* coming to Jeval every two weeks. That's why you traded pyre with me and only me. Saint had you checking on the daughter he abandoned across the Narrows. I didn't know you were working for him until we were in Dern."

I could see by the looks on their faces that they knew it was true. It was too insane not to be true.

"I was part of his deal with West when he gave him the *Marigold*. And you were right." I looked to Willa. "You've sold your soul to a man who doesn't have one. You'll never buy out the *Marigold*. He'll always find a way to keep you owing him. That's what he does."

"If Saint is your father, then . . ." Willa's voice trailed off.

"Isolde was my mother. That's why I can do what I do with the gems."

"You're a gem sage."

I nodded.

"You're not dredging for the *Marigold*." West spoke evenly, but he looked as if he was using every ounce of energy he had left to do so. "Saint would never allow it. And even if he did, he'd cut all our throats if something happened to you. Taking you on is a death wish."

But beside him, Auster looked amused. "What's in it for you?"

I shifted on my feet, swallowing down the shame of it. "I don't have anything else. Saint doesn't want me."

They all stared at me.

"If you take me on, I'll get the *Marigold* back on the water and fill the hull with enough coin to pay every debt you have. That's my offer."

"How are you going to do that?" Hamish asked, careful not to look at West.

"I have something. Something no one knows about. It's just waiting underwater for me to come get it."

"What is it?" Paj finally spoke.

"I'm not telling you unless you agree to the deal."

Paj sighed. "Dredging a reef isn't going to get us out of this mess, Fable."

"It's not a reef. And it's more than enough to buy you out from Saint."

A smile pulled at Willa's mouth, her eyes sparkling.

"Leave us." West turned back to the window. When the crew didn't move, he shouted. "Leave us!"

The others filed out without another word. I clicked the latch closed and leaned into the door, watching him. The stitches snaked over his shoulder, breaking before they picked back up below his shoulder blade. Even like that, he was beautiful.

"How did it work?" I asked softly.

He looked out to the street, only half of his face catching the light. "How did what work?"

"You buy pyre from me on Jeval, sell it in Dern, and give Saint the profit?"

He shook his head. "I didn't give him the profit. He didn't want it."

"So, you kept it?"

"It's in the cache. Every copper. The coin I gave you when we got to Ceros is part of it."

So that's why we stopped at the coral islands on the way to Dern. "All this time, I thought I was making my own way. I thought I'd found a way to survive," I whispered.

"You did."

"No, I didn't. The only reason I didn't starve to death on that island is because of you." The words seemed to embarrass him. His eyes dropped to the ground between us. "You could have lied to Saint about going. He would have never known."

"I wouldn't do that to him."

"But you'll run your own side trade and pocket off his ledgers?"

"That's different," he said simply.

"Don't tell me you admire the man who's got you pinned under his thumb?"

"You wouldn't understand," he muttered.

"Are you sure about that?"

He seemed to really consider the question before he answered. "A trader picked me up out of Waterside and put me on a ship when I was nine years old. He taught me everything I know about sailing and trading, but he was a bad man. Saint bought me off that ship and put me on his. He's a rotten bastard, but he's the only reason I'm not scraping barnacles off hulls down on the docks or rotting at the bottom of the sea."

I didn't want to imagine what West meant when he said the trader was a bad man. I could see by the way he swallowed between the words that he was ashamed of it, whatever it was.

"That's how he knew he could trust you," I said. "He's good at that—making sure everyone owes him *just* enough."

"He's smart."

I shook my head. "How can you defend him after what he just did? He cut you loose."

"Because he was right. I'm responsible for my crew and my ship. I messed up. And he didn't cut us loose; he's just not going to bail us out."

I stared at him, speechless. West was actually defending him.

"You're right—I admire him. The traders in the Unnamed Sea think the Narrows is eventually going to fall into their hands. Saint is showing them that we can stand on our own."

I would never admit it, but there was a part of me that felt proud, even if the rest of me hated him. And I realized in that moment that West was maybe the only other person who could understand how both of those feelings could exist together.

"How long until you buy out from under him?"

He didn't answer.

"How long?"

West reached up, pressing one hand to his side again as if it hurt. I wasn't sure how he was still standing. "Sixteen years."

I took a step toward him, waiting for him to meet my eyes before I said it. "Sixteen years or one night?"

"What?"

"You can spend sixteen years scraping to buy yourself out from under Saint. Or you can do it in one night. With me. No more shadow-ship work. No more reporting and spying or orders like the ones you had in Sowan."

He stiffened, and I could see the words hurt him. He didn't want me knowing about whatever happened in Sowan.

"I can't take you on, Fable," he said again, running a hand through his hair and holding it back from his face.

"You think I can't handle myself."

"You lived on Jeval for four years. I know you can handle yourself."

"Then what is it? Saint?"

He stared at his boots, his jaw ticking. "Saint is the only operation in the Narrows running routes to the Unnamed Sea since Zola's ships were banned. He's the only legitimate competition for the traders in Bastian. It's a position any trader in the Narrows would cut their own hand off for, and if anyone finds out who you are, every one of them will be looking to take leverage against Saint."

It was a fair point. But before I could even argue, he was speaking again.

"But more than that, I don't trust you."

"What?"

"You just tried to sway my own crew against me."

My mouth dropped open. "I—"

"You manipulated the only people I trust with my life. I depend on them."

"You wouldn't even hear me out. I knew that if they knew who I was, they would listen to what I had to say."

"That's not how a crew works."

I let out a long breath. "Then teach me."

West slid his hands into his pockets, falling quiet for a moment. "If it comes down to choosing us or Saint, you'll choose Saint."

I laughed. "Why would I? He's never chosen me."

"The only reason you want to crew on the *Marigold* is because Saint turned you away," he tried again.

"And the only reason you're helmsman of the *Marigold* is because Saint made you helmsman of his shadow ship. It doesn't matter why we're here, West. We're here. I need someone to trust with *my* life."

His mouth pressed into a hard line.

"You don't trust me, but I trust you." My voice lowered.

"You have no reason to trust me."

I crossed my arms, looking away from him. "You came back."

"What are you talking about?"

"I sat on the cliffs above the beach on Jeval every night, imagining the sails of my father's ship on the horizon. Hoping he'd come back for me." I paused. "He didn't—you did."

He looked up then, his eyes meeting mine.

"I want to dredge for the *Marigold*. I want to get you out from under Saint."

He leaned into the wall behind him, scratching the scruff at his jaw. "I never should have let you onto the *Marigold* in the first place."

"What does this have to do with what happened on Jeval?"

"Everything."

"You just told Saint that you gave me passage to save your own neck."

"I took you off Jeval because I didn't want to leave you there," he breathed. "I *couldn't* leave you there." It was the first thing he'd said to me that had the heavy weight of truth in the words.

I tried to read him, studying the shadows that moved over his face, but only fragments of him were visible, as always. He was only pieces, never a whole.

He was quiet for a long moment before he took a step toward me. "I'll cast my vote to bring you on as our dredger." The heat of him coiled around me. "If you tell me that you understand something."

"What is it?"

His eyes ran over my face. "I can't care about anyone else, Fable."

His meaning filled the small bit of space between us, making me feel like the walls were creeping in. Because I knew why he'd said it. It was in the way his eyes dropped to my mouth sometimes when he looked at me. It was in the way his voice deepened just a little when he said my name. West was taking a different kind of risk by voting me onto his crew, and in this moment, he was letting me see it.

"Tell me you understand." He held his hand out between us, waiting.

This wasn't just an admission. This was a contract.

So, I met his eyes, not a single hitch in my voice as I took his hand into mine. "I understand."

TWENTY-NINE

A single lantern glowed up on the *Marigold* as I walked down the dock in the dark.

The empty ships floated in the harbor like sleeping giants, the crews drinking their weight in the city, and only the harbor workers they'd paid to watch the bays were out. Even Waterside looked empty, the little faces that usually lined the alleyways gone. Ceros looked so much smaller in the dark, but I felt less small within it.

When I reached the slip where the *Marigold* was anchored, my boots stopped at the bloodstain on the dock where the two bodies had been that morning. It was scrubbed clean, but the hints of red were stained into the wood. I could still see them, their crumpled frames lying in the sun, and I wondered who they were. Probably poor men spending their nights for hire to make extra coin. It was a pathetic way to die, caught in the middle of someone else's feud.

The ladder was unrolled, waiting for me, and I looked up,

fitting my bandaged hands onto the rungs. I thought I'd stood on the decks of the *Marigold* for the last time, but now, this ship would become my home. This crew would become my family. And like the turn of the wind before the most unpredictable of storms, I could feel that everything was about to change.

I lifted myself up over the railing, and the others were already gathered on the deck, standing in a circle before the helm. The naked masts towered over us like skeletons, reaching up into the dark until they disappeared. The torn canvas now lay rolled up in the hull.

West stared at the deck as I found a place beside Willa, the tension visible in the way he stood. He'd agreed, but he wasn't happy about it, and that wounded me more than I wanted to admit.

"You sure about this, dredger?" Willa's arm pressed into mine as she leaned into me.

I looked at West, and for just a moment, he met my eyes. "I'm sure."

And I was. It wasn't just that there was nowhere else for me to go. It was that since that first night sleeping in the empty hammock below deck, there seemed to be a place for me here. I fit. Even if West didn't want me on the crew, I could make my own way with the five of them. I could trust them. And that was enough. That was more than enough.

Auster pulled the wool cap from his head, letting his unbound hair spill over his shoulder, and held it upside down in the middle of the circle.

A lump rose in my throat as I stared into it.

Willa took a single copper from her belt. "I say we let this good-for-nothing Jevali dredger crew for the *Marigold*." She flicked the coin into the air, and it flashed against the lantern light as it spun, landing in Auster's hat. "Even if she *is* a bad luck charm."

"Fine by me." Paj snapped a copper between his fingers, shooting it in after Willa's.

Auster followed, giving me a wink. "Me too."

Hamish took a copper from his vest, eyeing me. The hesitation wasn't hidden on his face. "What was Saint's daughter doing on Jeval?"

I shifted on my feet, my hands sliding into the pockets of my jacket. "What?"

"If we're going to trust you, I want to know the story. How'd you end up on Jeval?"

"We don't need to know." West gave Hamish a warning look.

"I do."

"He left me there," I said, my throat tightening. "The night after the *Lark* sank, he left me on Jeval."

They fell silent, their eyes finding the ground. I didn't know their stories, but I imagined they couldn't be much better than mine. I wasn't foolish enough to feel sorry for myself. The Narrows was the edge of a blade. You couldn't live here and not get cut. And I didn't have it in me to be ashamed of where I'd come from. Those days were gone.

Hamish gave me a nod before he flipped his coin in, and

they all looked to West. He stood silent as the seabirds called out in the dark behind him, and I wondered if he would change his mind, letting the crew outvote him.

When he finally lifted his hand, the glint of copper shined between his fingers. He dropped it into the hat without a word.

His words echoed in the silence. He'd take me on. He'd take my coin to save the *Marigold*. But that was it.

"Get the rye, Willa." Auster pushed the hat into my hands, and I looked down into it.

It was tradition for every member of a crew to give a copper to the newest member as a show of good faith. I'd seen my father's crews do the same many times. But in the years since I first set foot on Jeval, I'd never been given anything. Ever. I didn't bother trying to hold back my tears. They streamed down my face one after the other as I hugged the hat to me.

Like a weary bird flying out over the most desolate sea, I finally had a place to land.

Willa uncorked one of the ink-blue bottles from the tavern, and Paj passed out the glasses as she filled them, the overflowing rye hitting the deck at our feet. All together, we knocked them back, taking the rye in one swallow, and they erupted in cheers. I coughed against the burn in my throat, laughing.

"How much?" I asked, turning the empty glass in my hand.

"How much what?" Willa refilled her glass.

"How much coin do we need for the sails?"

Hamish looked a little surprised at the question, but he

pulled the book from inside his vest. He took the lantern from the mast and set it on the deck between us, opening to the last marked page, and we all crouched down around it, our faces lit in the dim light. His handwriting scrawled across the parchment in rows with the numbers on the right side organized into sums.

"After paying the repair crew and making up the losses from the storm, we'll need at least eight hundred coppers for the sails."

"Eight hundred?" Paj looked skeptical.

"I'm pretty sure that's what we'll have to offer to get a sailmaker to do it. No one will want trouble with Zola."

"He's right," West said.

The rye in my veins didn't dull the sting of the number. I knew it would be expensive, but I hadn't guessed the cost would be that high. I hoped my plan would still hold against it.

"Can you get it or not?" The light reflected off of Hamish's spectacles as he looked up from the page.

"I can get it."

Willa twisted the cork back into the bottle and set it between us. "You never said how."

"Does it matter how?"

"Not really." She shrugged. "But I'd like to know all the same."

"Saint's going to pay for the sails."

West's eyes snapped up to me, and Paj cleared his throat. "Saint?"

"That's right."

"And how are you going to get him to do that?" Willa was clearly entertained.

"I have something he wants. Something I know he'd give anything to have back."

They didn't ask what it was, but I could see on their faces that the idea made them nervous. Saint was already angry with them about Zola. As soon as he figured out I was playing him to repair the *Marigold,* he'd likely want all of our heads.

"You're playing with fire, Fable," Willa said, but the wicked smile on her lips reached her eyes, making them twinkle.

I could see that West was thinking the same thing, but the amusement was missing from his face. He stared into his empty cup, the light catching the green glass. The cut that ran along his forehead was hidden beneath his hair, but the entire left side of his face was still swollen, one of his eyes bloodshot.

This crew had already been in trouble when I stepped onto their ship, but I couldn't help wondering if I was going to be the storm that finally sank them.

THIRTY

I'd broken my promise to him, but I was still living by
Saint's rules.

Dawn swelled behind the land as I stood between two
buildings, watching the bridge. If I was right, Saint's boots
would be knocking on the wood planks any moment as he
made his way to Griff's tavern. When I was a girl, if we weren't
out to sea, he took tea at Griff's every single morning before
the sun rose.

I'd thought maybe Saint had changed in the years since
I'd last seen him. But if he was still the same ruthless trader
who cut the knees out from everyone around him so that he
stood taller, then maybe he was still the same bastard who
took tea at Griff's before sunup.

The distant sound of footsteps made me look up to the
only bridge that led out of the Pinch. Even though they were
empty at this time of morning, Saint didn't like to walk in the
muck of the streets.

A shadowed figure moved against the dark sky, and I could tell by the way his coat rippled in the wind that it was him. I stood up off the crate I was sitting on and stepped onto the street below, following. He took the same turns he always did, heading to Waterside, and I walked with my hands tucked into my pockets, watching the shape of him slip over the buildings as he passed. That was like Saint too—casting his shadow on everything around him.

When he started down the ladder near the harbor, I pressed myself against the wall of the nearest building and waited, holding my breath. The pale light made his coat glow like the blue coral snakes that slithered over the east reef of Jeval. His boots hit the ground, and he started down the alley just as the lanterns of the city were flickering to life. The street would be busy with dock workers and bakers in a matter of minutes, the wheels of Ceros starting to turn.

I waited for him to disappear around the corner before I followed, keeping my footsteps light. The sign for Griff's tavern hung out over the alley, the words scratched off by the brunt of sea winds. But I knew the place. The block stone walls were framed in by huge timber beams, the roof so steeply slanted that even the birds couldn't land on it.

Saint disappeared through the door, and I stopped in front of the window, watching him. The place was empty except for Griff standing behind the counter, tying a cloth around his waist. He didn't bother looking up as Saint slid a chair back from a table and took a seat.

A woman appeared from the back, a tray of tea in her

hands, and she set it down carefully, arranging the pot at the corner of Saint's table as he pulled a roll of parchments from his coat. The teacup looked tiny in his hand as he took a sip, his attention on the pages.

I put my hand on the latch, steadying myself before I pushed the door open.

Griff glanced up from the counter and the woman reappeared in the doorway, both of them startled. But it was Saint's gaze that fell heaviest on me. He looked up from his teacup, his thick brows arched over his bright blue eyes.

"Morning." I gave a nod to the woman. "I'll take a pot of tea, please."

She looked to Griff, as if to get permission before she moved, and he nodded, clearly suspicious of me. But his eyes widened as I took the chair opposite Saint, sitting before him with my hands folded on the table.

"What are you doing here?" Saint's gaze fell back to the parchment, but the way he shifted in his seat told me that I'd surprised him.

"Ledgers?" I leaned over them, feigning interest.

"That's right. Two ships came in late last night." He picked the cup back up, and a ring of tea was left on the corner of the parchment. "What do you want?"

"I want to have tea with my father." I smiled, my voice dropping to a whisper.

But every muscle in Saint's body tensed, his hand gripping the cup so tightly that it looked as if it might shatter between his fingers. His eyes slid to meet mine as the woman set down a second pot of tea between us, rearranging the table to fit everything.

"Milk?" she asked.

"Yes, please."

"What about sugar, my dear?"

"Sure." I looked to Saint. "I haven't had sugar in years."

He set his tea down a little too hard, and it sloshed out as I filled my own cup. The woman returned with a little dish of cream and a few sugar cubes in a linen napkin. Saint ignored me as I stirred them in.

"Did any of your ships get damaged in that storm a few days ago?"

"Everyone's ships were damaged in that storm," he muttered.

"Zola's too?"

He dropped the parchment. "What do you know about Zola?"

"Nothing much, other than the fact that he's got some kind of feud going on with that gem trader from the Unnamed Sea." I watched him. "And the *Marigold*. I heard their sails got slashed."

"The less you know about his business, the better."

I picked up the teapot on his side of the table and refilled his cup. "You've got trouble with him too?"

"Your mother did," he said, and my hands froze on the pot. "So, yes. I have trouble with him."

"He knew her?" I took care not to say her name. The last thing I needed was for him to get angry.

247

"She dredged for him before I took her onto my crew."

I stared at him, shocked at his candor. Saint always spoke in riddles, but he was giving me bits of information I hadn't even asked for. It made sense that Isolde would have dredged for other crews before she worked for Saint, but she had never talked about the time between leaving Bastian and joining the crew on the *Lark*.

"What kind of trouble?"

He leaned over the table toward me. "It doesn't matter."

I gritted my teeth, resisting the urge to take hold of his lovely coat and scream.

You weren't made for this world, Fable.

He didn't think I could take care of myself. He'd given me the *Lark*, but he didn't think I could make my own way. Not really.

I filled my lungs with the air that always seemed to hover around him. The proud, hardened demeanor that was always lit in his eyes. I pushed down the ache in the center of my chest that just wanted him to reach across the table and take my hand. The small, broken part of me that wished his eyes would lift from the parchments and look at me. Really *look* at me.

"When are you going to tell me why you came here?"

I took a sip of my tea, the sweet bitterness stinging my tongue. "I need some coin."

"How much?" He didn't sound the least bit interested.

"Eight hundred coppers."

That got his attention. He leaned back in his chair, smirking. "You want me to give you—"

"Of course not," I interrupted. "That would break one of your rules. Nothing is free." I recited it to him the way I had when I was a child. "I want to make a trade."

His curiosity was piqued now. "A trade."

"That's right."

"And why do you need eight hundred coppers?"

"You told me to make my own way. That's what I'm doing."

He nodded, conceding. "And what could you possibly have that I would pay that much coin for?"

I reached into my jacket before I could change my mind, pulling the sea dragon from my pocket. I set it on the table between us, and even Saint couldn't hide the shock that cracked through him in that moment. He turned to stone, his eyes widening as they fell on the necklace.

"Where did you get that?" he croaked.

I knew it was wrong. That there was something truly depraved about using my mother against him. And it was monstrous to leverage her most prized possession to barter. But the necklace had called me to it as I stood before the mirror in Saint's post, as if Isolde knew I would need it. For this very moment.

He picked it up carefully, the abalone sea dragon swinging beneath his fingers.

"That's why you went back to the *Lark*," I said. "You went back for her necklace."

He didn't answer. He'd had that pendant made for my mother in Bastian by a jeweler who made one-of-a-kind pieces.

The abalone was rare, the unmistakable green of the kind that only came from the Unnamed Sea. She never took it off.

"So?" I looked up at him, tears burning in my eyes.

He closed his hand around the necklace before he dropped it into the breast pocket of his jacket. He cleared his throat. "Eight hundred coppers is fine."

I held my hand out and he took it, shaking on the deal. He didn't look up as I stood, and the sinking knowledge of what I'd just done settled within me. I knew what mattered to him, and I had used it against him. I had become the reason he needed his rules.

I turned my back before a single tear could fall.

"And Fable?"

I froze, one foot already outside the door.

The cool, calm set of his mouth returned as he sank back into his chair, looking up at me. "You ever try to shake me down using your mother again, and I'll forget you ever existed."

THIRTY-ONE

I felt her pull away from me as I walked out of Griff's tavern, leaving the necklace behind. That feeling of Isolde's presence had followed me like a ghost in the air since I'd taken it from Saint's post.

Paj tied two full coin purses to my hips, knotting the leather around my belt. "Once we start walking, you don't stop."

I nodded, fastening the buckle tighter so the weight didn't pull it loose.

"You don't stop," he said again, waiting for me to look up at him.

"I understand."

Behind him, Willa stood in the shadow of the alley, watching the street. Saint's coin master showed up in the middle of the night with the copper, escorted by two men carrying knives in both hands. They'd watched me with narrowed eyes as I signed the parchment in my room at the

251

tavern, but neither of them said a word. If they worked for my father, they knew not to ask questions.

Hamish urged us to make the deal with the sailmaker first and not risk carrying any copper through the city, but West thought our chances were better at getting him to take the commission if he saw all that coin with his own eyes.

There's no persuasion like the shine of copper, he'd said.

"We'll get you to the doors and we'll wait outside." Auster checked the purses again.

"You're not going in with us?" I looked between him and Paj. I didn't like the idea of being in the sailmaker's loft with so much coin and only Willa to raise a blade against anyone who tried to take it.

"Tinny doesn't like us much." Paj smirked, leaning into the wall beside Auster.

"Why not?"

"He doesn't do business with Saltbloods."

My eyes widened, looking between the two of them. "You said you're from Waterside." My gaze landed on Paj.

He went a little rigid, perhaps uncomfortable with Auster telling me something about them that was true.

But Auster didn't seem bothered. "We were born in Bastian."

The gleaming, wealthy city on the shores of the Unnamed Sea was also the place my mother was born. It was rare to meet anyone who'd taken up the life of the Narrows if they'd had one in a place like Bastian. The only people who did were running from something.

There was more to whatever story had brought them here.

And I didn't miss what Auster was doing by telling me. He was giving me just a little bit of trust to see what I'd do with it.

"Time to go," Willa said, looking over her shoulder.

I closed up my jacket as Auster and Paj took their places at either side of me.

Willa pulled the dagger from her belt. "Ready?"

I nodded in answer.

She stepped out onto the street, and I followed, walking in step with Auster and Paj, who stayed close enough to hide me between them.

The sailmaker's loft was one of twelve piers that reached out over the water on the east side of Ceros. The framed glass windows spanned an entire side of the building, overlooking the city. The red brick was covered in thick green moss, the mortar crumbling. I walked with my hands in my pockets, my fingers curling around the heavy purses to keep them from jingling.

I didn't miss the way everyone who passed us took a long look at Willa's scarred face, but she kept her head up, as if she didn't notice. I hadn't seen her try to cover the scar once, and I wondered if it was of use to her now, letting the Narrows know that she'd seen her share of its brutality. It wasn't uncommon for women to crew ships, but they were definitely outnumbered. And the softer you looked, the more likely you were to become prey.

By now, word about the *Marigold* and West would have travelled to the other traders. The feud with Zola had turned into something more—a war—and it was obvious to anyone paying attention that the crew was bleeding out. But no one knew anything about the girl from Jeval who'd fleeced Saint for coin to save the ship.

We reached the steps of the pier, and Auster took a position on the side of the building with a good vantage point, pulling a pipe from his pocket. Paj followed, slipping his hands into his vest. They both watched from the corners of their eyes as Willa pulled the huge iron doors open and we stepped inside the sail loft, where the light from the windows lit the bottom floor.

A maze of folded canvas in every size and thickness was stacked covering the floor so that only a stairway was visible ahead. Along the wall beside the door, finished orders were packaged and ready for the merchant's house, wrapped in brown paper with the names of ships scrawled across them.

A man's bald head popped up from a curtain of canvas, watching us as we climbed the stairs that led to the second floor. It was one big, open room where the sailcloth was laid out, cut, and constructed by hand. The windows let in the light from every direction, and the billowing white fabric covered every inch of the floor, where apprentices sat nested with their wooden tool boxes. Ropes strung with shining grommets hung from the ceiling above them like chains of silver.

"Tinny!" Willa called out, and a man appeared from behind a stack of crates on the other side of the loft.

His eyes widened, his mustache bouncing as he mumbled a curse. "Oh, no you don't. Not a chance, Willa!"

The apprentices scrambled to pull the canvas back,

clearing a path before she could step on the sails as she marched toward Tinny.

"Not in a million years!" He shook his head, driving the pointed end of a fid into the corner of the sail in his hand. He twisted it, widening the hole, and the light reflected off his ring. The rust-colored carnelian stone was set into a thick silver band stamped with the seal of Ceros, identifying him as a certified merchant by the Sailmakers Guild. Everyone in the loft worked beneath him, putting in their years of apprenticeship in hopes of one day getting their own ring. "There's not a sailmaker in Ceros who's going to outfit the *Marigold*, so there's no point in even asking."

"Zola's been here?" Willa set a hand on the window beside him, leaning into it.

"He's been everywhere."

Willa met my eyes behind his back. Hamish and West had been right.

Tinny took a grommet from his apron and fit it into the hole he'd made. "No one needs a fight with the *Luna*'s crew, all right? Zola may not be the fleet he once was, but he fights dirty. I'm sorry for what happened to the *Marigold*." His eyes lifted, running over Willa's face. "And I'm sorry about what happened to you and West. I don't know what you did to catch the eye of a sea demon like Zola, but I don't need the business bad enough to cross him."

Behind us, one of the younger apprentices sat listening as he pulled his needle along the tight stitching, his eyes going to the shape of the purses beneath my jacket.

"We've always done right by you, Tinny," Willa said. "We've always paid fair."

"I know that. But like I said . . ." He sighed. "You'll have better chances in Sowan. If Zola doesn't get there first."

She glared at him, but he wasn't budging. "And how do you suggest we get to Sowan with no sails?"

"Look, I shouldn't even be seen talking to you." His eyes lifted to the loft behind us. "People talk."

"We have coin. A lot of it." Willa dropped her voice low. "We're willing to pay twice what the sails would normally cost."

Tinny's hands stilled for just a moment as he looked up at her.

"Show him," she said, meeting my eyes.

I stepped behind the crates and unbuttoned my jacket, opening it up to reveal the two full purses.

The set of Tinny's mouth wavered, the thoughts racing over his face. He shifted on his feet, glancing out the window. He was tempted, but I could see before he even opened his mouth to speak that he wasn't going to risk his neck, no matter how much coin we gave him. "I'm sorry, Willa." He turned away from us, working the fid into the next corner.

"Traitorous bastards," Willa muttered as she walked back out into the loft. The apprentices gathered up the canvas in her path again, but she didn't slow, the soles of her boots striking the floor like a heavy heartbeat.

"Someone in this city has got to want eight hundred coppers," I said, following her down the stairs to the door.

"If anyone was going to do it, it would have been Tinny."

Paj stood up off the wall as we pushed through the doors. "That was fast."

"He won't do it." Willa groaned, setting her hands on her hips and looking out to the crowded street.

Auster pulled a long drag off of his pipe, blowing the smoke through his nostrils. A mischievous smile was playing at his lips.

Paj studied him. "Don't even think about it."

Auster didn't say a word as he rocked back on his heels.

"What is it?" I eyed him.

"We might know someone who will do it," he said, avoiding Paj's gaze.

I looked from Paj, to Auster, and back again. "Who?"

"We're not going to Leo." Paj glared at him.

"Who's Leo?" Willa was growing impatient.

"Someone we know from the old days. He'll do it," Auster answered.

But Paj didn't look like he was going to give in.

"No one would ever find out. In a way, it's safer." Auster shrugged.

"How do you know no one would find out?" Willa looked between them.

"Because this sailmaker isn't supposed to exist."

"Don't you think you should have mentioned that before we went in there and started rumors about the crew of the *Marigold* going to Tinny for sails?" Willa's voice rose.

Paj sighed. "It's kind of a last resort."

"That sounds about right," I said, turning on my heel. "Let's go."

THIRTY-TWO

Wsat in the window of the cramped teahouse,
waiting.

North Fyg was the only district of the city where the
cobblestones were dry and children didn't run barefoot in the
streets. Many of its residents were Bastian-born, stationed in
Ceros to represent their guilds or oversee their employer's
interests outside the Unnamed Sea. They were used to a
different way of life than the one we led in the Narrows. The
smell of Ceros didn't exist here, where the sun reflected off
stone-faced houses trimmed in bronze ornaments that had
turned green with the passing of years.

I'd never been in North Fyg, because my father refused to
step foot anywhere west of Waterside. When he had meetings
with city officials or guild masters, he made them come to
the heart of the city, where he could negotiate and conduct
business on his own turf.

Every eye on the street had followed us as we made our

way to the teahouse, and I wondered when the last time any of them had been down to the docks was. Our kind wasn't exactly welcomed in North Fyg, but they weren't going to turn down our copper either. We paid extra for our seat at the window, where we could watch the red door across the street.

"What the hell is this?" Auster picked up one of the small cakes on the tiered platter, holding it before him. The layers of thin, brittle pastry were covered in a crumbling powder the color of blood.

A woman stopped beside the table with a rolling silver cart and laid the tea, setting two hand-painted pots on the table. She kept her eyes down, as if we weren't there, and I realized it wasn't disapproval that kept her from looking at us. She was afraid. And for a fleeting moment, I found that I liked the feeling.

I turned the teapot before me, studying the intricate purple flowers and painted gold along the rim. The matching cup alone was worth more than my entire belt of tools.

"Is he going to show or what?" Willa huffed impatiently, filling her cup with the steaming black tea.

"He'll show," Paj said, his eyes still pinned on the red door.

"How exactly do two Bastian-born crewmen know an affluent tailor in North Fyg?" Willa watched Auster over her cup.

"He's a Saltblood." He looked to Paj before he answered. "And Paj did him a favor once."

"What kind of favor?" I asked.

259

"The kind that needs repaying," Paj cut Auster off before he could speak.

They'd already said more in front of me than I would have expected them to. I wasn't going to push it.

Willa picked up a cake from the platter, taking a bite and talking around a full mouth. "What if he refuses?"

Auster smirked. "He won't. He'd do it for one hundred coppers if that's what we offered."

"How do you know?"

"Because he hasn't made a set of sails in years. He'll jump at the chance."

I leaned back in my chair. "Then why aren't we offering him one hundred coppers instead of eight hundred?"

"We'll pay him one hundred for the sails. And seven hundred for his silence," Auster said.

Willa laughed. "Saltbloods don't stick together, then, huh?"

"Here we go." Paj stood, leaning into the window as a man with a white mustache in a speckled scarf appeared across the street, a bundle of packages in his arms. He fumbled with his pockets until he found a key and unlocked the door, pushing inside.

I finished my tea as the others stood, and Auster opened the door for me, Paj at my side as we stepped out into the sunlight.

He looked up and down the street before he gave me a nod, and we moved together, crossing in lockstep. But there was no going unnoticed in North Fyg for a ship crew. Our leathered skin, sun-streaked hair, and worn clothes gave us away. A woman leaned out her window in the next building, watching us with a scowl on her face. Everyone else on the street stared as we stopped in front of the tailor's door.

Paj lifted the latch, letting it swing open, and we went up the steps. Inside, the walls of the small shop were painted the palest shade of lavender, bolts of fabric in every color lining the shelves.

"One moment!" a voice called out from the back.

Paj took a seat in the armchair beside the window, where a threefold mirror stood in the corner to catch the good light. Beside it, a tray of crystal decanters filled with amber liquids sat on a small table, and Paj unstopped one of them, filling a little etched glass before he brought it to his lips and took a sharp sip.

I reached up, touching the fraying edge of unrolled white silk, dotted with tiny yellow flowers, curling my fingers into my fist when I realized how dirty my hand looked next to it.

Footsteps trailed toward us, and Auster leaned on the counter with both elbows, waiting. The man rounded the corner, stopping short when he saw Willa, but his eyes widened when he caught sight of Paj. The scarf around his neck was tied into a neat bow, his white mustache curled up at both ends with wax.

"What do you think you're doing here?" His thick accent unraveled the end of each word.

"I thought you'd be happy to see me, Leo." Paj smiled.

He huffed. "My customers will not be happy when word gets around that a bunch of urchins were in my shop."

"If you remember, it was an urchin who saved your ass back in Bastian. You wouldn't have this fancy shop if it weren't for me," Paj said, tipping his head back to empty his glass.

Leo went to the window, pulling the lace curtains closed before he pulled a pipe and a small round tin from his apron. We watched in silence as he filled the chamber with crushed mullein leaves, and he lit them, puffing until the white smoke was pouring from his lips.

"Isn't it dangerous to wear that?" Auster looked at the ring on Leo's middle finger. It was a merchant's ring, set with carnelian. I looked around the shop again, confused. If he was a sailmaker, why was he running a tailor shop?

"Worried about me? I'm touched." Leo spread his fingers before him, eyeing the stone, and when I looked closer, I saw the seal of Bastian imprinted into the silver. So, he was a sailmaker, but he hadn't been given a merchant's ring by the guild in Ceros.

"We need a set of sails," Auster said simply.

Leo's mustache twitched. "I'm not supposed to make sails. You know that."

"That doesn't mean you won't."

His eyes squinted. "Why not go to one of the sail lofts on the other side of the city?"

Paj refilled his glass. "We did. They won't do it."

"So, you've found a bit of trouble." Leo chuckled to himself.

"What do you care? Will you do it or not?"

"That depends on how much coin you'll give me to make risking my neck worth it."

"Eight hundred coppers," I said flatly.

Willa looked at me with a stern reproach.

But we were beyond negotiation. We were desperate, and there was no point in acting like we weren't. "We don't have time to barter. We need sails and we need them now."

Leo looked over us, thinking. "What kind of ship?"

"A double-mast lorcha," Auster answered. "It should take you no time."

"This wouldn't be the lorcha that had its sails slashed two days ago, would it?" A twinkle lit in Leo's eye.

Willa glared at him. "How fast can you have them done?"

I watched him think. If he was caught making sails without a merchant's ring from the Ceros Sailmakers Guild, he was as good as dead. And he wasn't hurting for coin if he worked in North Fyg. If he did it, it was because he wanted to. Not because he needed anything from us.

"Two days." He smiled, the pipe clenched in his white teeth.

"And how are you going to make them in two days?" Paj cocked his head to one side. The light coming through the window shadowed his face, painting his skin ink-black.

Leo shrugged. "I have people."

"Well, they better know how to keep their mouths shut." I untied both leather purses from my hips and tossed them to him. "There's two hundred. You'll get another two when the sails are finished, and the last four when they're strung up."

"Deal."

Willa took a step closer to him. "You don't deliver, and I don't need to tell you what we'll do to you."

His smile faltered a little. "I said I'd do it."

Paj stood, setting down his empty glass. "I think we can call it even, then."

Leo nodded, opening the door. "It's about time."

We filed back out into the street, the weight of the coin now missing from my belt, and Paj and Willa walked ahead of us as Auster and I followed.

"What did Paj do for him?" I asked, speaking low so only Auster could hear me.

He checked to see if Paj was listening before he answered, "Paj crewed a ship out of Bastian before we came to the Narrows. Their trade route ended in Ceros, and he smuggled Leo into the cargo when he needed to disappear."

"Disappear from Bastian?"

He nodded.

"So, he was a sailmaker in Bastian."

"Not just any sailmaker. He was Holland's sailmaker."

I stopped midstride, gaping at him. Holland was the same trader Willa said had it out for Zola. The same trader whose coin controlled the gem trade.

"He fell out of her good graces. It was leave Bastian without a trace, or meet whatever end Holland had planned for him," Auster said. "He paid Paj sixty coppers to get him on the ship to Ceros. It was more money than we'd ever seen, so he did it. But no trader or merchant would touch him when he came to the Narrows, so he set up shop as a tailor."

That's what Auster meant when he said that Leo wasn't supposed to exist. He'd found a desperate kid to hide him in the belly of a cargo ship and ran. As far as anyone in Ceros knew, he was just a tailor.

"So, you've been with Paj a long time," I said, looking ahead.

He knew my meaning. I wasn't just asking how long they'd known each other. I was asking how long they'd loved each other.

A crooked smile twisted on his lips, his eyes meeting mine for a moment before he nodded. But then his hand absently went to the sleeve of his shirt, tugging it down over the tattoo on his arm and a shadow passed over his face.

Two intertwined snakes coiled together, each eating the other's tail. It was the kind of mark that had meaning, and the symbol was one of infinity. Forever. But as far as I knew, Paj didn't have one.

"The crew knows about you two?"

"They're the only ones."

And now I knew too. "That's a long time to keep a secret."

He shrugged. "You know how it is. It's dangerous for people to know."

The thought made me happy before it made me sad—the idea that you could find love in this world the way Saint and Isolde had. Even if you had to keep it hidden to protect the one you loved. When I was alone on Jeval, I'd thought many times that love was no more than folklore. And that my

265

mother had only been able to give it flesh and bone because she wasn't like the rest of us. She was mythic. Otherworldly. Isolde seemed connected to the sea in a way that no one else was, as if she belonged beneath the surface of it instead of up here, with us.

But in the next breath, I thought of West.

I hadn't spoken to him since I shook his hand, agreeing to his conditions for taking me on. I'd dredge for the *Marigold,* but I was to keep my distance.

West said that Saint taught him everything he knew. That's why he was dealing in debts and running side trade. Pocketing from the ledgers and dumping men in crates into the sea. There was a certain amount of darkness it took to live this life. Saint had always told me that, but I didn't really learn it until Jeval. I'd done plenty of wicked things to survive on the island, but I couldn't find it in me to feel badly about any of them. It was the way of things. Maybe that made me more like my father than I wanted to admit.

And though West had said again and again that he didn't do favors and that he didn't take chances, he'd done both. Over and over.

For me.

THIRTY-THREE

Two days felt like twenty.

We kept our heads down in the city, drinking too much rye and sleeping late to avoid notice as Leo worked around the clock to finish the sails for the *Marigold*. But I could feel Zola's eyes on us at the docks. He wasn't stupid, and we weren't rid of the *Luna*'s crew yet. They turned up at every tavern we drank at, their footsteps following ours on the bridges and in the alleyways.

He was waiting for our next move.

But no one could guess what was coming. In another two days, the *Marigold* would be anchored in Tempest Snare, and we'd be bringing in the haul that would buy us out of West's debt to Saint. The crew would be free to scrape the crest off the floor of the helmsman's quarters, and for the first time, the *Marigold* would be beholden to no one.

West holed up in his quarters, refusing to leave the ship while he healed, the injuries that Zola's crew had left him with still covering almost every inch of him. The bruises had begun to yellow, the skin puckering along the stitches, but it would be weeks before he fully regained his strength.

Leo sat high on the mast, the striped silk scarf that was tied around his neck fluttering in the wind. Willa was perched beside him, holding the rolled sail in her arms. Since the moment the sun went down and the fog rolled in, they'd been working, Leo's hands moving so fast at the riggings that it was difficult to even see what he was doing. When we told him he would have to fit the sails in the pitch-dark to keep from being seen, he looked excited by the added challenge. By the time the sun rose, we'd be out of the harbor and on our way to Tempest Snare.

The others were already waiting when I came into the helmsman's quarters, the map Saint had given me clutched in my hands. West stood at the head of the desk and I didn't miss the way he avoided meeting my eyes.

"Almost finished," I said, closing the door behind me.

West looked to Hamish. "What else?"

He pushed the spectacles up his nose with the tip of his finger as he answered, "I've called in all our debts. It took one or two broken noses, but we're paid up, and it should be enough to cover us until we can trade in Dern."

"And the cargo?"

"Auster and I have offloaded everything we don't need. We had to sell it at a loss, but by the time we meet back up with our merchants, we'll be able to pay them. They never have to know what we lost in the storm or what we dumped here in Ceros."

It had taken us an entire day to get everything out of the hull. The *Marigold* would have to ride lighter than ever before if we were going to get through Tempest Snare without sinking.

"Now, we just need to chart the course," Paj said, eyeing the map in my hands.

I hesitated, for just a moment, feeling the weight of it baring down on top of me. The *Lark* was the only thing I had in the world. By giving it to West, I was putting my life in his hands. The thought made my stomach roil, the beat of my heart quickening.

Paj reached out, and I set the map into his hand before he unrolled it on top of the others scattered over the desk. "All right. Take us through it."

I touched the scripted letters that ran along the edge and followed the line of the shore, remembering the feel of the parchment under my fingertips. They moved up and away from the coast and past Jeval, stopping on the thin slices of land encircling one another in the middle of the sea.

"Tempest Snare." West leaned on the table across from me, his voice low.

Paj ran his hands over his face, sighing. "That's where this haul is hiding? Tempest Snare?"

I nodded.

"You've got to be kidding me," Hamish muttered. "What's down there?"

"Gems. Metals. Coin. Everything," I answered.

"A shipwreck." West stared at the map.

"And how are we supposed to get to it?" Auster looked at me. "There's a reason no one goes into the Snare. It's a death trap."

"Unless you know how to navigate it," I said.

West looked up, then, both hands planted on the desk before him. "*You* know the way through Tempest Snare?"

I didn't take my eyes from his as I unclasped my jacket and let it fall from my shoulders. It dropped to the floor, and I rolled up the sleeve of my shirt. The gnarled, puffed scar looked up at us, dark red in the lantern light. I set my arm on the table, lining it up over the map.

Paj pressed his fist to his mouth. "Are you telling me . . . ?"

Hamish shook his head, unbelieving.

I pointed to the farthest right point of the scar beneath my wrist. "It's here."

"What is? You still haven't told us what's down there," Auster said.

I swallowed hard. "The *Lark*."

All at once, they collectively stepped back from the table, a hush falling over the cabin.

I put one finger on the center of the reefs and put the other in the sea above Jeval, repeating the words just as I'd heard Clove say them after the storm. "The storm that hit the *Lark* came from the north." I pulled my finger down toward the reefs. "It pushed her into the reef, but then it turned."

I moved my finger that was on the reef back into the sea. "Then it shifted west. It dragged the ship here, before it sank. She's there." I stared at the small atoll sitting in the maze of reefs.

Hamish looked up at West over the lenses of his spectacles. "If we do this, that's it. Our ties with Saint will be cut for good."

"He could come after us." Paj looked worried.

"He won't." I paused. "The *Lark* belongs to me."

"Belongs to you? How?"

"He gave it to me."

"He *gave* it to you," Auster repeated.

"It's my inheritance."

They all stared at me. Everyone but West.

"It's only forty or fifty feet down."

West was quiet, his eyes still running over the map.

"I can get us through," I said. "I know I can."

"All right," West finally said, and the others looked relieved, a nervous smile on each of their faces. "We'll dredge the *Lark* and sell what we can in Dern to fill our hull with coin. Then we come back to Ceros and give it to Saint to pay for the *Marigold*."

"If the sea demons don't get us first," Auster whispered, his smile spreading wider.

They'd crewed the ship for more than two years, but it had never been theirs. It never would be, if Saint had anything to say about it. He'd brought West on under the debt because he knew he'd never be able to pay it. He had no reason to think that he'd ever actually lose his shadow ship.

"We better get out of here before this whole damn city starts wondering what we're up to." Paj went for the door and Auster followed him.

"One-third," West said, still looking at the map as the door closed.

"All right. One-third to the *Marigold*'s ledgers and the rest—"

"No," he cut Hamish off, "she'll take one-third."

Hamish nodded.

"But why?" I asked. Taking one-third of the haul for myself meant after coin for the ledgers, only one-third would be left for the crew to split. It wasn't fair.

"When we made the deal, you didn't tell me it was your inheritance," he said.

"You didn't ask. It's mine and I can use it however I want."

"You don't have to do that," Hamish said.

"Yes, I do."

West let out a long breath. "You may never get another chance like this again, Fable."

"I know. That's why I'm not going to waste it." I hoped he could hear what I wasn't saying. That even though I'd said I didn't owe him, I did. And I wanted to pay him back tenfold. "Two-thirds to the *Marigold*'s ledgers, and we'll split the rest between us. Evenly." I rolled up the map and tucked it back into my jacket.

West's eyes moved back and forth on mine, his jaw ticking like he was working up the courage to say something.

But just as he opened his mouth, footsteps pounded on the deck, coming into the breezeway.

"West!" Willa appeared in the doorway, her eyes wide. "We've got trouble."

THIRTY-FOUR

The six of us stood at the railing side by side, the only sound the ring of grommets sliding onto rope above us.

In the distance, torches bobbed beneath the iron archway that led into the harbor below Ceros. The fog had thinned in the cool wind, uncovering the *Marigold* from her hiding place.

"Well." Willa sighed. "That's not good."

I looked up to the foremast, where Leo was finishing the last of the new sails and he froze when his eyes landed on the harbor. Zola's crew was coming to finish what he started.

"What is it?" Leo called out.

The torches were almost to the docks, and I could just barely make out the throng of men carrying them. The weight of a stone pulled at the center of my stomach as I realized what they were going to do.

They were going to set fire to the *Marigold*.

"Make ready!" West shouted, his voice echoing as he ran

to the starboard side where Auster was already unlocking the crank for the anchor.

"If you're not off this ship before we shove off, you're going with us!" I yelled, and Leo's eyes widened. He pulled a tool from the back of his belt and went back to work, fastening the corner of the last sail with shaking hands.

The sharp click of the crank rang out as Auster and West raised the anchor, and I went for the lines, untying them with one eye on the harbor. Zola had thought the sails would finish West, but they hadn't. Now, there was only one thing to do if he wanted to put an end to the *Marigold* and its crew—he'd have to sink it.

Leo slid down the foremast, landing too hard. His legs buckled and he fell to the deck, groaning, before he got back up with his arm pinned to this side.

"Are they ready?" I looked up to where the clean, white canvas was neatly folded, the grommets gleaming.

"As ready as they'll ever be!" He limped toward the railing. "Hey!"

He turned back, his bag of tools slung over his shoulder. "You want your coin or not?"

He cursed, running back, and I picked up the sack at the top of the steps. He took it from me before he ran back to the ladder and disappeared over the side.

Willa untied the sails on the foremast, and the wind picked up, blowing in from the south. We'd need it if we were going to get out of the harbor before those torches hit our deck.

Once the lines were free, I jumped out from the mast

with the ropes wrapped around my fists. They slid open in one smooth motion, and I landed on both feet, looking up to their crisp, angled shapes against the black sky. They were beautiful, with lacquered wooden rod boning that fanned out from the bottom corner like two wings, ready to take flight.

Hamish took the ropes from me, and I swung myself over the side, making my way down the ladder to the dock. With the sails open and the anchor up, the *Marigold* was already drifting. I released the heaving lines from the first post, and they slapped against the hull as Paj wound them up.

Shouting sounded behind me, and I worked at the second one, but the rope was wedged too tightly in the knot. I fit my fingers into the loop and sank back, yanking with all of my weight and screaming, "Come on!"

The rope slipped, and I fell flat on my back, hitting the ground so hard that the impact made my lungs curl like fists. Zola's crew was already on our bay, running straight for me. I scrambled back to the post, unwinding the lines, and Paj pulled them up, but the ship was already too far. I couldn't reach the ladder.

"Fable!" Willa shouted as I came to the edge of the dock, swung my arms back behind me, and threw myself forward, leaping for the rungs.

I caught the ropes with both hands and hit the hull, my boots dragging in the water, but the glare of a torch was already flying overhead.

"Climb!" West appeared at the railing, his hand reaching for me.

I pulled myself up the swinging ladder and just as I made it halfway, it jerked and snapped, almost throwing me from the ropes. Below, a man had hold of the last rung. He launched himself up out of the water and grabbed my boot, pulling me back down. I kicked until the heel of my foot caught his jaw and he groaned, but he was already climbing. My elbows hooked into the ropes, and I grunted, trying to hold on against his weight as my fingers reached for my belt, but it was no use. I couldn't get to my knife, and if I let go, I would fall.

A shadow fell from overhead and a body dropped through the air, splashing into the sea below us. When I looked down, West surfaced in the black water. He swam back toward the ship as the man wrenched me back by my shirt.

West climbed up the opposite side between the ship and the ladder, and when he was face-to-face with me, he reached around my waist, taking the knife from my belt. He swung his arm out wide, bringing the blade from the side, and sank it into the man's ribs. He screamed, his hands trying to grab ahold of me before he slipped, but West kicked him in the chest, sending him backward.

The ladder swung, and I pressed my face into the ropes, gulping air as my arms shook.

"Are you all right?" West reached through the ropes, pushing my hair back from my face and checking me over.

I turned, the harbor drifting away from us, the silhouettes of at least a dozen men standing on the dock. When Zola heard about the sails, he'd sent his crew for blood. By morning, every trader in Ceros would know that we'd made it out of the port. And after his public display of putting the crew of the *Marigold* in its place, the humiliation of it would fall at Zola's feet.

In the distance, the *Luna* sat anchored without a single lantern lit on its deck. But he was there, watching. He had to be. And now, he wasn't just West's enemy. He was mine.

But the flash of something on shore made me look up to the shadows of Waterside, where the deep blue of a coat almost glowed in the dark.

Saint.

He leaned into the post on the street, unmoving, except for the hem of his coat blowing in the wind. I couldn't see his face, but I could feel his eyes on me. And if he was watching, then he knew. His own copper had paid for the sails that now stretched out over the *Marigold*, pulling us out to sea. And it didn't matter who I was or what had happened between us. For the first time in my life, we were on opposite sides of a line.

"Fable." West's voice shook me from the thought, and I blinked, finding his face before me again. Seawater still ran down his skin, his hands clamped onto the ropes below mine, where the bloodied blade of my knife caught the moonlight between us. "You all right?" he asked again.

I nodded, looking down into his face and letting the calm in his eyes steady me. That same smooth expression that was always there. Since we left Jeval, we'd come through a storm that almost swallowed us, and Zola had nearly killed him before stripping and almost sinking the *Marigold*. Nothing ever seemed to shake him.

"I'm fine," I answered.

He nodded, sliding the wet knife back into my belt. "Then get your ass on the ship."

THIRTY-FIVE

The sun shined on the sea in a slithering beam to the east like a lantern lighting our path.

I stood at the prow with Auster, rigging the crab traps into hauling baskets we could use to bring up the cargo of the *Lark*. I tied off a knot, watching the calm water, the sounds of sailing plucking at every memory I had from before Jeval. My father bent low over his maps, a pipe in his mouth and a rye glass in his hand. The splash of ropes and the glow of light on the shining deck.

My eyes trailed up the mast, to where my mother would be, lying back in the nets high up above the rest of us. She told stories of diving the remote reefs in the farthest reaches of the Unnamed Sea, but she'd never told me about her life in Bastian or her time crewing for Zola before she joined up with Saint. She'd never even told me what brought her to the Narrows. And since I sat across the table from Saint at Griff's tavern, I couldn't help wishing I'd asked more questions about her.

The first time Isolde took me diving, I was six years old. My father was waiting on the quarterdeck of the *Lark* when we surfaced, that rare smile reaching up one side of his face beneath his mustache. He lifted me up over the railing and took my hand, pulling me into the helmsman's quarters where he poured me my very first glass of rye. That night, I slept in my mother's hammock, curled against her warmth as the wind howled against the hull.

Tempest Snare was the last stretch of water before the Unnamed Sea and a favorite landing place for the storms that had made it into a graveyard. I could feel the Narrows widening around us, making the *Marigold* feel small in the vast sea. Soon, we would be at the edge of it, leaving us with no reachable land.

Paj appeared in the breezeway with his instruments, unpacking the octant carefully before he got to work, making notes into the open book set on the piles of rope. I watched him slide the arms until the light caught the mirror just right.

"How long?" I asked, setting the trap down at my feet.

"We should be there by morning if the wind picks back up."

I squinted against the light to see Auster at the top of the mainmast, a cloud of seabirds flying in a circle around him as he pulled another perch from his bucket. "What's with the birds, anyway?" I asked.

Paj lifted his eyes, a soft smile pulling at his lips before he laughed. "He likes them."

"Looks like they like him too," I said.

He worked a few more minutes before he opened the box and set the octant inside. "You were really on the *Lark* when it went down?" he asked suddenly, slipping the book back into his vest.

I nodded, looking out at the pink and purple clouds, the sun seeming to grow and swell as it began to sink down the sky. I didn't know if they'd heard stories about that night, but I wasn't going to be the one to tell them. It was a tale I was afraid would come alive within me if I spoke it aloud. There was a distance between the girl I was, standing on the deck of the *Marigold,* and the one who'd jumped from the *Lark* in Clove's arms.

West came up the steps in the passageway, rolling the sleeves of his shirt up to his elbows. He and Willa had been working in the hull since we left Ceros, seeing to the last of the damage from the storm that we couldn't afford to hire repairmen for. He hadn't said a word to me since we pushed off the dock. He hadn't even looked in my direction.

"Let me see," he said, coming to stand beside Paj.

Paj obeyed, taking the book back out and opening it to the last page he'd written on. West's eyes ran over the numbers slowly, and a piece of his hair loosed itself, blowing across his face.

"Let's drop anchor while the wind is weak. We'll make up the time."

Paj nodded.

"And the crates?" West asked Auster, even though it was clearly my job.

282

"Done," Auster answered for me.

"Check the knots again." And again, he didn't meet my eyes. I gritted my teeth.

I came around the mast. "West—"

But he turned on his heel, walking across the deck to the breezeway. I followed him to the helmsman's quarters, where he began working the compass over the map, checking Paj's measurements against his own. His mouth twisted as he bit the inside of his cheek.

"What's wrong?" I came to stand beside him, looking over the parchments.

"Nothing," he said in a breath, dropping his compass.

I eyed him, waiting.

He thought for a moment before he came to the other side of the desk, setting a finger on the map. "This."

The turn that sat at the center of Tempest Snare was a hard right angle, a difficult maneuver for any vessel bigger than a fishing boat. It would take expert precision to pull it off.

"Is there a way around it?" He studied the shapes of the reefs.

"I don't think so," I answered. "Not without scraping bottom."

"It will have to be perfect," he murmured.

"Then it will be."

He leaned into both hands, the muscles in his arms surfacing beneath his gold-painted skin. "We need to be back in Dern in the next few days if we're going to make this trade without notice."

He was right. We'd have to work fast, but if Paj's calculations were good, we could get the haul up onto the *Marigold* before the next day was out.

"That's how he did it, isn't it?" West sat in the chair, looking up at me.

"What?"

"Tempest Snare. That's how Saint built his fortune and started his trade."

"Yes," I answered. "He spent years mapping the Snare before he started his first route. He used the coin from dredging shipwrecks to buy his first vessel."

West was quiet, as if he was picturing it. As if he was imagining himself in Saint's shoes.

The string of white adder stones chimed together as they swayed in the open window behind him. "Do you think they really bring luck?" I asked.

He looked amused by the question. "They've worked so far."

The set of his mouth changed, pulling up on one side, and I could hear an unspoken answer in the words, but I didn't know what it was.

I picked up the white stone at the corner of his desk. "What is this?"

"It's from Waterside."

"Oh." I set it back down, feeling suddenly embarrassed.

His eyes flickered up to me. "Saint gave it to me when I got the *Marigold*. To remind me where I came from."

I sat on the edge of the desk, smirking incredulously.

Saint had wanted West to remember his place. And for some reason, West had kept it.

"I know that you know Willa's my sister," he said, his voice hardening again. "And I know you went to see our mother."

I tried to read him, looking for any trace of the anger that was usually lit on his face. But he still looked up at me with eyes that were full of words he wasn't saying.

"I didn't mean to. I didn't know where we were—"

"It doesn't matter." He set his elbows on the desk, scratching at his jaw, and I wondered why he said it. It did matter. It was likely one of the only things that really mattered to him.

"How have you kept it from the others all this time?"

"Maybe they do know, but they aren't going to say it. They don't ask questions. But Willa and I agreed a long time ago to never tell anyone we knew each other."

I nodded. To tell someone that Willa was his sister was to give them power over him. And her. It was the same reason why no one outside of this ship knew about Auster and Paj.

"Willa had a better chance crewing on a ship than staying in Waterside, so I made it happen." He said it as if he had to justify it. As if he knew it had come at a cost to her.

"What about your father?" I asked, my voice small.

But that pushed too far. And I wasn't sure why I'd even asked except that I really wanted to know. "We'll lose the light in a few hours." He stood, going to the trunk against the wall and opening it.

"What else needs doing? I'll help you."

He looked over his shoulder at me, and for a moment, I thought he smiled. "I've got it." He pulled a wide, flat scraper from the trunk, sliding its handle into his belt.

If he was using that tool, then he was going to clean the hull. Barnacles, mussels, seaweed, and a number of other creatures made their homes on the bottom of ships, creating their own kind of traveling reef. But in the Snare, we couldn't afford to catch on anything. We needed the hull to slide over the seafloor.

It was a disgusting, tedious job. One that West either thought I couldn't or wouldn't do.

"Are you worried about the draught?" I asked. The depth at which the ship sat in the water was the first thing that could take us down on the reefs. But the *Marigold*'s hull was empty and with the new sails, she was moving smooth over the sea.

"Right now, I'm worried about everything." The lid to the trunk fell closed, and he pulled his shirt over his head, wincing against the pain that erupted in his body as he lifted his arms. It dropped to his cot before he pushed past me, going out onto the deck.

I stared at the open doorway, thinking, before I followed after him. Just as I came around the corner, he stood on the rail and stepped off, disappearing over the side. A splash sounded below, and I peered back through the open door of his quarters, eyeing the white stone that sat at the corner of his desk.

I went back into the breezeway, turning the lock of the

cabinet on the wall and riffling through the shelves until I found another scraper and a mallet.

Willa watched me from the quarterdeck as I kicked off my boots and climbed up onto the rail, filling my chest with air. I jumped, falling into the sea with my arms up over my head and the tools clutched in my fists. The water stirred around me, and I spun, turning under the surface until I spotted West, floating near the stern in the vast blue expanse that reached out around us. Long ribbons of seaweed trailed beneath the ship and his hands stilled on the hull as I swam to him.

The hiss and snap of the mussels adhered to the ship clicked around us, and I took the place beside West, fitting the scraper against the thick crust of barnacles and hitting it with the mallet. It broke into pieces, erupting in a white cloud before drifting down into the deep below us.

He watched me work for a moment before he lifted his tools again. He wasn't going to let me in, like the others. He'd told me as much when he agreed to vote me on. But if I was going to be on this crew, I had to find a way to make him trust me.

Even if it meant breaking another one of Saint's rules.

Never, under any circumstances, reveal who or what matters to you.

I was taking a risk when I jumped into the water. I was showing my hand. That I didn't just care about the *Lark* or joining a crew. I cared about West. And I was becoming less and less afraid of what he might do if he knew it.

THIRTY-SIX

Tempest Snare rose above the calm water like the ridged backs of submerged dragons.

Paj stood at the prow, a wide grin on his face, the early sunlight reflecting in his eyes. His calculations had been perfect, to the hour, and we'd spotted the reefs just as dawn broke on the horizon. The labyrinth sprawled out before us for miles, the water so clear that the sand on the bottom seemed to shimmer.

Willa, Auster, and Hamish stood portside, shoulder to shoulder, and silence fell over the ship, leaving the *Marigold* quiet. I looked up to West, standing on the quarterdeck alone. His arms were crossed, his cap pulled low over his eyes.

The same unreadable expression was cast over his face that had been there since we'd left Ceros. And it was only now that I was beginning to see beneath it.

West stood at the edge of something. In a matter of hours,

everything was going to change. For him. For the crew. The day he'd come to Jeval through that storm, he hadn't known where it would lead. He didn't know that when he agreed to give me passage, the winds were shifting.

There was so much about this world that couldn't be predicted. And yet, we all knew exactly how it worked. Now, West would have choices before him that maybe he thought he'd never have. And that was enough to shake even the most stone-faced in the Narrows.

Paj took the helm, turning into the wind, and the path of the *Marigold* angled until the sails began to flap above us. When she began to lose speed, he let the handles spin over his fingers one way and then the other so that the rudder hinged from side to side. In a matter of moments, the ship slowed to a crawl.

"What's our way in?" Paj called out to West.

West studied the reef ahead before he looked over his shoulder at me. I climbed the steps to the quarterdeck and went to the railing, pulling the map from inside my jacket. I unrolled it before me and West took one side, holding it in place.

His eyes ran over the parchment before he pointed to the opening in the reef to our left. The ridges lifted above the surface unevenly before they disappeared, making an opening.

"Once we go in, there's no going back. Not till we get to the atoll," he said, almost to himself.

I followed our path on the map, understanding what he

meant. There would be nowhere wide enough to turn about until we made it to the *Lark*. If we ran aground, we were stuck, with no way out of the Snare.

"Get up there, dredger!" Auster looked up at me from the main deck, Willa at his side.

"You ready?" West's deep voice sounded beside me, and I looked up, meeting his eyes.

Suddenly, I was overwhelmed with the need to know he believed I could do it. That I could keep my promise. To all of them. I'd thought he didn't trust me, but what he was doing now had required every bit of his faith. He was putting the fate of the crew and the *Marigold* into my hands.

"Ready," I whispered.

He rolled up the map and followed me down the steps from the quarterdeck, and I went to the mainmast, taking hold of the pegs and pulling in a deep breath before I began the climb. My heart ticked unevenly in my chest as I rose higher into the wind.

West took the helm from Paj, looking up at me as I settled against the ropes and cast my gaze out over Tempest Snare. The last time I'd seen the Snare, it was seething with the storm that sank the *Lark*. Now, it was sparkling beneath a clear blue sky, as if it didn't hold the corpses of countless ship crews beneath its surface. The blue-green waters were filled with walls of craggy reef, narrow passageways winding under its façade in infinite veins. It was a maze—one that only I knew the way through.

I rolled the sleeve of my shirt up above my elbow and

held my arm out before me. The scar was an almost perfect rendering of the reef's arteries, and I marveled at Saint's ability to compose it by memory. He had sailed these waters so many times that he didn't need a map to cut its path into my skin.

My fingers trembled as I lifted one hand into the air. The warm wind slipped through my fingers as I measured the opening to the Snare below. "Bear starboard!"

Without hesitating, West turned the helm, and Hamish, Auster, and Willa reefed the sails, making the pockets tight so that the *Marigold* began drifting slowly. We moved toward the mouth of the reef, and Paj leaned over the bow, watching the prow cut through the shallow water.

I leaned over, calculating the side of the ship against the reef. "Come right!"

West guided the ship straight into the Snare, and silence fell, a chill running over my skin like the buzz in the air before lightning struck. Tempest Snare had taken more ships than anyone knew. In the distance, more than one mast breeched the water. But the sky was still clear, the movement of the water calm.

I looked down at my scar, following its shape to where the first fork was coming up. "Bear port, West. Five degrees."

He tilted the helm gently until we were cutting east, just enough to slip into the next vein, and the reef narrowed.

"Careful," Paj called out from the bow, his eyes on the depth as it grew shallower.

We inched along, passing the outcroppings of rock on

either side, where birds were leg-deep in the water, plucking their breakfasts from the coral. Schools of fish swirled like clouds of smoke beneath the surface, breaking off as the ship drifted forward and the reef widened again before the next split.

"Bear starboard. Fifteen degrees," I said, trying to sound sure.

West let the spokes rotate just slightly, and the mast vibrated under my hands as the keel slid along the sandy bottom. Willa met my eyes from where she was perched on the foremast, and I tried to slow the race of my heart, curling my fingers to calm the shake. One buried rock and we'd have a breach. But below, West looked calm, his hands light and careful on the helm.

I looked over my shoulder to the open sea. We were well into the Snare now. If a storm blew in, we were finished. Fear sang silently in my blood, its invisible tentacles wrapping around me and squeezing as we met fork after fork in the reef.

"It's coming up," I said, eyeing the hard turn ahead. Our speed was good, but it would all come down to the timing and the direction of the wind. If we turned too soon, we'd scrape the starboard side. Too late, and we'd crash the prow straight into the sharp corner of the reef.

"Steady . . ." I held a hand out to West, looking up to the sail above my head just as the wind suddenly changed direction, a gust rolling up off the water from nowhere. It pushed us forward, filling the sails, and the *Marigold* turned.

Too fast.

"Reef the sheets!" I called out.

Hamish, Auster, and Willa let the lines out and the ship slowed. But it was too late. We were too close.

"Now, West!"

I wrapped my arms around the mast and held on as he let the helm spin. "Drop anchor!" he shouted to Paj, who was already unlocking the crank.

If we were going to keep from smashing into the reef, we needed it to drag us. The others dropped the sails in unison and Paj kicked the lever of the anchor, sending it plummeting into the water.

The *Marigold* heeled, the stern swinging as we wheeled starboard. A sound like thunder erupted beneath us as the hull grazed the embankment, and Paj ran to the side, crashing into the railing as he peered over.

I pinched my eyes closed, every muscle constricting around my bones, my heart in my throat.

"It's all right!" Paj shouted through a panicked laugh.

I looked up to the sky, gasping, as hot tears sprung to my eyes.

Hamish jumped down to help him raise the anchor back into place, and West set his forehead on the helm, letting out a deep breath.

But we were still moving. I studied the scar, my eyes running over the reefs below as the sails unfurled again. My heart swelled in my chest, a lump rising in my throat as we made it to the end of the next pass.

The opening between ridges came to a stop in the middle of a semicircle of reef—the atoll. And there, beneath the jewel-blue waters rippling like glass, a faint shadow glimmered.

The *Lark*.

THIRTY-SEVEN

I raked my hair up on top of my head, tying it in a knot as Auster stacked the baskets against the railing before me.

The *Lark* sat only forty or so feet below, and I guessed it would take almost an entire day of diving to get what we came for. The sun was nearly overhead, and it would be impossible to navigate out of the Snare in the dark, so we had to be fast if we didn't want to spend the night on the atoll.

Paj checked the huge iron hook on the end of the line and slung it over the side. The rope uncoiled as it fell, sinking to the seafloor and pulling taut in the water.

The familiar weight of my belt around my waist calmed my nerves. The only thing we hadn't accounted for was the fact that in the last four years, someone else could have found the *Lark*.

I checked my tools, running my fingers over the picks, chisels, mallet, and hammer twice. I'd only need them if something had gotten lodged or buried from the wreck, and I hoped that wasn't the case. I needed every minute of daylight to get the haul into the baskets and get them aboard.

The water was crystal clear, the mainmast just below the surface, and I blinked away the image of my mother on its top, watching the moon. The thought of her pulled at the pit of my stomach, the feel of her like breath on my skin. I shivered, looking back down into the water. There was something about the stillness that made it feel as if she were still down there.

West came from his quarters as Auster hauled the last basket over the side. He dropped a belt on the deck beside me, pulling his shirt over his head. I followed the patchwork of stitching on his skin with my eyes. They added to the collection of scars that was already mapped over him.

"What are you doing?" I looked at the belt beside my bare feet, confused.

He kicked off his boots. "It'll go faster with two."

I glanced up to Willa and the others, but they didn't seem the slightest bit surprised by the sight of West fitting a dredger's belt around his waist.

"You never told me you dredge," I said, staring at him.

"There are a lot of things I haven't told you." He grinned, a crooked smile turning one side of his mouth up, where a dimple appeared.

I dropped my eyes, the sudden flush in my cheeks warming my skin. I didn't think I had ever seen him smile. Not ever. And I didn't like the way seeing him like that made me feel. Or I did. I didn't want to disentangle the difference between the two.

He worked the buckle of the belt absently, as if he'd done it a hundred times. I'd never heard of a helmsman who dredged. But this was no ordinary ship and no ordinary crew. It seemed there was no end to their secrets.

I held on to the rail and lifted myself up, balancing on the side of the ship to stand in the warm wind. West climbed up beside me, and I looked down into the water before us, where the ropes disappeared.

"I'd like to put forth for reconsideration by the crew, my standing as a bad luck charm." I called out to Willa, grinning.

She laughed, leaning into the mast. "We'll take a vote, dredger."

I looked up to West, asking him without words if he was ready. For the *Lark*. And for everything that came after.

The same smile pulled at his lips that had been there on the deck, and together, we stepped off the railing, falling through the air before we plunged into the sea. I sank, kicking against the weight of my tools until I broke the surface, West beside me.

He shook the hair back from his face, looking up to Willa and the others, who peered down at us from the *Marigold*.

I dragged the air in to fill the space between my ribs and pushed it back out, stretching my lungs until they stung inside me. The blood warmed in my arms and legs, and I kept at it until I could hold the amount of breath that I would need.

West waited for me to give him a nod before he tilted his head back to take in the air, and I did the same, filling my belly first, then my chest, and taking a last hissing sip into my throat.

He disappeared beneath the surface, and I followed, sinking down after him. When I saw it, I pushed my hands out before me to hover over the view of the *Lark*. She sat below us, the split in the hull half buried in the pale, soft sand, and the bow of the ship pointing to the sky. But the rest of the ship looked just as I remembered it.

The *Lark*.

The place where my mother's story ended. The place where mine began.

West looked down at it and then up to me.

I hesitated for a moment before I dove, kicking toward the stern of the ship, and the pressure pushed in around me, my ears popping as we went deeper. The reef that encircled the wreck was alive with life, swarms of bright fish twisting around one another and scattering in every direction. We swam into a cloud of butterfly fish and the sunlight caught their iridescent scales, twinkling like stars at twilight. I stopped, reaching out to touch them with my fingertips as they skittered past.

I smiled, turning back to West. He was a drifting, golden form before the infinite blue, watching me before he reached out and did the same. They whirled around him like little sterling flames before they jutted ahead, leaving us.

We swam the rest of the way to the ship and Saint's crest came into view, the paint depicting the white triangle sail almost completely gone. But the breaking wave was still there, brushed onto the wood in the same rich, vivid blue of his coat. I pressed my hand to it as we swam past, and when we made it to the deck, my skin went colder.

The algae-covered helm stood ahead untouched, like a ghost. I could almost see my father standing behind it, his big hands resting on the spokes. The broken mast towered overhead, and the sunlight wavered on the surface in the distance, where the *Marigold*'s shadow floated far above.

I pushed off, drifting toward the steps that led below deck, the beam of wood fallen from where it had hung above the passageway. We swam into the darkness, passing the doors that lined the long hallway, headed for the one that sat at the very end.

The water clouded with sediment as we reached it. I tried the door, but it was jammed, the swollen wood wedging it into the frame. West fit his back against the wall of the passageway and kicked until it gave, and it swung open before us.

Rays of sunlight cascaded through the cargo hold, emerald glowing beams illuminating stacks of toppled crates and overturned barrels. I floated over them, headed for the back corner. The lockers were still there, bolted to the wall, and I could feel them like a chorus of a thousand voices. The gems sang in a harmony that wrapped around me like the pull of wind.

I brushed away the sand until I could see my father's crest inlayed with pearl on the black tarred wood. I chose the smallest pick from my belt at my back and felt for the keyhole in the dim light. It took only a few tries before the mechanism clicked, and I fit my fingers under the lid, looking up to West before I opened it.

Suddenly, I wished I could speak. I wished I could say

something. Anything. Down here, in the deep, with the *Marigold* floating above, it was quiet. No Saint or Zola or Jeval. No secrets or lies or half-truths. Down here, we were only two mortals in an upside-down world.

The only world where I'd ever belonged.

West's gaze met mine, and I blinked slowly, hoping I would remember it forever. Exactly as it was, his sun-painted hair waving in the green light and the complete quiet of the sea. I gave him a smile before I looked back to the locker, lifting its lid with a creak. But his hand came down, holding it closed.

His callused fingers slid over the wood before they wound into mine slowly, pulling my hand from the trunk. I stilled, my heartbeat breaking into an uneven gait, the feel of his touch moving up my arm and spreading like the feel of sun on my skin.

He looked at me with a hundred stories lit behind his eyes.

Then he was coming closer. The air burned hot in my chest as his hands lifted and touched my face. His fingertips slid into my hair as he pulled me toward him and before I could even think about what he was doing, his lips touched mine.

And I disappeared. I was erased.

Every day on Jeval. Every night in the belly of the *Lark*. It all flickered out, leaving only the hum of the deep. Leaving only me and West.

Bubbles ran up between us as I opened my mouth to taste the warmth of his, and the whole sea fell silent. It swelled. I kissed him again, hooking my fingers into his belt and trying to pull him closer. Trying to feel him in the cold water. When I opened my eyes, he was looking at me. Every speck of gold in the green glimmered, the sharp angles of his face softening.

His arms slid around me, and I folded myself into him, finding the place beneath his jaw, and he held me. So tight. Like he was keeping me from unraveling. And he was. Because that kiss broke open some dark night sky within me filled with stars and moons and flaming comets. That darkness was replaced by the blazing fire of the sun racing under my skin.

Because the most deeply buried truth, hidden beneath everything my father taught me, was that I had wanted to touch West a thousand times.

THIRTY-EIGHT

We made it out of the Snare just before sunset, with soft winds and clear skies.

Auster pulled the kelp from where it was caught on the corners of the last basket and tossed it overboard before he opened it. Inside, the last of the small chests were stacked carefully.

I braided my wet hair over my shoulder, feeling West's eyes on me for just a moment before he disappeared into the passageway. As soon as he was gone, I turned toward the water, touching my mouth with the tips of my fingers as the tingle on my skin resurfaced.

Since we'd come back up onto the ship, I hadn't dared to even look in his direction, not wanting the memory to fade from exactly as it was still living in my mind. I wanted to remember it the way I remembered the gleam of my father's rye glass in the candlelight or the shape of my mother's silhouette in the dark.

I wanted to remember him kissing me in the deep. Forever.

I'd keep my end of the deal we made when I came onto the crew. I wouldn't bring the moment up here, to this world, where it would be crushed beneath the weight of the Narrows. But I also wouldn't forget it. Not ever.

Auster stacked the chests into my arms, and I followed him down the steps, where West was standing in the doorway of the cargo hold. He moved aside, pressing his back against the wall so I could pass, and he looked over my head, careful not to touch me as I sidestepped into the room.

The hull of the ship was alive with the light and hum of the gems, their individual songs blending together until it was just one deep, reverberating sound. Hamish sat in the center of the floor beside Willa, parchments strung out around him as he made notes in his book. I found a bit of empty space in front of them and set down the chests, opening the first one. The lantern light fell on dozens of large peacock pearls, still glistening wet.

Willa started the count, and I opened the next lid. Inside, crude, misshapen pieces of gold and palladium were mixed together.

"Is that . . ." Willa's mouth dropped open, picking up a single stone from a smaller box beside her. She held it between two fingers.

"Black opal," I finished, leaning forward to examine it. I hadn't seen one since I was a little girl.

West crouched down beside me, taking it from her, and his arm brushed against mine, making me feel like I was tipping to one side. When I looked up, Willa was looking between us, her brow wrinkling.

"What do you think it's worth?" he asked.

I didn't know if he was asking me or Hamish, so I didn't answer, picking out the pieces of palladium one at a time and setting them before me.

"More than two hundred coppers, I think," Hamish said, making another note in his book.

West reached in front of me for a purse Willa had filled with polished serpentine, and the smell of him washed over me, making me unsure whether the pricking moving over my skin was the gems or if it was him. I pressed my lips together, watching his face as he leaned over me, but he didn't look up.

"So, how does it look?" Willa asked, peering over Hamish's shoulder, to the filled page he was writing on.

"It looks good." He smiled. "Very good."

West let out a relieved breath. "What's the plan?"

Hamish slapped the book closed. "I think we can get away with trading a quarter of it in Dern if we're careful. We should end up with more than we need to pay the debt to Saint and square up with the merchants at each port. The rest, we can drop at the cache and trade bit by bit over a longer period of time. We'll have to keep it small at each port to avoid notice. Go in two groups so that we don't leave the ship." He reached into his jacket, pulling out the red leather purses I'd seen them use in Dern. This time, there were six instead of five. "No more than six hundred coppers' worth in each purse.

Not too many gems, not too many metals, and make sure to put a few low-value pieces in each one. We have to be smart if we want to keep the merchants and the other crews from getting curious."

We got to work, filling each purse strategically. We'd have to spread out and vary our timing, so we didn't hit the same dealer too many times. Dern was the safest port to try and pull it off. Not so big that there would be many other ships in the harbor, but big enough to have the number of stalls we'd need in the merchant's house.

It was a good plan. But like most good plans, it wasn't without risk. If someone reported us to the Trade Council, we'd lose our license to trade. And if Saint or Zola got wind of what we were up to, we'd find ourselves dead in the water again. Part of me wondered if Saint would be in Dern, waiting for us. He'd seen us leave Ceros, which meant he knew I helped the *Marigold* get their sails. He could guess we were going to the *Lark*. What I didn't know, was what he planned to do about it.

"So, how does it work?" Hamish asked, turning the black opal in his hand. "Can you . . . talk to them?"

I realized then that he was talking to me. I'd guessed that they had their suspicions about me being a gem sage, but the question embarrassed me. "I don't know how to explain it, it's just something I can do."

"Can you feel them?"

West seemed to still, as if he, too, was waiting to hear my answer.

"Kind of. It's more like I just *know* them. Their colors, the way the light hits them, how they feel when I hold them in my hand."

Hamish stared at me, clearly not satisfied.

I sighed, thinking. "It's like Auster. With the birds. How they're drawn to him. How he understands them."

He nodded then, seeming to accept the explanation. But I wasn't even sure if I understood it. If my mother hadn't died, I would have apprenticed as a gem sage under her for many more years. With her gone, there were things I'd never learn.

"Should come in handy," Hamish said, piling the full purses into one of the chests before he stood. "But best to keep it to yourself." He waited for me to agree with a nod before he followed West up the stairs.

Willa picked up a small basket of raw garnet, setting it into her lap. "What's with you and West?" She looked at me from the top of her gaze.

"What?" I frowned.

She counted out the faceted stones in silence, making a note before she set her eyes on me again. "Look, I don't make a habit of asking questions. The less I know, the better."

I set my hands into my lap. "Okay."

"He's my *brother*."

I looked up at her, then, unsure of what to say. She wasn't stupid. And there was no point in lying.

"If he's getting himself into trouble, I want to know about it. Not because I can control him. No one tells West what to do. But because I need to be ready to protect him."

"From what?"

Her leveled gaze held the answer. She was talking about me.

"You're not just some Jevali dredger, Fable. You matter to someone who has made our lives very difficult. Someone who could do a lot more damage than he already has." She handed me the garnet, and I set it into the open chest beside me. "I knew something wasn't right the night you showed up on the dock and he agreed to give you passage."

"He never told you who I was?"

"West doesn't tell me things unless I need to know them." Her irritation wasn't hidden. "I wasn't worried until he asked me to follow you in Ceros."

"You don't have anything to worry about, Willa." The words hurt me to say, but they were true. West had made it clear that we were shipmates. Nothing more.

"I don't?"

"I'm on the *Marigold* to crew."

"No, you're not." She sighed, getting to her feet. "You're on the *Marigold* to find a family."

I bit down on my bottom lip, blinking before tears could gather at the corners of my eyes. Because she was right. My mother was dead. My father didn't want me. And Clove, who'd been the closest thing to family I had other than my parents, was gone too.

"I'm leaving the *Marigold*," Willa said suddenly.

My hands closed over the purse in my hands. "What?" I whispered.

"I'll wait until things are settled and West has found a new bosun." She said the words methodically. As if she'd recited them to herself a hundred times. "But once he's paid Saint and set up his own trade, I'm going back to Ceros."

"Have you told West?"

She swallowed hard. "Not yet."

"What will you do?"

She shrugged. "Apprentice with a smith maybe? I don't know yet."

I leaned into the crate behind me, remembering what Willa said about not choosing this life. I wasn't only buying West's freedom with the *Lark*. I was buying hers too.

"I like you, Fable. It was my idea to bring you on, and I'm glad you're here." Her voice dropped low. "I'm not saying I don't want you to love him. I'm only saying that if you get him killed, I don't know if I'll be able to keep myself from cutting your throat."

THIRTY-NINE

In the pitch-black, Dern was no more than a few flickering lights on an invisible shore.

I stood out on the bow, watching it come closer as West guided the *Marigold* into the harbor, where a dock worker was standing with a torch to log our arrival.

Paj threw out the heaving lines, and I headed below deck to the cargo hold. The haul from the *Lark* was organized and stowed, every gem and precious metal and pearl accounted for in Hamish's book. It was enough to pay West's debt to Saint and help the *Marigold* settle into their own operation, maybe even one that would reach the Unnamed Sea one day.

The possibility made me feel something I rarely did. It made me hope. But it was quickly followed by the swift and brutal reality of what life as a trader was. A constant game of strategy. The never-ending maneuvering to get ahead and the insatiable hunger to want more.

More coin. More ships. More crews.

It was something that ran through my own veins. I was no different.

Soon, the sun would be rising behind the land, and I would have moved the only piece I had on the board. But taking Saint's payoff and using it to bail out the *Marigold* in exchange for a place on a crew was a move even Saint would admire. That's what I told myself, anyway.

Hamish came from the helmsman's quarters, setting one of the purses into my hand, and I closed my fingers around the soft leather. It would be my first time trading with the crew as one of them, and I was suddenly nervous.

The others came out onto the deck with their jackets buttoned up, and Willa folded her collar down, letting the scar on her face show.

West pulled on his cap. "Paj and Fable with me in the first. Auster and Willa with Hamish in the second. Let's go."

Auster let the ladder down, and Paj went over. On the next ship, a woman sat on the mast, watching us. Maybe news of what happened to the *Marigold* in Ceros had already reached Dern. If it had, there would be more attention on us than we could afford.

"Stay away from that gem dealer." West spoke low beside me, handing me an extra knife. I nodded, sliding the blade into my boot.

He went over the rail, and I followed as the others watched from the quarterdeck. I pulled the hood of my jacket up and shoved my hands into my pockets, staying at West's back as he led us up the docks. The crews of the ships in the harbor were just beginning to wake, and I scanned the crests, looking for the *Luna*, but she wasn't there. If Zola stayed on course after Ceros, they'd likely be in Sowan now and moving farther north before they came back to this part of the Narrows. That would give us the time we needed, but not much more.

The merchant's house doors were already open when we came up out of the harbor, and we disappeared into the flood of people inside. The warmth of bodies broke the chill of the wind, and I dropped my hood, keeping my scarf pulled up over the bottom half of my face.

"You good?" West turned back, looking at me and then to Paj.

"I'm good."

"Good," Paj echoed.

"All right, one hour."

We split into three directions, shoving into the aisles, and I moved to the southeast corner of the warehouse, meandering through the stalls. Merchants selling mullein leaves and other herbs were gathered at the end of the row, but on the other side, I spotted a case of silver. I slipped between two men to the front of the line, and a man with long red hair beneath a black knit cap looked down at me.

"What can I do for you, girl?" He tapped his hand on top of the case, his merchant's ring clinking on the glass. The face of the onyx stone was so scratched that it hardly shined anymore.

I reached into the purse inside my pocket, finding two pieces of the sharp-cornered metal, one gold and one palladium. "Ran across a few pieces in Ceros. Not sure what they're worth," I lied, holding them out before him.

He leaned in close, fitting a rusted monocle to his eye. "May I?"

I nodded, and he picked up the lump of gold, inspecting it closely. He took the palladium next, taking longer to check it. "I'd say thirty-five coppers for the gold, fifty for the other." He dropped them back into the palm of my hand. "Sound fair?"

"Sure." It wasn't a great price for such good pieces, but I was only just getting started and I couldn't waste time haggling with him. I'd take what I could.

He counted out the coppers into a small purse and handed it to me. "So, where in Ceros did you say you—"

"Thanks." I shouldered back into the aisle before he could finish.

I found a quartz merchant next, taking my time to peruse her stones before I plucked three from my purse. The woman's eyes went wide when she saw the size of the bloodstone in my hand, and I bristled, wondering if I'd underestimated the merchants. Maybe we should have put smaller pieces into the purses.

She stuttered over her words as she held it to the light. "Haven't seen one like this in quite some time."

It took her only seconds to make a good offer, and I made the two other gems part of the deal to get rid of them faster, walking away with another ninety coppers in one trade.

I lifted myself up on my toes, looking for West's green cap. He was bent over a table along the opposite wall of the warehouse. Paj was in the next aisle ahead of me, arguing with a sharp-eyed old lady over a piece of red tiger's eye.

The weight of the purse grew lighter, and my pockets grew heavier as I traded the gems in pairs of two or three, saving the most conspicuous for last—the black opal.

I eyed the merchants in the stalls, looking for someone who carried rare gems and might be less curious about a girl trading such a precious stone. When I caught sight of a man with a large green beryl in his hand, I moved toward him, listening to the deal he was making. He gave a fair price without much fuss for the beryl, and when the woman trading it walked away, he dropped it into a locked chest behind him.

"Yes?" he grunted, not bothering to look up at me.

"I've got a black opal I'm looking to trade." I picked up a piece of jadeite on the table and turned it over, pressing the tip of my thumb into its sharp point.

"Black opal, you say?" He set a hand on top of the case, eyeing me. "Haven't seen a black opal in the Narrows for at least a few years."

"It was part of an inheritance," I answered, smiling to myself. Because it was true.

"Hmm." He turned around, fetching a gem lamp from a case behind him and set it down on the table between us. "Let's see, then."

They were the tools used by the gem merchants because they couldn't feel the stones like I could. They didn't understand their languages of light and vibration or know how to unravel their secrets. Once, the Gem Guild had been full of gem sages. Now, most merchants were just ordinary men with fancy tools.

I took a deep breath, watching around me before I pulled it from the purse and set it on the mirrored glass. It was the largest black opal I'd ever seen, and it would take only seconds for the people around us to notice it.

He looked up at me from beneath his bushy eyebrows and I tried to smooth my expression, wondering if maybe I'd misjudged him. But he didn't say anything as he sat on his stool and lit the candlewick.

The little flame reflected off the glass, and the light poured through the black opal, filling the entire black, inky stone and the colors suspended inside. Flecks of red, violet, and green danced like spirits in the darkness, their shapes almost seeming to writhe.

"My, my . . ." he murmured, turning the stone slowly so the lamp's light illuminated his face. "Inheritance, huh?"

"That's right." I leaned into the table, speaking quietly.

He didn't buy it, but he didn't argue. He set his hand over the opal as a man passed behind me and blew out the lamp. "Two hundred and fifty coppers," he said in a lowered voice.

"Deal."

His eyes narrowed on me, no doubt suspicious at how quickly I'd taken the offer. He pulled a full purse from his belt and grabbed another from the locked cabinet behind him, setting both down before me. "That's two hundred." He snatched a smaller one from his belt. "And that's fifty."

I picked up all three purses and dropped them into my deep pockets. The weight felt right. Counting them would take time I didn't have. On the other side of the warehouse, Paj and West were already waiting for me beside the door that led to the harbor.

"Don't know what you're up to, but you'd better be careful," he whispered, reaching out a hand to me.

I shook it before I stepped back into the aisle and disappeared, unleashing the pent-up breath in my chest. West's eyes found me as I neared the door, and we stepped out into the morning fog.

"All right?" West spoke over his shoulder, waiting for me to pass him.

Paj nodded. "I held back the smoky quartz when I started getting looks but sold the rest. What about you?" He looked to me.

"All gone," I breathed.

It had worked. It had actually worked.

I smiled beneath my scarf, pulling the hood of my jacket up as the *Marigold* came back into view. In another day, she would be free.

FORTY

Flames flickered on the candlesticks in the breeze, the white wax dripping down and landing like raindrops on the deck between us. Auster set an entire roasted goose in the middle of our makeshift table, and Willa clapped her hands, whistling out into the night.

The crisp, golden skin still sizzled as she reached forward with a piece of torn bread, soaking it into the juices pooling in the bottom of the tray. Baked plums simmered in cinnamon honey steamed inside the bowl in front of me beside a slab of pungent cheese and a row of smoked pork pies with flaking crusts. Paj had even gone to the gambit to buy a set of hand-painted porcelain plates and real silver cutlery. Everything was laid out under the night sky that glittered with starlight above us.

The smell made my mouth water, the hollow in my stomach aching as we all watched Auster carve into the goose and set two medallions on my plate. Paj poured the rye, filling my cup until it overflowed onto the deck, and I fished two plums from the crock.

West sat beside me, tearing the round of bread and setting a piece into my hand. His fingers touched my palm and that same flash of heat reignited inside me, but he kept his eyes down, reaching across the table for the bottle of rye.

"I'd like to make a toast." Willa raised her glass into the air, and the candlelight made it glow like an enormous, glistening emerald in her hand. "To our bad luck charm!"

I laughed as every glass raised to meet hers, and they shot down the rye in one simultaneous gulp. Willa slapped the deck beside her, her eyes watering, and I broke a piece of cheese off the hunk in my hand and threw it at her. She leaned back, catching it in her mouth, and the crew cheered.

They hovered over their plates, laughing between bites, and not ever using the finely engraved knives and spoons beside their plates. The sound of the wind grazed the drawn sails, and I looked down at my plate, picking at the buttery crust of a pie and putting a small bite into my mouth.

I wanted to stop time and stay there, with the sound of Hamish singing and the sight of Willa smiling. Auster wound his pale fingers into Paj's before he brought his hand to his lips and kissed it. Side by side, they were coal and ash. Onyx and bone.

Willa pushed another filled glass toward me and looked up to the sail flying over the bow. The white canvas bearing the crest of the *Marigold* fluttered and curled in the soft wind.

"Why *Marigold*?" I asked, counting the points of the star. "Why is she named *Marigold*?"

Willa's eyes flitted to West, who stiffened beside me. The others continued chewing, as if they didn't hear the question.

"What do you think he'll say? When you pay the debt?" Hamish changed the subject, looking at West over the greasy bone clutched in his hands.

"I don't know." West's voice was rough with the weariness that pulled at his face as he stared into the candle flame. The saltwater from diving in the Snare had dried in his twisting hair.

We'd pulled it off. We'd made it to the *Lark* and filled the coffers with coin, but he was worried.

He was probably right to be. Saint would never see it coming, and there was no telling what he'd do. The man who was always three steps ahead would lose a shadow ship and an entire crew in the span of a moment that he hadn't predicted. And there was nothing he hated more than losing control. The only thing we could count on was the fact that Saint was a man of his word. He'd cut the *Marigold* loose before he broke a deal, but he wouldn't forget. And there would be a price to pay.

West drained his glass before he stood, and I watched him disappear down the ladder to the main deck.

The sound of the crew's voices rang out over the quiet harbor, and the lanterns on the other ships went out one by one, leaving us with only the dim glow of our little candles until their flames were extinguished in the clear melted wax. Hamish picked over the goose carcass for the last of the meat, and Willa lay back, her arms stretched out around her like she was floating on the surface of the water. She looked up to the sky, and in another moment, her eyes were closed.

Hamish threw the last bone into the tray, getting to his feet. "I'll take first watch."

Paj and Auster climbed up into the netting of the jib, curling up together, and I followed Hamish down the ladder. Before us, Dern was silent, the smoke from the three chimneys of the tavern catching the moonlight as it rose up into the sky.

I stopped before the archway, where the light from West's quarters was coming through his open door. His shadow was painted onto the deck, the angles of his face touching the wood planks beside my feet. I hesitated, one hand on the opening to the passageway, before I walked with quiet steps into the breezeway and peered inside.

He stood over his desk, an open bottle of rye and an empty glass on the parchment before him.

I knocked lightly, and he looked up, straightening when I pushed the door open.

"You're worried," I said, stepping into the light.

He stared at me for a long moment before he came around the desk to face me. "I am."

"Saint made a deal, West. He'll keep it."

"That's not what I'm worried about."

"Then what?"

He seemed to think about how to say it before he spoke. "Things are changing in the Narrows. In the end, it might be better to have him on our side."

"But you'll never be free."

"I know," he said softly, pushing his hands into his pockets. He suddenly looked so much younger. For a moment, I could see him running along the docks of Ceros like the children we'd seen in Waterside. "But also . . . I think I'll always feel like I owe him. Even if I pay the debt."

I tried not to look surprised by the admission, but I understood that feeling. We weren't supposed to owe anyone anything, but that was just a lie we told to make ourselves feel safe. Really, we'd never been safe. And we never would be.

"Marigold was my sister," he said suddenly, picking up the white stone that sat at the corner of his desk.

"What?" The word was only a breath.

"Willa and I had a sister named Marigold. She was four years old when she died, while I was out at sea." His voice grew timid. Apprehensive.

"How? What happened?"

"Whatever sickness that kills off half the people on Waterside." He leaned back onto the desk, his hands clamped down over the edge. "When Saint gave me the ship, he let me name her."

"I'm sorry," I whispered.

That was what West meant when he said that Willa had better chances on a ship than in Waterside. It was the reason he'd risked both their lives hiding her in the cargo hold, hoping the helmsman would take her on.

The weight of the silence grew in the small room, making me feel like I was sinking into the floor. He wasn't just telling me about his sister. There was something else beneath the words.

"I've pocketed on Saint's ledgers from the first day I started sailing under his crest, but I've never lied to him."

"What?" I tried to read him, confused.

"The last time we were in Sowan, I set fire to a merchant's warehouse on Saint's orders. He was a good man, but he was making another trading outfit rich, so Saint needed him to stop supplying. He lost everything."

I took a step backward, watching him. "What is this? What are you doing?"

"I'm answering your questions," he said.

I held my breath as his eyes lifted to meet mine, so green that they could have been carved from serpentine.

He set the stone back down and stood up from his desk. "What else do you want to know?"

"Don't." I shook my head. "The moment you tell me anything, you're going to be afraid of me."

"I'm already afraid of you." He took a step toward me. "The first helmsman I ever crewed for used to beat me in the hull of the ship. I caught and ate rats to survive because he didn't feed Waterside strays who worked for him. The ring you traded for the dagger belonged to my mother. She gave it to me the first time I went to sea. I stole bread from a dying man for Willa when we were starving on Waterside and told her that a baker gave it to me because I was scared she wouldn't eat it. The guilt of it has never left me even though I would do it again. And again. The only thing I know about my father is that his name might be Henrik. I've killed sixteen men, protecting myself or my family, or my crew."

"West, *stop.*"

"And I think I've loved you since the first time we anchored in Jeval." He grinned suddenly, staring at the floor, and a bit of red bloomed on his skin, creeping up out of the collar of his shirt.

"What?" The breath hitched in my chest.

But his smile turned sad. "I have thought about you every single day since that day. Maybe every hour. I've counted down the days to go back to the island, and I pushed us into storms I shouldn't have because I didn't want to not be there when you woke up. I didn't want you to wait for me. Ever. Or to think I wasn't coming back." He paused. "I struck the deal with Saint because I wanted the ship, but I kept it because of you. When you got off the *Marigold* in Ceros and I didn't know if I would ever see you again, I thought . . . I felt like I couldn't breathe."

I bit down on my bottom lip so hard that my eyes watered and the vision of him wavered before me.

"The only thing I feel truly afraid of is something happening to you."

This wasn't just enough of the truth to be believable. It was whole and naked, a first spring bloom waiting to wither in the sun.

"I kissed you because I've thought about kissing you for the last two years. I thought that if I just . . ." He didn't finish. "We can't do this by the rules, Fable. No secrets." He stared at me.

"But in Ceros, you said . . ." The words trailed off.

"I underestimated my ability to be on this ship with you and not touch you."

I stared at him, hot tears rolling down my cheeks as he lifted a hand between us, his palm open before me. I lifted mine to meet his, and his fingers closed between mine.

He was opening a door that we wouldn't be able to get closed again. And he was waiting to see if I was going to walk through it.

What he was saying—the things he told me—was his way of showing me he trusted me. It was also his way of giving me the match. If I wanted to, I could burn him down. But if we were going to do this, I would have to be his safe harbor and he would have to be mine.

"I'm not going to take anything from you, West," I whispered.

He let out a long breath, his hand squeezing mine. "I know that."

I lifted onto my toes, pressing my mouth to his, and the boiling heat that had flooded into me underwater found me again, racing beneath every inch of my skin. The smell of rye and saltwater and sun poured into my lungs, and I drank it in like the first desperate sip of air after a dive.

His hands found my hips, and he walked me back until my legs hit the side of the bed. I opened his jacket and pushed it from his shoulders before he laid me down beneath him. His weight pressed down on top of me and I arched my back as his hands caught my legs and pulled them up around him.

I closed my eyes and tears rolled down my temples, disappearing into my hair. It was the way his skin felt against mine. It was the feeling of being held. I hadn't been touched by another person in so long, and he was so beautiful to me in that moment that I felt as if my chest might crack open.

My head tipped back, and I pulled him closer so I could feel him against me. He groaned, his mouth pressed to my ear, and I tugged at the length of my shirt until I was pulling it over my head. He sat up, his eyes running over every inch of me and his breaths slowing.

I hooked my fingers into his belt, waiting for him to look at me. Because it was a wave that would retreat if I didn't say it. It was a setting sun unless we could really trust each other.

The words wound tight in my throat, more tears sliding from the corners of my eyes. "Don't lie to me and I won't lie to you. Ever."

And when he kissed me again, it was slow. It was pleading. The silence of the sea found us, my heartbeat quieting, and I painted each moment into my mind. The smell of him and the drag of his fingers down my back. The taste of salt when I kissed his shoulder and the slide of his lips down my throat.

Like light cast over the morning water, it became new. Every moment that lay ahead, like an uncharted sea.

This was a new beginning.

FORTY-ONE

The seabirds calling out over the water woke me from the deepest sleep I could remember.

I opened one eye, and the window in West's quarters came into view, only one of its shutters closed. Outside, the gray morning was cloaked in fog, the cool mist creeping into the cabin. I rolled over, and West was sleeping beside me, his face softer than I'd ever seen it. He still smelled like saltwater, and I brushed an unruly strand of hair back from his forehead before I pressed my lips to his cheek.

The air was cold as I slipped out from under the quilt and walked to the window. I stood before the view of the silver water, eerie and calm before the warmth of sunlight touched it. West didn't open his eyes as I pulled my clothes on, his breaths still deep and long.

His face was only half-lit in the pale light, and he looked so peaceful in that moment. So untouched.

I stepped with bare feet across the room and opened

325

the door slowly, slipping out into the breezeway. The deck was empty except for Auster sitting at the prow beside a line of perched seabirds, as if he were one of them. I stopped midstride, looking back at West's closed door, and a knowing smile spread on Auster's face as he dragged the blade of his knife down the piece of wood in his hand, but he didn't look up. He would pretend, the way everyone pretended not to know West and Willa were brother and sister. The same way they didn't draw any attention to him and Paj. And in that moment, I felt more a part of the crew than I had guiding them through the Snare.

My face flushed again as I leaned against the mast and pulled my boots on.

Auster jumped down, coming to meet me. "Where are you going?"

I untied the ladder, and it unrolled against the hull with a slap. "There's one more thing I have to do before we shove off." I swung one leg over and climbed down, jumping onto the dock when I reached the bottom.

The fog was so thick that I couldn't even see the ships in the bays, their masts emerging from the white mist here and there and then disappearing as it rolled in. I pulled my scarf up over my mouth, still smiling beneath it as I passed under the harbor's archway. I would replay the night over and over, drowning in the memory of the way West looked in the candlelight. The way his bare skin felt against mine.

The village was quiet, with empty streets snaking between the cluttered buildings, and my footsteps were the only sound as I walked. It would be another hour before the sun was in the sky, burning the fog off the land, but its light was already beginning to bleed into the dark.

Three chimneys with billowing smoke appeared ahead, and I climbed the steep hill that led up to the tavern. As I passed, my reflection in the window made me stop, turning back to the bubbled glass. I pushed my hood back and stared into my own face, my hands raising to press against my pink cheeks.

I looked even more like her than I did when I was at Saint's post. The cut of bone in my face and the deepest shade of red in my hair. It almost glowed in the mist, spilling out from the buttoned collar of my jacket and falling down over my chest.

A flash of blue lit behind the window, and I stilled, my eyes focusing beyond my reflection. I pressed one hand to the glass, the burn already lighting behind my eyes.

On the other side of the window, Saint sat at a table before a white teapot. He looked up at me, the look on his face stricken, as if he could see her too.

Isolde.

I pushed open the door and stepped inside, where the fire in the hearth was blazing, filling the room with a dry heat that crept inside my jacket and warmed me. The collar of Saint's coat was unfolded up around his jaw, hiding half his face, and I pulled the chair beside him out from the table, taking a seat.

"I didn't see your ship in the harbor," I said, realizing

suddenly that the feeling bubbling up inside me wasn't anger. I was *happy* to see him, though I wasn't sure why.

A woman shuffled in with another cup and set it down before me with three sugar cubes nestled on the rim of the little plate.

"May I?" I looked at the teapot, and he hesitated before he nodded. "What are you doing here, Saint?"

He watched me fill my cup, the light coming through the window brightening his crystal blue eyes. "I came to see if you did what I thought you would do."

I glared at him, gritting my teeth. "You can't take credit for this. Not this time."

"That's not what I meant."

"Then what did you mean?" I lifted the cup to my lips, and its fragrant steam hit my face, the smell of bergamot and lavender filling my nose.

"You're going to get yourself killed, Fable," he ground out as he leaned on the table, looking at me. "Just like she did."

The tea burned in my mouth as I sipped, and I set it down, folding my shaking hands into my lap. I was glad in that moment that he didn't say her name. I knew she was dead. I'd felt it in my bones when we rowed away from the *Lark*. But on my father's lips, it became a different kind of truth.

I sniffed. The only thing worse than the pain that had carved a home inside me was knowing that he could see it.

"You don't have anything to prove, Fay. Go back to Ceros and—"

"You think I'm doing this because I'm trying to *prove*

something? I'm doing this because I have nothing else." The words were bitter, because they weren't entirely true. The *Marigold* and West were also what I wanted. But hopes like that were too sacred to speak aloud to a man like Saint.

"You don't understand anything."

"Then explain it. Tell me!" I shouted, my voice echoing in the empty room. "I know you don't know how to love me. I know you're not built for it. But I thought you loved *her*. She would have hated you for leaving me on that rock. She would have cursed you." A cry slipped from my chest, but I kept myself from slamming my fists into the table.

He stared into his tea, his body rigid. "I swore to your mother that I would keep you safe. There is nowhere more dangerous in this world for you than being with me."

My fingers coiled around each other in my lap, and I turned to the window, unable to keep the tears from falling. I'd always wanted to hear him say he loved me. I'd wanted to hear the words so many times. But in that moment, I was suddenly frightened he would. I was terrified to know how badly they would hurt me. "You were wrong. About so many things. But most of all, you were wrong about me." I breathed.

"What does that mean?"

"You said I wasn't made for this world." I spit his words back at him, the ones that had echoed over and over in my mind since the day he left me.

He smiled just enough for the wrinkles to appear around his eyes. "And I meant it."

"How can you say that?" I glowered at him. "I'm *here*. I made it off Jeval. I found my own crew. *I* did that."

"You don't know him."

I bristled, realizing he was talking about West.

"He's not who you think he is."

My jaw clenched, and I swallowed, uneasy. Because that wasn't like Saint. There was a heavy truth to his voice that I didn't want to hear.

He looked up then, his eyes meeting mine, and I thought I could see the glimmer of tears in them. "You were made for a far better world than this one, Fable," he rasped. "I was young. I hadn't learned the rules yet when Isolde came asking me to take her onto my crew." The words turned to a whisper. "I loved her with a love that broke me."

He brushed the tear from the corner of his eye, dropping his gaze back down to the table. I didn't think about it before I reached across the knotted wood and covered his hand with mine. I knew what he meant because I'd seen it. Everyone had. Isolde was the wind and sea and sky of Saint's world. She was the pattern of stars that he navigated by, the sum of all directions on his compass. And he was lost without her.

We sat there in the silence, watching the village come to life outside the window, and in the time it took us to finish our tea, everything felt like it did back then. The smell of mullein smoke on my father's coat. The clink of glasses with a fire at our backs. And as the sun rose, so did the unspoken goodbye between us.

When we got back to Ceros, West would repay his debt and the *Marigold* would be ours.

I set my chin on my hand, twisting my fingers into my hair, and I looked at his face, memorizing every wrinkle. Every silver streak through his mustache. The way his eyes matched the blue of his coat so perfectly. I tucked the picture into my heart, no matter how badly it would make it ache.

The chair scraped over the stone floor as I stood, and I leaned down, kissing him on the top of his head. I wound my arms around his shoulders for the length of a breath, and two tears slipped down his rough cheeks, disappearing into his beard.

When I opened the door, I didn't look back.

Because I knew I would never see my father again.

FORTY-TWO

The roof of the village gambit appeared at the end of the alley as I rounded the corner. It sat shrouded in the last of the morning mist, the sign that hung above the door reflecting the light.

I came up the steps, banging my fist on the window as the street behind me filled with carts on their way to the merchant's house. When there was no answer, I peered through the grimy glass until the gambit appeared in the shadows. He hobbled toward the door, his eyes squinted against the light, and when he opened it, I pushed in.

"What the—" he grumbled.

I went straight for the cabinet in the back, sinking down onto my heels and looking inside. Rows of velvet-lined trays were stacked side by side, filled with silver chains and glittering baubles. But it wasn't there.

"I traded you a gold ring for a jeweled dagger and a necklace the last time I was here." I stood, going to the next case.

"Do you have any idea how many gold rings I have, girl?"

"This one was different. It had notches imprinted in the metal, all the way around."

It wasn't until I looked up that I realized the gambit was almost naked. His long shirt fell over his bare legs like a skirt. He huffed, making his way around the counter, and he pulled a black wooden box from another case. He dropped it on the counter before him and leaned into it, glaring at me.

I lifted the lid, and the light coming through the window fell on the shine of a hundred gold rings. Every size, some with stones, some without. I raked through them with my fingers until I saw it.

"There." I held it up before me, turning it in the light. "How much?"

"Ten coppers if you get the hell out of here."

I smirked, dropping the coins onto the counter. The bell chimed above me as I opened the door, and I went down the steps, pulling the leather string from where it was wound tightly around my hair. I slipped the ring onto it and tied it around my neck, clasping the jacket at the top.

The fog finally cleared as the sun peeked up over the first rooftops, and I looked out over a sun-soaked, shimmering Dern. So many memories crept through the alleyways, so many ghosts. I followed them back the way I'd come, and when I passed the tavern, Saint's table was empty, the two teacups left sitting alone.

The bell for the merchant's house rang out, and I cut

through a side street to the docks, not wanting to see any merchants or traders from the day before. If we wanted to outrun the talk that had probably already started, we needed to get on the water. By now, the crew would be readying the ship, waiting to shove off.

"A real shame."

A voice came from the opening of the next alley, and I stopped, staring at the shadow that crept over the cobblestones before me. It stretched and grew as Zola stepped out from behind a whitewashed brick wall, his black coat pulling around him in the wind.

"It's a real shame to see you waste your time with the likes of that crew, Fable."

My hand slid around my back for the knife at my belt. I'd never told him my name. "How do you know who I am?"

He laughed, his head tilting to the side so that he could see me beneath the rim of his hat. "You look just like her."

My heartbeat skipped, a sinking feeling making me feel off-balance.

"And just like your mother, you've made some really stupid choices."

Three men stepped out of the alley behind him.

I looked over my shoulder, to the empty street that led back to the gambit shop. There wasn't a soul to see whatever Zola had planned, and it wasn't likely I'd come out the other side of it.

I stepped backward, the trembling in my hands making the knife shake. I wouldn't be able to make it past all four of them, but if I went backward, I'd have farther to run before I reached the docks.

There was no time to think. I turned, pivoting on my heel and launching myself forward to run with the knife at my side. My boots hit the wet stone and the sound multiplied as the men took off after me.

I looked back to where Zola still stood, his coat blowing in the wind, and slammed into something hard as I turned, the air leaving my lungs. The knife flew from my grasp as I fell forward and arms wrapped tightly around my shoulders.

"Let go of me!" I screamed, shoving into the man who had me, but he was too strong. "Get off!"

I reared my foot back and brought my knee up in a snap, driving it between his legs and he fell forward, a choking sound strangling in his throat. We tumbled backward, and my head hit the wet cobblestones, making the sky above me explode with light.

My hand reached for my boot, sliding West's knife free, and as another man came over me, I swung it out, grazing his forearm. He looked at the blood seeping beneath his sleeve before he reached down, taking my jacket into his hands and the third man wrenched the knife from my grip.

When I looked up again, his fist was in the air, and it came down with a crack across my face. Blood filled my mouth and I tried to scream, but before I could, he hit me again. The light swayed overhead, the black creeping in, and with another, it flickered out.

FORTY-THREE

I t was a love that broke us all.

My mother was high on the mast, just a slice of black against the glimmering sun overhead. It glinted around her and the dark red braid swung at her back as she climbed. I stood on the deck below, fitting my small feet into her dancing shadow.

She was the sun and the sea and the moon in one. She was the north star that pulled us to the shore.

That's what my father said. The sound of his voice faded in the ripple of wind over the sails, the canvas snapping.

But I wasn't on the *Lark* anymore.

The iron taste of blood was still on my tongue when I opened my eyes. But it was too bright. Every inch of my face throbbed, the corner of my eye so swollen that I could barely see out of it. I looked up to the rows of sheets reaching overhead, my heart wrenching in my chest. I couldn't see over the railing, but I could hear it—the water lapping against the hull of a ship.

The deck beneath me was warmed in the sun, and when I looked up to find it in the sky, my stomach dropped like a stone in my gut. Tears stung in my eyes as I looked up to Zola's crest burned into the ornate wooden archway.

My arms were pulled behind me, bound around the foremast, and the ache in my back shot into my shoulders, down to my wrists in a quick pulse. I tried to breathe through it, looking for anything nearby I could use to cut free.

Shadows slipped over me as the crew went about their work, their eyes not meeting mine, and I looked for Zola. But he wasn't at the helm. Men worked the lines on the masts and a woman with cropped hair sat in a pile of nets on the quarterdeck.

Behind me, on the boom, I spotted one figure I knew.

The pain in my body was nothing compared to the slice and sting of recognizing him. The set of his shoulders and the ears that stuck out beneath his cap. The way his hands hung heavily at his sides—hands that had held me as we leapt from the sinking *Lark* into the churning sea.

I shook my head, blinking to clear my vision. But when I looked up again, he turned, jumping down from the foot of the sail, and I caught sight of the profile of his face. The bridge of his nose and the curl of his blond mustache.

A feeling like frost inside my lungs crept up my throat, the name frozen in my mouth.

Clove.

ACKNOWLEDGMENTS

Writing this book truly did feel like an adventure, and I couldn't have done it alone.

I always give my thanks to my own little crew first—Joel, Ethan, Josiah, Finley, and River—because they are the ones who see me through the restless fever dream that is drafting a story. Thank you for the early morning coffee runs, the meals carried into my office, and the late-night glasses of wine that appear beside my laptop. Most of all, thank you for the imagination that keeps my stories alive.

To my father, who this book is dedicated to, this story came to me only days after you left this world. Sometimes, it felt as if you were watching over my shoulder as I typed the words on its pages. There are messages in a bottle throughout this book for you. I have no doubt you'll find them.

And thank you to the rest of my clan and kin, Mom, Laura, Rusty—king of the Rustyrita—Brandon, Rhiannon,

Adam, and Chelsea. I just honestly don't like anyone as much as I like you guys.

All my gratitude to my agent, Barbara Poelle, and my editor, Eileen Rothschild. I feel like you both had so much unflinching belief in Fable's story and I'm so glad we could bring her to the shelf together. To my incredible team at Wednesday Books: Sara Goodman, Tiffany Shelton, DJ DeSmyter, Alexis Neuville, Brant Janeway, and Mary Moates—thank you for everything you do. I couldn't keep this ship afloat without you.

Yet another acknowledgment to my critique partner/ work wife/codependent storyteller, Kristin Dwyer. I have never wanted to throttle you more than when you made me delete the first six chapters of this book and rewrite them. Thank you for not ever letting me give less to a story than my absolute best.

To my writer friends, I could not navigate the waters of publishing without you! A huge thank-you to Stephanie Garber, who somehow always has the words that will keep me believing wholeheartedly in my work. Thank you also to my soul sister, Shea Ernshaw, for whom I don't even need to add specifics because she can literally read my mind. You are a gift. Thank you to Isabel Ibanez, Rachel Griffin, Stephanie Brubaker, Shelby Mahurin, Adalyn Grace, Shannon Dittemore, and the rest of my local writer gang.

Perhaps the most important contributor to this book was Lille Moore, who served tirelessly as my sailing expert on this project. I can't believe how lucky I got when you answered my request for someone who sails! I am endlessly grateful for the time, energy, and dedication you gave to *Fable*. Thank you.

Thank you to my beta readers, Natalie Faria, Isabel Ibanez, and Vanessa Del Rio. I don't know what I would do without you.

And a heartfelt thank-you to my non-writer-world supporters—the A's, the Ladies, and everyone else who has been there for me along this journey.

ABOUT THE AUTHOR

Adrienne Young is a born and bred Texan turned California girl. She is a foodie with a deep love of history and travel and a shameless addiction to coffee. She lives with her documentary filmmaker husband and their four little wildlings beneath the West Coast sun. Adrienne is the author of the *New York Times* bestseller *Sky in the Deep*, *The Girl the Sea Gave Back* and the Fable duology.

For more fantastic fiction, author events,
exclusive excerpts, competitions, limited editions and more

VISIT OUR WEBSITE
titanbooks.com

LIKE US ON FACEBOOK
facebook.com/titanbooks

FOLLOW US ON TWITTER AND INSTAGRAM
@TitanBooks

EMAIL US
readerfeedback@titanemail.com